Run To You

Erosa Knowles

Men of 3X CONStruction Series

Run to You,
Copyright November 2011, Knowles, Erosa
Printed in the United States of America
Published by Sitting Bull Publications, LLC

This is a work of fiction. Names, places, characters and incidents are either the product of the author's imagination or are used fictitiously, and any resemblance to any actual persons, living or dead, businesses, organizations, events or locales is entirely coincidental. All trademarks, service marks, registered trademarks, and registered service marks are the property of their respective owners and are used herein for identification purposes only. The publisher does not have any control over or assume any responsibility for author or third-party websites or their contents.

Copyright 2011 by Erosa Knowles

2011 All Rights Reserved
ISBN: 978-1-937334-13-0

All rights reserved under the International and Pan-American Copyright Conventions. No part of this book may be reproduced or transmitted in any form or by any means, electronic or mechanical, including photocopying, recording, or by any information storage and retrieval system, without permission in writing from Erosa Knowles.

WARNING: The unauthorized reproduction or distribution of this copyrighted work is illegal. Criminal copyright infringement, including infringement without monetary gain, is investigated by the FBI and is punishable by up to 5 years in Federal prison and a fine of $250,000.

Run to You

Brenda and Roark lived the "Happily Ever After" part of the fairy tale. He'd rescued her from the bad guys, swept her off to his home, and loved her like a madman. Brenda was in heaven, until she went to visit her dying aunt and disappeared. Roark, his brothers and the men of 3X Construction race against time to find the woman Roark refuses to live without.

This book is a part of the *Men of 3X CONStruction* series. Although it can be read as a stand- alone book, the reading is more enjoyable when the other books in the series are read first. Visit the men of 3X construction website for updates and free reads.

www.menof3XCONStruction.com

Other Books by **Erosa Knowles**:

Secrets
Special Forces
Nikki's Challenge
The Ultimate Breed
Have I Told You Lately?*
Ready for Love*
Where There's Smoke*
Not This Time*
Run to You *

* *denotes Men of 3X CONStruction series*

Dedication

There are so many people I'd like to thank for all their help with this book. Wow, this is the fifth book of this series and there are so many more interesting characters left at the company and in the family tree.

A special shout out to Vicki, Linda and Karen for putting their eyes and editorial talents on the words of these pages.

All the members of the men of 3X CONStruction website, you guys push me hard, but I wouldn't trade you for anything. You're the best support group any author could ask for.

I also want to thank my family who allows me to do what I love to do, which is write.

And most importantly, I thank my Creator who blesses me with all my abilities.

Chapter 1

Morning sunlight tickled Brenda's forehead. Her arm lay over her eyes in a vain attempt to stay hidden in the shadows of her dream. A grin tugged on her lips as she rolled over and snuggled into the warmth of Roark's loose embrace. For so many years, she'd wanted one thing, for someone to love her just like in the fairy tales. Although life was no dream, dreams did come true. Roark starred as her prince, rescuing her from her lowest point, and then taking her away from her problems to his castle. Brenda grinned at her mental ramblings. The idea of Roark sweeping her into a dashing romance warmed her heart. She, Brenda Washington, was Lady of his castle.

Slowly, in protest of the rising sun, her eyes opened, and her heart warmed at the sight of her lover lying asleep. Thick straight hair, a mixture of browns, reds, and gold, covered part of his forehead and sculpted cheek. Whenever he smiled, a dimple winked in his right cheek. Normally, men and dimples didn't mix, but his worked, softening his masculine features. Dark eyebrows slashed over widely-spaced sherry-colored eyes. Eyes that softened in pleasure and spit nails in anger. The cleft in his chin reminded her of Ben Affleck, a modern day Cary Grant.

The part of his face that always captured her attention, made her knees weak and panties wet, were his lips. Full, firm, and a nice dusky red color. The thought of nibbling on his lips and slipping her tongue into the warmth of his mouth, sent a shaft of arousal through her.

As she listened to his even breathing, she relaxed, secure in the knowledge that this was where she wanted to be. Taking care of this man, his home, and building a future with him blanketed her with a sense of purpose and well-being.

There were days when fear wracked her body. Visions of waking to discover her life was a sham, a cruel joke, and it shook her to the core. But when she looked into Roark's eyes and saw his caring, compassion, and what she wanted to believe was love, she realized she'd won the lottery. Whatever it took, she'd make sure Roark never regretted bringing her into his life and home.

Shifting her thighs to make contact with his, she licked her lips as his eyes opened in slow motion, followed with a naughty grin. She winked and he returned the gesture.

"Mornin' sunshine." His voice held remnants of sleep.

Brenda giggled and settled closer. Wide, rough palms smoothed her outer thigh, sending tingles of pleasure up her spine. Inhaling deeply, his natural male scent curled inside her heart, and teased her nostrils, beckoning her to play. After six months of living together, her heart still raced whenever he touched her.

"Sleep good?" he asked, his lips next to her ear. His eyes roamed over her face, and then pulled the sheet down to gaze at her naked breasts.

"Um hmm," she moaned as his hand moved up her thigh and cupped her breast. Her body had been on low simmer since she woke, but as he pulled her taut nipple, heat flowed to her core.

"You smell good." He breathed deep and long.

She smiled as his fingertips tweaked her other nipple. "You always say that," she chuckled, although she was pleased her diligence in taking better care of herself had paid off.

"Because it's true." His hand moved into her hair and massaged her scalp, a major weakness for her. He bent forward, brushing his lips against her forehead, triggering a tremor that shot through her body. Eager for him, she rubbed against his morning hardness. The sun wasn't the only thing rising. A wicked sigh escaped his mouth as he pressed forward, his thick erection staking its claim on her ass. Intoxicated by his touch, she turned toward him as soft lips grazed her ear. His arm tightened around her waist. Gentle nips on her earlobe sent zings of pleasure between her legs.

"Roark." Inherent in her husky voice was a plead for more. Indistinct words of pleasure escaped her mouth as his fingertips tapped against her wet entrance. Without thought, her legs spread, allowing him the greater access they both craved. Eyes closed, she joined him as they journeyed to a place where nothing mattered, a world of their making. Each sojourn bound their souls tighter.

The man knew how to make her scream, and right now, an opera worthy performance seemed likely. "You're ready for me," he said, a smug note in his tone.

If she could move, she'd smack him for stating the obvious. Luckily, he didn't expect an answer. Instead, he pulled up her leg, and slid into her warmth. Her muscles tightened around him in welcome. He groaned and laid his forehead on top of hers.

Nothing compared to the way he made her feel. It was like coming home. For a moment she basked in the sense of fulfillment as they lay, content, connected.

"Love me," Brenda whispered into the quiet of the room. He pulled her closer to him, rubbing her stomach.

Months ago, when she'd first said those words, he'd tensed. Now, he understood she couldn't say the more vulgar term. What she did with him wasn't fucking. Not the way her heart reacted whenever he was near, or whenever he touched her, or whenever he loved her. For her, they made love, always had.

"Whatever my lady desires."

He started with smooth, gentle strokes. He always started their morning love-fest this way. The beat of her heart picked up, anticipating the next phase. In a few moments he'd become more aggressive. Then, he'd hit his groove and take it up another level. That's when she'd be transported to a realm he'd created for her alone. There was no thought or conversation. Their bodies communicated sublime pleasure, yoking them together in a way she couldn't explain and didn't bother to try. Quite simply, the man freed her from some unknown prison deep within herself. He pistoned into her, his hips flexing, pounding. She lost focus as her orgasm erupted and flung her past reason into a pool of bliss. Stiffening as the sensations spiraled and tightened; she released herself to his care, knowing they'd make the crossing together. Gasping for air, waves of pleasure rolled through her, leaving her shaking. Hearing his shout of passion, she tightened her vaginal walls to give him an extra jolt of satisfaction. He shuddered as his hand tightened on her toned thigh in appreciation. It was a moment before either of them could talk.

Chest heaving, she rolled to her stomach as he slipped from between her thighs. His palm stroked her ass, providing comfort and keeping them physically connected. She sighed, enjoying her early morning post-coital glow. Slumberous, she wondered if she had time for a nap before starting her day. A stinging slap on her butt made her jump. Turning around, her eyes squinted as Roark left the bed. Watching his tight ass flex as he walked away erased the glare she'd meant to send him. This was one view she never tired of seeing. The man had a perfect body and delicious cheeks. And for this space in time, he was all hers. Fingers crossed, he'd be hers for a lot longer.

"What're you doing today?" He asked, pulling clothes from the closet. Roark stood two or three inches over six feet; his wide muscular chest and thick arms were football-player worthy. Seriously, the man could compete with the best of them. It never failed to amaze her how graceful he was for such a big man. His clothes always fit just right, accentuating his physique. His thick mahogany colored hair stuck out all over his head, but after he finished dressing he'd look as though he just stepped out of the pages of GQ.

"I have some class work, and then some things I need to take care of around here," she answered in her best neutral tone.

One of the reasons she would always love this man was his encouragement that she finish college. Even though her classes were with an online university, she felt a sense of accomplishment from getting her education back on track.

A knot formed in her throat; she was so happy, it scared her. She had a good man who appreciated her, she was on track to complete her education, and she had a safe place to live. Goosebumps rippled over her skin when her thoughts skipped sideways. An irrational spike of fear touched her, as though her situation wasn't real, as though it were a simple fairy tale. Pushing back the scalding panic, she swallowed hard while picking at lint on the sheet.

Roark frowned. "What do you plan to do here? I told you not to worry about cleaning and stuff, I have someone who comes in and takes care of that."

"Pfft." She dashed under the cover, cutting him off. This was an old argument between them. For some reason he didn't, or wouldn't, understand her need to contribute something, anything. She didn't work and had no money to pay even a portion of the rent or buy groceries. And despite his argument that he'd invited her to live with him, she didn't want to feel like she was a guest. This meant she couldn't just lie around and do nothing.

Besides, she enjoyed taking care of him. Cooking his meals, washing and folding his clothes, and making sure things were comfortable when he came home. It fed her fantasy of her as Lady of the Castle. Of course, the sex was the crème de la crème and she'd offer herself to him on the dining room table, legs up, complete with an apple in her mouth, to make sure he didn't stop giving it to her on a regular basis. A woman had needs, and Roark met every one of them.

"I feel like baking. I want to try a recipe I found last week." Pushing the covers back, she rose up on her elbows so she could watch him in the bathroom mirror. His sexy silhouette in the shower tempted her to join him. Experience had taught her he'd love her company, and would blow her mind with his creative flexibility. However, some days her voyeuristic nature came out, and she just liked to watch the byplay of his muscles on his arms, chest, stomach, and long legs. Sometimes, when they had time, he'd allow her to touch him all over with the pads of her fingers.

He grinned as he walked out the shower drying his hair, and then his chest. "Get an eyeful?"

At ease with his teasing, she whirled her fingers around, signaling for him to turn. He complied, giving her a better view. Releasing a loud whistle, she licked her lips and rubbed her stomach. "Um, um, um. That's a serious side of beef right there." She rolled to the side when he threw the towel at her. "I want that ass." She deepened her voice, mocking him. Recently, he'd been hinting for anal sex.

"I want your ass." He turned and gazed at her, his eyes turned dark as they swept over her nude body from head to toe. "One day, I'mma get it."

Heat, like a warm wind, blew across her skin at his determined look. Swallowing hard, she pulled the sheet up her waist slowly. "We'll see," she said feeling bashful all of a sudden. She might start the teasing, but he always seemed to finish it.

He smirked and winked. "I want to take you out to dinner tonight, so don't cook."

Shyness forgotten, she squealed as she jumped up. "Really? Where?"

He shook his head and pulled on a pair of dark dress pants. "We go out every week, and you still get excited." Pouting, she slapped his chest.

"Ow." He leaned back, caught her hand and placed a kiss in the middle of it before releasing it to finish dressing. She shrugged and sat on the side of the bed, waiting for him to finish.

"We've had Italian, Mexican, Chinese, and what else?' He glanced at her. She unknowingly enticed him as she sat with her legs crossed and the sheet draped haphazardly across her thighs as she tried to remember all the places they'd gone.

"Eeep." The startled sound escaped her mouth. Her hands flew to his shoulders for stabilization when he dropped to his knees, snatched away the sheet, and pulled her, naked and willing, towards him. His face dipped between her legs and kissed her crotch. Watching him stirred a fluttering sensation in her chest. They didn't talk about feelings, she wasn't exactly sure how he felt about her, but she knew this man had her heart locked up tight.

His tongue teased her, and despite their vigorous romp a few minutes ago, her body reacted to the need stamped on his face. Within seconds, she ached in places only he could assuage. A deep-seated hunger roared to life as he stroked her dripping pussy.

"I don't really care where we go, I just want to take you somewhere. Maybe go see a movie before or do some dancing after." He glanced up at her, his eyes twinkling at her quick breaths. Unable to talk and not willing to be teased, she scooted backward.

He pulled her forward. "I just need a snack to tide me over until tonight." He pulled her legs apart and licked her clit again.

Her breath hitched. Frozen by her need, she couldn't move. Roark pushed her back and lifted her ass. "You won't deny me that, will you?" He kissed her crotch again.

"N-n-nooo." Her eyes rolled back, her head thrashed as he licked, suckled and finger-fucked her. Over the past months, he'd become adept at mastering her body. He knew exactly where and how to touch her body to make her cum. Within minutes, she shuddered under the force of her orgasm while he continued licking and lapping up her juices.

After Roark finished dressing, he kissed her good-bye. Inert, her hand flopped to the bed in a semi-wave goodbye as she fell asleep. *Man, what a way to start the day.*

****

Brenda closed the oven with her hip and placed the pan of walnut-filled brownies on the counter-top. The warmth of the kitchen, coupled with the aromatic smell of chocolate, filled her with a sense of completeness. She'd taken a chance moving in with Roark, the man had been a stranger of sorts, but the attraction between them had been immediate and bone deep. She was no psychic and didn't claim God had told her he was safe, but somehow, she knew he'd be good for her. Turns out, she was good for him, too. They meshed.

The melodic sounds of Jennifer Hudson blared from her cell. Wiping her hands on a paper towel before grabbing her phone, she grimaced at the mess she'd made in the sink.

"Hello." She ran the water to clean the bowls and utensils without glancing at the caller ID.

"Hey, how's it going? I figured I'd call you, since you're too busy getting laid to call your girl."

Brenda laughed. "Don't start. I didn't want to bother you. I know you're planning your wedding and everything." She knew that wouldn't fly and wasn't surprised when Denise called her on it.

"Riiiiight. Last I checked, you were *in* my wedding. But I'd never know since you haven't returned my calls or emails with your shoe size. Don't get mad at me if you're wearing boats walking down the aisle. All you had to do was send me the damn size! I know you ain't had no real loving in a while, but Bren, it's been six whole months. You gotta let your cat breathe girl, give her a break. Take her for a walk or something. You can't be on that pole all the time!"

Laughing, Brenda collapsed onto a chair. Denise had saved her sanity on more than one occasion with her wacky humor. They'd met in college their first year and had hit it off immediately. The night Denise met her fiancé Irish, better known as Red, who was also Roark's older brother, the two of them had been in the club hanging out. She'd been happy Denise had given Red a chance, and despite a bunch of challenges, the two were finally getting married after eight years and two beautiful little girls.

"I know, but damn, the man is seriously fine. I can't help myself." Brenda took the brownies out of the pan and placed them on a plate.

"If he's anything like his brother, and no, I don't want to know if he is, then I understand why it's hard to come up for air. Shit, they ruin you for anybody else. Can't many men flip and then floss you with one hand. To be so big, they're flexible as hell."

Brenda wondered what Denise and Red got into. "Flip, floss? Girl, you got a kinky side to be a preacher's kid."

Denise laughed. "After eight years with an O'Connor male, I'm doing good to only be into kink. You remember Red's brothers, the twins?"

Brenda snorted. "Hell, yeah. Fine, but I can't imagine the stuff they get into. Bondage and spanking." Although she enjoyed the love taps Roark gave her, she wasn't sure if she'd be interested in more. Shrugging off the visual, she remembered Roark's older twin brothers. The men lived an alternative lifestyle in a huge house near the Pennsylvanian mountains. Denise had told her they had servants and were seriously into BDSM.

"Well, they're in the wedding and everyone's waiting to see who they bring to the wedding."

"Everyone?" she asked, her tone dry. Denise had a dramatic flair. Brenda doubted anyone cared who the twins brought to the wedding, certainly not Red, Roark or their older brother.

"Don't you want to know?"

"No. I don't know them that well. It doesn't matter to me."

"Well, it might if you and Roark are next." Twins forgotten, Brenda's heart tripped at Denise's words. Had Roark said anything to Red? Everyone knew Red couldn't hold water, if he knew something he would've told Denise.

"We're not there yet." She spoke softly, with a hint of inquiry in her voice. It wouldn't pay to be too eager for information, even though her heart beat a fast melody in her chest.

"But you want to be, don't you?" Brenda could imagine the sly look on Denise's face, fishing for information.

"Who wouldn't? Roark is…he's perfect." She ended the last word on a whispery sigh, taken up with the wonder of their relationship. The men in her past took her for granted, worse, she allowed it. For some reason, whenever she tried to break up with the dead-beats she'd dated, a switch would flip in her mind, she'd become terrified of being left alone. Worse was the obsession that if she didn't go along, put up with the bullshit, she'd have nobody.

"No man is perfect." Denise's swift correction sounded harsh, shattering her bubble.

Grumbling, she slumped in the chair at the table, her mood soured. "I know he's not perfect, he's human. I meant he's perfect for me. I really like him."

"I know." Denise dragged out the two words, making them sound like some part of a chorus. "Everybody knows you like him. Hell, even the twins know how much you like their Uncle Roark. Question, what're you going to do about it? Where do you see this going?"

Oh no, Brenda groaned, straightening and then placing her forehead on the tabletop in dismay. Detective Denise was on the prowl. She glanced at the clock and released a breath. Denise should be picking up the twins in another hour. All she had to do was stall, change the subject, or create a nuclear bomb. Her chances of achieving any of those things had similar odds of success.

Nil. Nada. Zero.

Her tone light, Brenda took the plunge and answered. "It's only been six months. Trying to plan a future might jinx what we have. I wanna enjoy each day to the fullest without thinking long term. That way, I get to be with him without stressing about tomorrow. It's good. I'm enjoying this time, getting to know him better. We get along great. He appreciates everything I do, cook, or decorate. He's neat, smart, and always considers what I want to do. Like I said, we're just taking our time, learning one another." Nerves frayed from the question, her rambling answers came out choppy, disjointed. Why couldn't she just say none of your business? Because she knew her friend was asking out of genuine concern, that's why. She needed to butch up and deal with the discussion.

"You love him."

Brenda's eyes widened a bit, her mouth opened and closed in silence. Since it was a statement, she didn't respond. Not that Denise gave her an opportunity before barreling on.

"I can tell you love him. Roark's a good man. At least you won't be spending your Mondays trying to get bail money to get him out of jail for being stupid over the weekend, or picking him up from the hospital because he got into a fight."

"Stop!" Brenda's voice rose. Her heart slammed against her chest, her jaw flexed in and out. The haze of her remembered anger and embarrassment had her teetering on the precipice of despair. She'd promised herself she'd never make that particular journey ever again. Yet if

Denise was right, she'd stepped into it again.

A few deep breaths helped stop the rage from consuming her. Teeth gritted, she lashed out. "You're my girl, and I know you mean well. I understand my past is a part of who I am; I want to believe I endured those experiences and came out better for it. But I don't reminisce on hard-ass lessons learned. What I want to build with Roark is clean and separate from that time in my life. I cannot afford to draw parallels; there are none because *I* was different then." She exhaled. Her head throbbed as she beat the memories back into their cage and put it away in a dark corner of her mind. "I don't talk about it. Okay?"

"I'm sorry, Bren. Zip it, lock it, and put it in my pocket." Denise's low voice thrummed with pain and humility.

The tension ebbed as Brenda laughed. "You're spending too much time at the twins' school."

"I know." Denise chuckled. "I'm happy for you. Believe that. It's definitely your turn to laugh in the sunshine. You're one of the nicest people I know. Beautiful inside and out, Roark's lucky to have you."

Brenda closed her eyes as they filled with tears. Her heart lurched at Denise's words. If anyone knew the hell she'd gone through with Bruce, aka Tex, her girlfriend did.

"Thanks." She sniffed. "Now tell me what I need to do to make sure my shoes are right for the wedding, because I'm not wearing any boo-boo shoes down the aisle."

Chapter 2

Roark drove to his office, whistling some off-key tune he'd heard on the radio the day before. If he had to give an accounting for his upbeat mood, he'd be hard-pressed to pinpoint one particular thing. Especially when all thoughts led to the beautiful sexy woman living in his home. *Brenda Washington.* Several months ago, he'd rescued Brenda from some bullies looking to hurt her because she'd warned Denise about some trouble about to go down. It'd been a good tip. Denise had gone looking for Red so they could leave, but found him lying on the floor instead, shot.

The moment Roark laid eyes on Brenda in the restaurant; her eyes wide with terror, his life had changed. He'd been hard-pressed not to push the blade further into the crotch of the asshole who'd placed that look on her face and threatened her in his presence. She had looked at him with a wealth of gratitude, and surprisingly enough, female interest. Her large doe-shaped eyes had spoken of her loneliness, and her apprehension at involving Denise in her troubles. From that moment, he made it his goal to erase the former and eradicate the latter.

After a few weeks with his Nubian goddess, he'd recognized the truth. Without trying, she'd enslaved his heart. There was nothing he wouldn't do to make her smile. After discovering she'd lost her home, he'd moved quickly to ensconce her in his world by inviting her to live with him. *The woman was his.* They connected on so many levels, he wondered if he'd ever been serious about a woman before.

Brenda understood him in ways that should've taken years, instead of months for her to know. Too many of his friends had settled for half-baked romances and later regretted rushing to the altar. He'd dated more than his share of women, but he'd never wanted to share his home with anyone before. There were lots of things in his past he'd change if he could, but he couldn't, so he made the best of his life. Each day cemented his decision to share the rest of his life with Brenda.

Minutes later, he pulled into a parking spot at the three-storied office building his brothers owned. He and his partner, Benjamin, aka Ben, owned an investment company on the second floor. They'd been roommates in college. After graduation, they'd worked at competing banks and investment firms for a few years to gain a little polish before finally deciding to open their own company. Things were rocky at first, but after a few years, they had built up a solid client base and reached some of their benchmarks. After nodding to the security guard at the entry desk, Roark accessed the elevator to his office floor.

"Good morning, Jeff." He nodded to one of his researchers as he headed to his office. He planned to accomplish quite a lot today. High on his list was putting the final changes on a surprise trip to the Cayman Islands with Brenda. The travel agent had sent over the final documents yesterday and he planned to spring it on her tonight at dinner. In less than ten days, they'd be laying in the sunshine on the beach, sipping wine; the perfect setting to speak his heart and ask her to share his life.

****

"Hey," Benjamin said, walking in his office later that day. "It's past time to grab a bite to eat, you interested?"

Roark nodded as he shut down his computer. "Sounds good, give me a minute." He'd made decent headway into his to-do list and felt comfortable giving his eyes a break.

His partner nodded at the vacation brochures sitting on Roark's desk, and sat in the stuffed chair near the desk. "Have you told her yet?"

"No. Tonight, at dinner." Standing, Roark checked his pocket for his keys and wallet. Satisfied, he walked toward the door. Benjamin stood and followed him out. They waited silently at the elevator, watching the activity on the floor. Roark enjoyed the busy atmosphere of his firm; it added to the illusion that things were constantly being done. For the most part, he was correct. They ran a productive company.

The elevator doors opened. Roark was surprised to see Blaine and Donald, his older brothers, inside. Although they owned the building, it was uncommon to see them together at work. Donald's law practice took up the first floor; and Blaine, a financial analyst, occupied the third floor.

"Hey, guys." Roark smiled and reached out to Blaine, who grabbed him in a bear hug, while nodding at Ben.

"Good to see you, lil' bro," Blaine teased, slapping him on his back.

"Younger, not little-ler," Roark corrected automatically as he grabbed Donald in an embrace. All three men were the same height. The twins might have been a tad heavier, but not by much, at least that was Roark's opinion.

"Definitely not smaller." Blaine slapped his back and nodded to Ben as the elevator doors closed.

"Where you guys heading?" Roark asked, genuinely glad to see his brothers. The last time he'd seen them had been right after they'd returned from the escapade dealing with Red in Michigan. Hell, that'd been a long time.

"Thought we'd grab a bite to eat. We were on our way to get you since we hadn't seen you in a while." Donald paused after glancing at Ben. "Are you heading to a business deal or something?"

Roark laughed. He knew Ben was curious about his brothers, and he had asked a few questions about their lifestyle. Obviously Donald's keen eye, which served him well as an attorney, had picked up something about Ben. Shrugging it off, he answered since Ben remained quiet.

"Just a late lunch, I got busy and forgot to eat. Where are you guys going?" He figured they'd eat together and catch up. Being the boss had its perks, especially when it came to taking long lunch breaks.

"Delmonico's. I'm hungry for something more substantial." Blaine looked at Ben. "What about you, Ben. You ready for something more?"

Roark stiffened, picking up on the undercurrents, but remained quiet. Ben was a grown man and if his reddening face was any indication, he understood the conversation just fine.

They all exited the elevator and headed toward the exit. Ben looked through the glass doors as he answered. "I'm not sure. But I think I'll have something light. I have plans for later tonight."

Blaine nodded.

Donald smiled.

Roark sensed something major had just happened, but was clueless to the particulars. In college, Ben had experimented a lot with his sexuality and was open to most things. They'd had only one discussion on sex. Roark had made it clear he was interested in women only, pain did nothing for him, games were a waste of time, and he couldn't imagine a relationship with more than one female at a time.

****

Donald patted his lips with the red cloth napkin, then placed it across his plate. "That was good. Nothing beats a well-seasoned steak cooked to perfection." He patted his trim waistline.

Erosa Knowles

Page 14

Blaine smiled, but remained silent as he placed his napkin on his plate as well. He'd eaten every bit of a large portion of grilled salmon and vegetables.

Roark was glad they'd come into town; the atmosphere at the restaurant was soothing and the food excellent. He refused Donald's offer of a beer or a glass of wine, since he planned to return to work. The beef medallions were excellent as always. "Thanks, this was a good idea." He patted his mouth with the cloth napkin before laying it on his empty plate.

"When are you leaving for Michigan?" Blaine asked, looking at Roark.

"I'm not sure. I think a few days after we come back from the Cayman Islands. Brenda made the reservations, so I'll have to check." He ignored Donald's raised brow and took a sip of his iced water.

"Brenda? Denise's friend from Michigan? From the restaurant?" Blaine asked.

Roark nodded before meeting his brother's eyes. "Yeah, that's her."

"She's still here?" Donald asked, his eyes wide.

"Obviously." Roark said in his driest tone. Both men watched him; he could hear the questions rumbling through their minds. If they asked him anything, he'd have been surprised. They didn't.

Ben broke the silence. "My steak was a little tough. I think next time I'll have it medium rare rather than well-done." All eyes turned to him as he wiped his mouth with his napkin.

Roark grinned. One of the reasons they got along so well was Ben knew when to charge and when to retreat. He also knew how serious Roark was about Brenda, and how nervous he was about being so serious so soon.

"I think we're flying out three days before the wedding. Since ma has got us doing some running around for her and daddy, we're getting out of here early so we can have a little down time." Blaine canted his head toward Donald, who nodded in agreement before speaking.

"She's so excited about one of us getting married, I think she'd shoot the sheriff if anything happened to stop her wedding." Donald snorted and glanced at Roark, his face a mask of disbelief. "She actually calls it her wedding."

Blaine picked up the sentence. "Denise just allows her to add anything she wants. This was supposed to be a small affair, but since mama took over, it's turned into a major pain in the ass." Blaine shook his head in misery. He glanced at Roark. "How much did she hit you up for?"

Confused, Roark stared at him. "Who?"

Both Donald and Blaine straightened, glaring at his confused face. "Mama. How much did she hit you up for the wedding?"

"Red's wedding?" The conversation had flipped from Brenda to the wedding, to paying for the wedding. He didn't grasp what they were talking about. They nodded. "Nothing," he said, confused. Why would his mama ask him for money to pay for his younger brother's wedding? If she'd asked, it wouldn't have been a problem. But she hadn't.

"What the hell?" Blaine whispered.

Donald's hand raked through his thick dark hair, yanking the ends as his lips pressed together in a tight line. He looked at Blaine. For a moment, Roark thought they were communicating mentally or something. When they burst out laughing, he gave the possibility a lot more consideration.

"At least she's backed off trying to get us to the altar," Blaine said in a relieved tone.

"Yeah, could've been worse," Donald agreed as he picked up his beer.

"What?" Roark asked. "What did mama do?" Still out of the loop.

Blaine chuckled as he leaned forward. "Between the two of us," he pointed to his twin, "ma hit us up for about twenty grand to help pay for the things she felt Denise and Red should have in their wedding. Never mind the fact Red is sitting on a damn nest egg, she decided the wedding would be her gift to the couple."

"Which means we're paying for it." Donald nodded.

"What about Frank? Did he help?" Roark asked, surprised he hadn't heard about any of this. He'd make sure to call his mom after he returned to his office.

Donald shrugged. "It's possible. Last time I talked to him he'd taken some time off." He paused dramatically. His eyes twinkled. "Personal time."

Roark choked on his water. "Whhhat?"Frank never took personal time unless it was for relatives. What had been going on in his family? No one kept him updated with the latest news. "Did you say Frank, my oldest brother, took personal time off from his job? His company. His baby."

Donald nodded. A smile split his face as he looked at Blaine. The two weren't identical, although you could definitely tell they were brothers.

"Must be something in the water." Blaine stared at Roark.

"Ma didn't ask me for money for the wedding," Roark said quickly avoiding Blaine's gaze. His brother waved off the comment.

"No biggie, as long as she's not hounding us about getting married it's worth it. But now I'm wondering if she's made you her target." Blaine's fingertips tapped the table-top as if he were weighing something. "Has she met Brenda?"

Roark nodded slowly. "Remember we flew Denise, Brenda, and Ross's lady to mom's while we handled things in Michigan." His eyes flew to Blaine and then Donald, cringing at the pity in their depths. Although he planned a future with Brenda, he wasn't up for outside meddling. His mama was a one-woman crusader whose mission in life was to see her sons happy. In her world that meant 'Married with Kids.'

"You don't think...."

The twins nodded.

"But I haven't said anything...."

"Mama knows everything. I bet she hasn't been bugging you about coming home for a visit, has she?" Blaine asked in a knowing tone.

Roark's heart raced as he realized the woman who'd birthed him was behaving completely out of character. Normally, she called him weekly for an update on his life. He'd been so engrossed with Brenda, he hadn't noticed they hadn't talked in at least two months. And that was *not* the way his mama operated.

"No." He wet his lips. "Actually, I haven't talked to her in a couple of months." He glanced at his brothers who shook their heads.

"You know better than that." Donald chuckled. "Even taking our money, she still manages to get her calls in. Nope, l'il brother, mama has you in her sites as her next project. She's giving you time to get used to the idea of having a woman around full time…"

"Getting the hang of married life." Blaine finished. "Be prepared for a talk at the wedding. If mama hasn't interfered by now, it means she approves of Brenda and wants you to make it work." Standing, Blaine clasped Roark's shoulder. "Don't fuck it up. As far as ma's concerned, Brenda's her daughter-in-law."

"But, but how?" He hated how his voice shook at the implications. He and Brenda hadn't even said the *L* word to each other yet. And even though he was sure of his feelings for her, he wasn't sure of hers for him.

Donald stood and looked down at him. "How many women have you lived with?"

Roark frowned. "None until now."

"Bingo. That means she's special. Remember when daddy told us how he knew mama was special, the one for him."

Thunderstruck, Roark could only nod.

"Well, welcome to their world. Mama believes in that. The fact that you haven't shown this kind of interest in any other woman tilted the scales. You say you're taking her away on a trip? And that she made the reservations for the wedding?"

"Yeah, but she's in the wedding. That doesn't prove anything." Roark tried to defend his actions, although with each word he saw exactly how his relationship with Brenda must look to his mom. He'd never been seriously involved with a woman before and no one had ever stayed in his home past a day or two. He valued his space and independence too much. Yet, he'd invited her to stay with him just a few days after meeting her.

"Did she use your credit card to pay for the reservations, or her own?" Donald dropped the question into the silence. Ben stood, threw some bills down and walked to the door, leaving the three brothers alone at the table.

"Does it matter?" Roark asked, watching as his brothers summed up the situation.

"It doesn't matter to me," Donald said, placing some bills next to the check. "I want you to be happy. Brenda makes you happy, that's great."

Blaine shrugged as he stuck his hands in his pockets after glancing at the check. "It only matters in the grand scheme of things. No man lets a casual interest use his credit cards, or live with him for months at a time. Looking at you, I'd say you're content, possibly happy. That's a good thing. Go for it. Just don't be surprised that people on the outside are watching and expecting certain things from your actions. Despite what you think, your actions scream even when your mouth's silent. If you don't plan to be with this woman long term, then know you're in for a battle," he paused with a grin, "from mama."

Roark stood and smiled, although it felt brittle on his face. No one liked being pushed and that's how he felt. "For the record, I really like her."

Blaine slapped his back. "I figured that."

"I mean a lot." He stared stubbornly at the twins. For a moment no one spoke.

Donald broke the silence. "Good to know and congratulations."

"Congratulations?" Roark frowned at the word. This talking in circles tired him.

"Yeah, finding the right one for you and falling in love is rare." Blaine added, walking slightly ahead.

Roark wondered at the wistfulness in his brother's voice. "Thanks for the heads up about ma, I completely missed that. I need to prepare Brenda. I don't want her to run." The three men laughed as they reached the door.

Chapter 3

The cavernous room smelled like rotten cabbage and old cheese. Tex and his men searched through rows of both opened and unopened boxes, tossing some to the side in their frustration. The tip he'd received had assured him his product had been stored in this warehouse that whoever was stealing music compact disks and new movie releases on DVD's didn't stop with just those two profitable items. Tex knocked aside boxes containing new text books, new baby clothes, items still in plastic, and cases of new shoes in all styles and sizes. He had no idea how they kept up with their entire inventory and after tonight, it wouldn't matter.

"Tex!" He looked up and saw Hector, one of his men, pointing to an open box on the floor. Sweeping his heavy black trench coat to the side, he strode in that direction. Anger raced through him when he saw the five missing cases of new music CDs and one case of movie DVDs. Those boxes had sent him and his men scurrying to comb the streets before his boss returned to town. Some asshole would definitely feel the bite of his rage for this infraction.

Silently, they removed the six cases from the warehouse and loaded them into one of their black SUVs in the side alley. Tex sent two of his men to return the merchandise to their warehouse, and to stand guard until he and the other six men returned. It would never be enough to tell Rafe, his boss and partner of sorts, that they had recovered the stolen merchandise; he'd also need to explain why it wouldn't happen again.

Fanning out around the large space, his men took positions. Tex planned his line of attack as he waited in the darkened building for the thieves to return so he could render his own brand of justice. It was critical that this breach never happen again.

Sitting in one of only three chairs in the warehouse, Tex eyed the rows of unwieldy merchandise and wondered how someone had managed to steal from him. Anyone in his tightly-held group of electronic engineers could have broken the rules and said something to someone. But everyone who worked with him downloading and copying music or movies received a percentage of the profits; he couldn't see them cutting off the source of their own money. Cracking his knuckles, his eyes slid to a darkened corner of the room. He thought he'd heard a sound. Another footfall. Using hand signals, he ordered his men to surround him and the group trying to sneak up on them. He could hear it was more than one. His brow furrowed deeply as he sat forward in his seat, his pistol in his hand.

"I'm not sure what they expected, but it wasn't what they got." The female voice sounded familiar, Tex listened harder as the voices came closer. The metal door scraped open, a second later the lights blinked a few times and then remained on.

"It didn't matter anyway. We got this." A masculine voice spoke. There was some laughter and the thud of the door closing. Tension coiled within him at the coming confrontation. Tex trusted his men to disarm anyone before things got too hot. The footfalls walked away from him, and then they split up. He could hear their voices, but couldn't make out their words.

Frustrated because things weren't going to plan, he moved to stand, then hesitated when he felt the cold metal of a gun pressed against his neck.

"Don't move." The husky, yet feminine voice came from behind him, pressing the weapon into his jugular. "Take his gun."

A short, Hispanic female walked in front of him, dark eyes flashing as she moved to pull the gun from his hand. He refused to let go, and instead reached out in a flash, grabbed the small woman, and pointed his gun at her head. From behind him, he heard the startled gasp of the woman holding the gun on him. Still holding her gun against his neck, she slowly moved into his line of vision.

"Tex?" she whispered, her light brown eyes wide with fear. Red-faced, she lowered her gun under his unwavering glare. "What?...what are you doing here?"

"Shut the fuck up," he growled at the woman he hated most in the world. His stomach clenched as rage boiled fast and furious in his gut. Memories of the havoc this bitch had caused him and the one woman he'd ever loved flew unchecked through his mind. He gut-checked his ire and focused on Anna, his ex-girlfriend's sister. The tiny woman in his arms scratched at his arms for release, trying to burrow beneath his coat with her nails. "Tell this wildcat to stop before I snap her neck." The seriousness of his tone caused both women to look at him, panic soaring in their eyes. The Hispanic woman whimpered as a shudder wracked her frame.

Loud voices grabbed his attention. He watched the calculating gleam reach Anna's eyes as she realized he wasn't alone.

"Please try something," he deadpanned, pointing his gun at her chest. "I couldn't do it before, but I'll damn sure put a bullet in your lying ass now and burn this shit to the ground. It'll be weeks before they identify your ass." A sweet calm came over him as her eyes widened and then squinted in anger. Finally, after all these years, he'd have his revenge on one of the people who'd made his life hell.

"Tex?" one of his men yelled. Voices rose, asking questions.

"Over here." He signaled for Anna to sit on one of the boxes near his feet. She rolled her eyes and plopped down on the cardboard. A moment later, four men and two women were corralled into the small area where he held court. He released the pint-sized Latina, pushing her toward Anna. His brow rose at the intimate manner in which Anna held and stroked the smaller woman.

"Which way did you come in?" Tex asked Anna. She rolled her eyes at him. He grinned and looked at Hector. "Take her. Make her show you how she came up behind me. I want every access point covered in this bitch."

Hector, a huge Asian-Hispanic male looked at Anna, his grin feral as he stepped in her direction. The pint-size Latina launched herself in Hector's direction. He sidestepped her and she landed in a heap on top of two of her teammates. The cocking sound of guns stopped all action except Hector's. With one hand, he lifted a fighting Anna from where she'd scooted between two large containers as Hector came toward her. She pulled her hand back, and swung. Hector caught her fist mid-air and squeezed.

"If you hit him, he will hit you back. You fight, he'll fight. As long as you do as he tells you, you won't get hurt…not too bad anyway." Tex enjoyed the fear that leapt into Anna's eyes before she banked it. Bullies always came up against someone bigger and badder than them eventually.

Tex smirked as Hector stalked off with a still-kicking Anna under his arm. His smirk turned into a full-fledged grin at the tell-tale sound of flesh smacking flesh. An ass whooping was long overdue for that bitch, she'd hurt others without thinking twice.

Refocusing on business, he sent two of his men to secure the exits they knew about. The remaining three men took positions around the small group as Tex asked his questions.

"Merchandise was stolen from my warehouse two days ago, I found it here. I want to know how it got here." His eyes hardened as he looked into the face of each person in the small group. There had to be more people involved, there was too much stuff in this warehouse for this small band to handle.

"What'd you lose?" A dark-complexioned man, possibly of Indian descent, asked as he pushed up his glasses.

Jaw clenched, fist balled, Tex glared at him. "I didn't lose a damn thing. Some asshole stole cases of music CDs and DVDs from my warehouse."

A gasp rent the silence.

He swiveled to locate the owner of the sound. The small Latina's face had reddened to the color of a cherry tomato. When he looked at her, she turned away, keeping her gaze leveled at the concrete floor.

"Now that you know what I lost, somebody'd better start talking." He infused a thread of deadly intent into his voice as he stood, legs braced apart, the pistol in his right hand lowered for the moment. The more he thought of the bold move to enter his domain and steal his shit, the madder he became. "Let me see if I understand this, you muthafuckers don't plan to explain why my shit was all up in your place?" His voice lowered as his fury rose. Heart slamming against his chest, his left fist clenched and unclenched. He raised his pistol.

"No!" The Indian-looking guy glanced at his comrades before speaking fast. "You don't understand how this works. We," he pointed to the others around him, "don't know the owners. We come in, catalog the stuff, put it in the computer, and then we leave. That's all. I've never been here during the day and have no idea where the stuff comes from or where it goes when it leaves here. We come in and count. That's it, I swear." His voice had risen to a pleading quality. Tex looked at the motley crew. The women's eyes were filled with tears, a couple of the guys' eyes were as well. The small Latina still hadn't looked at him.

"Who's the night-time supervisor?" he demanded, tired of wasting time. He needed to get back to his warehouse and make sure things were straight.

Before anyone could speak, the Latina's eyes flashed at him. "I am."

The look she gave everyone else dared them to contradict her. He had a feeling that's exactly what would happen if he talked to them one by one.

Tex pointed to the large, black female sitting behind the woman who'd just spoke. "Come here." Her eyes widened in fear, but she pushed herself up and moved in his direction. The entire time the smaller woman's eyes threw daggers at him. He waved his men to tighten the circle as he walked a few feet away.

When he was sure they couldn't be overheard, he asked, "How'd my shit get here?"

Her lips trembled and tears rolled down her dark cheeks. She brushed at them while trying to speak. "I don't know." Her words were so warbled, he barely made them out. She licked her thick lips. "I…I never saw CDs or DVDs. We, we don't usually see those." Tex thought back, the cases had been sealed until he'd had his men open them. He half-listened as she told him how she'd only taken the job for extra money.

"Who's your supervisor?" He cut off her rambling.

Her eyes blinked in surprise. "Anna," she whispered.

Inwardly, he smiled. The tension in his back eased, he could legitimately deal with Anna in a manner his boss would approve. Someone would pay for what happened tonight. He knew, without asking, Anna was aware the CDs were in the building. She probably had no idea who they belonged to, but that was beside the point.

"Who owns this company?"

The woman looked at him with a blank expression.

"The name on your pay check? Who pays you?" He glanced at the group behind her, irritated that this was taking so long.

She swallowed so hard, he thought she'd gag. When she spoke, her eyes filled with rebellious tears. "We get paid in cash."

Damn. He turned and strode back to the group, intent on calling one of the males when a weeping Anna and grinning Hector returned. The moment Hector released Anna, she hastened to her group. The large woman he'd just interviewed returned as well.

Tex met Hector halfway.

"There was a side door we missed." Hector spoke in a lowered voice, his back to the others. Tex watched Anna and the Latina spitfire. There was definitely something going on between those two. "I secured it and found the office. Nice set up, a bit tedious if you ask me, too much overhead. Everyone's paid in cash, no one knows who owns the set-up. She claims she got the job through a friend, but doesn't know much more."

"She's lying," Tex said with absolute certainty. "What I need to know is how she got our shit over here. Is there a threat we need to deal with?"

Hector shrugged before turning, his gaze cold. "She and the small one will have more answers. I can take them to the office and find out what we need to know."

Tex was tempted to allow Hector to use his form of interrogation on his nemesis. A euphoric feeling filled him at the thought of her broken and beaten. A similar image of Brenda flashed in his mind. He stiffened.

"You okay?" Hector stepped in front of him.

It took him a moment to focus, to rein in the horrible pictures polluting his psyche. Taking a deep breath, he reassessed the situation. First off, he had no idea who they were dealing with. One thing for sure, this was no small-time operation. Secondly, he needed to know the mechanics of the breech in his own operation. He assumed the only person in this room who might be able to answer that question was Anna. But he couldn't take any chances and overlook the other employees.

"I'm good." He waved off the big guy's concern. "I want you to take each person into the office and ask them who owns this joint, how they get paid, and what exactly they do."

Hector's brow rose in question.

"I don't want to torch the building without knowing who we're dealing with."

Hector nodded and stepped to the side.

"Another thing, I don't think they know a lot, so no violence unless it's provoked. They'll be interviewed again by whoever owns this place, make sure you say we just want to know who stole our shit and move on."

Finally, Hector understood the sensitivity of the situation and strode away to take the next person to the back.

Tex and his people were within their rights to ask questions and reclaim their shit. But not to mess over staff or destroy merchandise that wasn't theirs, at least not without knowing who or how big the operation was. Cash pay-outs, computerized databases, no heavy management, constant movement of merchandise; he was beginning to think this whole operation was too organized to be small.

Tex watched Anna lean heavily on the smaller woman as Hector walked off with the Indian male. Pointing to the other black female, Tex motioned for her to follow him. He took her to where he'd interviewed the first woman. It didn't surprise him that her answers were similar to the first woman. He and Hector finished at the same time and took the next two males. Anna's lips tightened as she watched him, and then Hector, leave the room. Within twenty minutes, they were finished interrogating everyone except Anna's friend. Hector pulled the small dynamo off Anna and bodily carried her to the back. Anna had jumped up to defend the woman, but sat back when one of his men pointed his gun at her.

Time passed and Tex still didn't know how his merchandise had magically moved from his secure warehouse to this place. He locked glares with Anna. She'd always been jealous of her younger sister and had gone out of her way to make Brenda miserable. His fist clenched with the need for retribution, not just for tonight, but for all of the nights he'd suffered because of this woman's lies and deceit. Thankfully, Brenda had stopped believing her sister and came to the realization of just how evil the bitch was. But the cost had been high, they'd still lost their son. His hackles rose again at the memory; his fists balled tighter. Anger suffused him again as he remembered her interference. Anna blanched at the look, possibly hate, that must've covered his face, and turned away.

Footsteps and light weeping sounds broke him out of the vicious funk enveloping him. Out the corner of his eye, he watched the small woman run to Anna, who held her tight, as a mother would a child. Was it possible? He searched his memory and couldn't remember her having any children that could be this age. Staring at the reunion between the two women, Tex waited for Hector to give him his take on the situation.

"You're right, there's someone big behind this. They get paid a grand a week, cash, to catalog this merchandise. If anyone comes in to watch them, they aren't aware of it. Although, someone could slip inside that side door and watch the floor by way of the cameras in the office, like I did. Anna is the supervisor, and Lola, the small one, is her assistant. The two are very close. One guy said he thought they were lovers. The only people allowed in the offices are those two women, but no one knows how the merchandise gets here during the day, not even Lola."

Tex nodded. He'd already made up his mind how he'd deal with Anna. That long overdue debt required payment. For now, he'd walk on the side of caution until he talked to Rafe. If they needed to do more, they could come back and handle it.

He moved forward a few steps and stared at Anna, the promise of her imminent demise in his eyes. That young, dumb man of his youth was dead; having been sacrificed on the altar of service when he gave his allegiance to the organization in which he now belonged. The past three years had shaped him into a cold, hard man his Brenda wouldn't appreciate or recognize. Very soon, Anna would discover the depth of his rage. Rage held in stasis since the day his son died.

Neutralizing his face, he turned to the assembled group. "Like I explained before, my merchandise was taken and I have retrieved it. I needed answers that none of you were able to provide." He paused as fear wafted off the people in the room. Eyes widened to ridiculous widths, jaws clenched, and sweat beaded up on shiny foreheads.

"I apologize if we made any of you uncomfortable, it was not our intentions. Thanks for your co-operation." He turned to look at Hector, who snorted. "You can go back to work now, if you want, we're done here." Tex ground out the words, his attempt at graciousness failing under the weight of his frustration.

"Oh, thank you." A sarcastic female voice said behind him.

Tex rolled his eyes at Hector before turning and motioning to his men to leave.

As they reached the front entrance, Tex looked up into the camera for a second. He knew Rafe would be hearing about this and wanted to be sure he covered his ass. His men brought up the rear as they stepped into the dark night. The rest of his team stood near the two SUVs and opened the doors. Piling in, they left the warehouse.

Tonight, Tex's past had caught up with him. It'd been two years since he'd seen Brenda. He'd finally stopped violating the restraining orders she'd been taking out against him. He'd made a stupid mistake, allowed himself to get caught up in Anna's web of lies, and done the unthinkable. Brenda had forgiven him much during their three-year relationship. But that night when he'd come home high, with Anna under his arm, had been the final straw. To this day, he didn't fully remember how Anna had gotten him high, or half-naked. What he did remember was pushing Brenda to the side when she tried to leave him. Even smashed, he knew life without her would be too difficult to bear. She'd fallen and lost their baby.

In the stillness of the night, when he allowed his mind to wander, he still heard her screams of pain, saw the blood and fluids running from between her legs. In the background he heard Anna's brash laugh, mocking them and their loss. He'd yelled at Anna to shut the fuck up and call the ambulance. He'd never forget what she told him.

"*I'm not doing shit for that bitch. I hope both she and that bastard in her belly die.*" He remembered clumsily swinging at her, but she laughed and ran out the room, taking his cell phone. One of their neighbors called the ambulance. When they were nearby, one of his friends pulled him to the side and told him Anna had been in his car before she left. Chances were good she'd planted some shit. That'd sobered him quickly. The sirens were coming closer. He glanced at the apartment where Brenda lay bleeding, losing his child, and then at the car that probably had enough illegal shit to send him to prison for a long time. As he drove off, he knew he'd made the biggest mistake of his life.

The next morning, Brenda refused to see him when he showed up at the hospital, a bunch of flowers in his hand and an apology on his lips. Their eyes locked that day and his heart dropped at the disappointment he read in hers. A block of ice filled his chest as she refused not only to listen to him, but to look at him as well. Something died within him that day.

True enough, Anna had left a couple of rocks of crack under the front seat of his car. His probation officer would never have believed the truth. He owed her big time, and finally he'd be able to pay.

****

The following night, Tex's eyes adjusted quickly to the darkened interior; the club was crowded. The band was finishing their set as he strolled to the bar. "Gin and tonic," he said to the harried bartender. The man nodded and a few minutes later, handed him his drink. Tex believed in rewarding good service, so he tipped the man heavily and walked off to track down information.

Searching the corners, he spied an old acquaintance and headed in his direction. Without speaking, he took the empty chair at the table. The smell of stale whiskey tinged his nostrils. The man sitting at the table was younger than Tex by a couple of years, but had been in and out of prison so many times, he drank alcohol to stay sane in a world not of his choosing. Pug was an asset; the man had eyes and ears everywhere, a veritable fountain of information.

"What's up, Tex?" The raspy voice could barely be heard above the loud noise in the room.

"Nothing much, Pug. Nothing much." Tex paused to ask. "Whatcha drinking?"

His table companion licked his lips, nodding. "Whiskey, straight up."

Tex signaled over a server and ordered a bottle of whiskey.

"Thanks, appreciate it man." Thin fingers grabbed the small glass of amber liquid as the waitress poured, and shakily brought it to his lips. Tex refused to watch the young man kill himself. At one time, they'd ran the streets together; that seemed a lifetime ago.

"Hey, whatever happened to that pretty young thing you dated a few years back?"

Tex tensed at the question. *What the hell?* Two nights in a row now someone had brought up Brenda, either directly or indirectly.

"What? I've dated a lot of women, you can't expect me to remember a particular one." Even as he finished speaking, Pug was shaking his head.

"Nah, she was special. I can't remember her name, but I remember being jealous of you at the time. She loved you. Not like these greedy bitches." He waved toward the dance floor. "I mean you had the real thing, you could see it in her eyes. That's not something a man sees every day." He sipped his drink. "Wonder what happened to her…" he whispered more to himself than Tex.

An explosion of goosebumps broke out on Tex's arms and a chill slid down his back, freezing him in place. He was glad for the darkness covering his surprised expression; he couldn't afford to show any emotions, not in his line of work. A longing to see Brenda again surged within him. The feeling buffeted him to the point his hand shook. He placed the shot glass on the table while staring straight ahead. The need to hear her voice, see her smile, to know once again that she believed in him, swamped him. The room shifted as panic replaced the goosebumps on his chest. She wouldn't like the path he'd taken and he didn't think he could deal with her disappointment again. The last time flattened him.

Brenda had seen the fledgling male he'd been, she'd always spoken to him about his potential. Knowing she saw something in him had made him want to be more, do more. Even when he'd begun flirting with the streets, dealing in shady avenues, despite her dislike of his choices, she had loved him unconditionally. Her faith in him had sent him soaring. In her eyes, he had stood ten feet tall.

"I don't know," Tex finally answered.

"Heard she ran into some problems with Irish's old lady a few months ago."

Tex was still zoned out and had missed most of the man's rambling. "Who? Who had problems with Red?" There were some people his people left alone. Irish and his band of construction workers had earned the respect of the street. Most people left them alone or died.

"The young beauty that loved you a long time ago. Heard someone tried to mess her over in a club or restaurant. Seems Irish's or Red's, whatever you call him," Pug snapped, "old lady took some fellas and rescued her from a restaurant. Think she left town after that."

"Wait." His heart slammed against his chest. He hated the dim light, he couldn't see Pug as clear as he wanted. Sitting forward, hands clasped tight, he stared at Pug. "Are you saying someone was messing with Brenda? Why?" He forced himself to breathe, forced himself to remain calm and not rip the answers he needed from Pug's throat, forced himself not to howl at the fucking moon that his woman had been hurt while he'd been elsewhere.

Pug shrugged. "Don't know. Just know it happened around the time Irish was shot in a club downtown near the old theatre. For some reason everyone was there that night."

Stunned, Tex couldn't speak. He remembered Rafe had sent him to look for the punks that'd shot Red that night, but couldn't find them. Later he heard Red's brother and partners had taken out the trash. He didn't realize Brenda had been anywhere near that place. It wasn't the type of place she'd hang out. A sense of urgency pulsed through him. He needed to find out what was going on. The thought of someone hurting her was unpalatable. He shushed the small voice reminding him how he'd hurt her.

Chapter 4

Brenda tried on three different outfits, still unsure about what to wear to dinner tonight. For some reason she wanted to look her best. Maybe it was because Roark had been mysterious about where they were going. She didn't know what was going on, but she liked that he enjoyed doing things with her.

Although Roark took her out often, each time it felt brand new. Maybe it was because he showered her with attention and affection whether they were at home or out in public. For someone as love-starved as Brenda, he was exactly who the doctor ordered. Each day, her confidence grew, old dreams resurfaced, and her battered ego raised its weak head from beneath the ground where it'd lain dormant the past two years.

She held a black dress in front of her, twisting from side to side in the mirror. Roark had picked it out last month for some fundraiser they'd attended and he hadn't been able to keep his hands off her. Then again, that was his M.O. most of the time. Roark wouldn't let her leave his side. She smiled at the memory.

The satin bodice hugged her breasts, the top of the sleeves just rested on her shoulders, leaving a good portion of her neck and chest bare. A black satin band was sewn in between the bodice and the rest of the a-line dress. Her fingers curled into the fabric of the dress, wrinkling the satin as old experiences rushed to the surface. There was a line between wanting to please your man and being consumed with a need to please him.

The habit she had of putting her men on pedestals had to stop. It was cruel and unhealthy. No one could stand under the weight of being another person's center. She had done it before, and when Tex fell, the disappointment had torn her apart. It'd taken years for her to pull it together again after that devastating experience. Never again would she submit herself to that kind of pain. She was no longer that needy, pathetic, caricature of a woman she'd been five years ago, willing to take scraps of fidelity rather than be alone. Desperate for a man's affection and attention, giving him so much of herself there was nothing but fumes left for her. Mentally, she shook off the rancid thoughts, refusing to allow them power over her anymore. *Safe*. The word ran through her mind like wildfire, releasing her tension and her hand from the dress. Roark was safe for her mind, her body and her bruised spirit. With him, she could be herself, and learn to love herself since he loved her so well. It was an amazing gift that he'd given her.

Stepping out of the shower, Brenda noticed the time. She had three hours before her man got home. After drying and curling her hair, that time whittled to one and a half. Bored, she went to check her email, read Denise's newest, and sent a reply. After deleting most of the mail, she saw one with the initials BJ in the signature line. Opening the mail, conflicting emotions flooded her.

Hey, Bren. Hope everything's cool with u. Take care. Tex.

Her stomach dropped at the sight of his name. For the briefest of moments, her mind balked at the note. It couldn't be him. The last time he'd spoken to her had been two years. She stared at the words, searching for hidden meanings. Minutes ticked by and as they did, reality kicked her into gear. Her anger soared.

"How the hell did you get my email?" she yelled, pointing at the computer. Her eyes widened as she looked around the empty room expecting him to jump out of a closet or knock on the front door. Chills raced up and down her arm, her heart thumped in her chest while she tried to breathe.

How dare he contact her now that her life was finally on track? Trembling fingers deleted the message before resting on her lips. The message appeared friendly, non-threatening. But she'd been taken in by that before. Fine tremors shot through her body in remembrance. Why couldn't he leave her alone? Too much had happened. Her dealing with the miscarriage alone, him rushing off after pushing her down, those incidents had been the conclusion of a relationship that should've died a year earlier. He'd begged for another chance, came up with a million reasons why they should reconcile; but at the end of the day, she'd found the last vestiges of her self-respect and made a clean break.

Tex had been like a dog with a damn bone, refusing to let her go. Although he'd never violated her physically, his ardent pursuit nearly drove her insane. The temptation to reconcile had been too great. She couldn't become a doormat again. Couldn't live with his lifestyle, the violence, the drugs or the fear of him not coming home. She'd move from place to place to escape him whenever it got to be too much.

Erosa Knowles
Page 32

In all honesty, there were a couple of times she almost gave in and took him back. Then she'd remember how he'd left her all alone when she lost their son. He'd chosen to run off to save his own ass, not caring one way or another about her or the baby, and her heart would harden against him to the point of hate.

She'd been so ashamed of her weakness or stupidity, either could be applicable, for all those years. Taking Tex back when she should've left him alone, ignoring stories of his actions in the streets, and taking his side. At times she'd behaved like some of those women you see on Jerry Springer, hissing and fighting over a bullshit man. Choking back the nausea in her belly, she pushed back those memories, which only triggered others. She'd never told anyone the entire story about her relationship with Tex. Denise had gotten edited tidbits for a while, but her shame made her back off from the best friend she'd ever had. That time with Tex set-off a new payload of guilt and shame. Without thinking, she picked up her cell and made a call.

"Hey girl." Denise's chipper voice soothed her wounded spirit.

"Hey." She paused, unsure if she should burden her friend with her problems. Denise was in the midst of planning her wedding and didn't need the weight of her dysfunctional lifetime drama. She changed her mind and tried to think of something else to say.

"I just called to see how things were going." She tried to infuse an upbeat note in her voice.

"Uhhuh. We talked earlier this morning, remember? You gushed about your perfect love," Denise teased.

"Gushed? I think not." Brenda glanced at the clock, time never moved fast when you wanted it to. Roark wouldn't be home for another hour.

"Okay, that was a stretch. The girls are over at Cherise's for the night. Red's at work. I'm here alone. Go ahead and unload." The serious tenor of Denise's voice smacked Brenda in the face. She'd forgotten how intuitive her friend could be.

"It's nothing much. How's the wedding going?" She tried to hedge.

"You'd have to ask Red's mama about that. She took it over a while back. Thank the Lord. The woman is a genius, but best of all, she's paying for it as part of our wedding gift. She claims she must have failed in his training somewhere since he made me wait this long. I love my mother-in-law!"

Brenda laughed at Denise's enthusiastic remarks.

"Sooooo, tell me what' up." Denise's abrupt change in tone disarmed Brenda.

"Do you think I'm like Mable?" The question came from the depth of her pain.

"What? No and hell, no. You're nothing like your mama. Go rinse your mouth out for talking filth."

Brenda's heart was too heavy to appreciate Denise's humor. "She uses men. Lives with them so they can take care of her. She told me to go back to Tex once she learned he made money. It didn't matter how he made the money. I kept taking him back after his bullshit, just like she does."

"Stop this. You are no Mable. First off, you love the men in your life. I may not understand it, but if you have a flaw, it's that you can't half do anything. Once you open your heart, it's out there. Don't bite my head off; Tex was too young to appreciate what you gave him. You were too young to rein it in to protect yourself. No matter what anybody said, you stood by him until he did something you couldn't forgive."

"Thanks for the pep talk," Brenda said with a dose of sarcasm.

"I wasn't finished, smart-ass. Money isn't the driving factor for you like it is with Mable. Can you imagine your mom going to court in support of any of the men she shacked with, or spending her money, if she had some, on medicine for some guy?"

Brenda snorted. Her mother wouldn't cross the street to help someone else unless it benefited her in some way.

Denise continued. "No. Mable is and will always be a selfish, pardon my language, bitch. The only person she looks out for is herself. Trust me, Bren. You and I would not be best girls if you were like that."

The seed of doubt blossomed, giving rise to her dark fears. "I live here with him for free. I don't contribute to anything in the house. Roark pays for everything. Sometimes, things get twisted inside and I feel cheap. Not quite like a prostitute, but something along that line. I mean, I'm doing for him the same things Mable did for the men she lived with. You're saying caring for the man makes a difference, I have to think about that."

"Is that what you really believe or are you in the middle of a pity party?"

"Both. I don't know why I'm still bugging with self-esteem issues, but some days, I look in the mirror and I see her." Her stomach tied in knots. She tried to swallow and stop from crying at the same time.

"I've lived with Red for most of our eight years. What do you think of me?"

The sober question sent her reeling. Brenda hadn't meant to imply her friend was loose like Mable.

"I think you're lucky to have a man who loves you."

"So are you. Roark loves you Brenda, even if he hasn't said it. This isn't about pussy-on-tap. No offense, but he had that when he met you. You're there because of the relationship the two of you have, not because of what he can give you. Or vice versa."

Brenda inhaled, struggling with granules of doubt. "I need to believe that, Dee. You have no idea how badly I need to feel this is real and not a game to him. I cannot afford to lose myself again. I may not make it back a second time."

"I know, Sweetie. You have to have faith in yourself and talk to him about your fears. If he's not on the same page, kick his ass to the curb. I'll help you."

"Thanks. You always know what to say." She meant it. Brenda had been her bedrock of sanity in the past.

"Back atcha, Chica. What brought all that on?"

"Tex emailed me and I got to thinking about some things," she said, waiting for the fallout. It didn't take long.

"What? No that…I'll be damned. Send it to me, I'd love to respond to his stupid ass." The heat of Denise's anger singed her ears.

"I deleted it." Her voice warbled. She was better than this. Her past would not cripple her again.

"You can still send it to me." Denise's voice hardened.

"No. I don't want him to know he reached me at all. Hopefully, he'll think the email got lost and give up." The idea had merit. Mentally she patted herself on the back as some of the tension lifted.

"How'd that ostrich thing work for you the last time?" Denise's dry tone and sarcastic comment hit its target.

Brenda cringed, she hadn't expected Denise's response to be so cold. Not everyone had a kick-ass-first personality. Not everyone grew up in a home with constant validation. Hell, not everyone was lucky enough to have two parents to pour love and affection into them so they weren't desperately seeking those things in the streets. Had she put her head in the sand and ignored Tex? Yeah, she had. It wasn't the first time she'd ignored potential land mines, and might not be the last. But she was able to function, and for her that was the critical thing.

"It's worked pretty well the past year, thank you very much," she said through tight lips, her tone just as sarcastic.

"He could've sent you an email a long time ago, why now?"

"I don't know, Detective." Releasing her anger, Brenda sighed. Everyone knew Denise lived for her police and crime television sitcoms, and it colored how she looked at things. In the emotional upheaval of Tex's message, she'd forgotten what a call to her friend would entail. Glancing at the clock, her jaw dropped when she realized only ten minutes had passed from the last time she looked.

"Seriously, Bren. The guy leaves you alone for two years, then all of a sudden you come back on his radar. He's probably had your email address for a while, but never used it."

Despite her annoyance with Denise, the question was a good one. One she had no idea how to answer. Surely, he didn't want to reconnect with her. She'd made her position quite clear when she'd screamed in his face that she didn't want him, numerous times.

"I honestly don't know. I'll talk it over with Roark later at dinner, get his take on it."

"I know you didn't just say you were going to discuss Tex with Roark." Denise sounded incredulous.

Brenda groaned, closed her eyes and dropped her forehead into her palm. "Yeah. He knows a little about it. But I think I'll tell him the rest."

"I hope you know what you're doing." Denise's tone clearly said Brenda did not have a clue what she was about to do.

"What do you mean?"

"Why would you tell him about Tex at this point in your relationship? Has the relationship gotten to the point where y'all are telling everything you've done in the past? Has he told you about the women from his past? Some of them were bat-shit crazy."

A flash of jealousy raced through Brenda at the thought of Roark with someone else. Green with envy, she asked without thinking. "What other women?"

Denise's long sigh ended on a whistle. "Has he told you about them? Do they still blow up his phone or send him emails? You want to tell the man you're living with, an ex-boyfriend sent you an email?"

"You're making it sound as though that's a punk move. Tex isn't a normal ex-boyfriend. He's stalker material, plus he was involved with illegal stuff." Her mind rebelled at the thought of Roark talking to his ex-girlfriends. The thought never entered her mind, although it should've. Living in his home, she was definitely exclusive with him, but that didn't mean he felt the same.

"Hey, do what you want. I just asked a question. I'll let you know if I hear anything about Tex around here. I thought he moved away, maybe he's in Detroit. I haven't heard anything about him in Flint."

Brenda felt bad about snapping at her friend. That was twice in the same day. "Dee, I'm sorry about that. It's just... I really like Roark. I don't want anything to come up and bite me in the ass. He's a good man."

"I know, he's perfect," Denise mocked before laughing. "Your nose is seriously wide open, he'd better not hurt you or I'mma have his mama kick his ass."

Brenda laughed and looked at the clock. Roark would be home in ten minutes. "I have to get dressed, we're going out to dinner when he gets home." A warm feeling filled her at the thought of seeing him, and later tonight, simply holding him. Yeah, her nose was wide open for this man, but she wasn't out of control, and that was okay.

"Oooo, that's a great idea. I think I'll get dressed so Red can take me out to dinner before he gets his dessert. I'll be sure to tell him it was Roark's idea." Brenda laughed as Denise hung up.

A part of her felt better after their conversation, another part was filled with new questions and more self doubt. Did Roark's former girlfriends still contact him? He never said. Should he have told her? Denise said some of his ex-girls were bat-shit crazy. Brenda couldn't imagine Roark dealing with anyone like that. But then again, she'd never thought she would've reacted the way she had against some of the women that'd tried to talk to Tex, either. For one insane moment, she'd had an out of body experience and cornered a woman she suspected had been with Tex. Would Denise call her *bat-shit* crazy? Probably.

Dressed in her black ensemble, she stood combing and styling her hair when Roark walked into the room. Her breath caught when he smiled and brushed his lips against hers. A light tremor worked its way down to her core as he brushed the back of his hand alongside her cheek. He snared her eyes and for a moment, she basked in the masculine appreciation she read in their depths.

"Good day?" he murmured.

Moving closer, her cheek brushed his. She delighted in the sensation of feeling the roughness of his five o'clock shadow. She whispered, "Much better now," and kissed his cheek before leaning back. "I talked to Denise. She gave me a hard time about the wedding."

Stepping back, his brow rose as he stripped off his tie, followed by his shirt. "Why?"

She filled him in about the shoes, the latest news on his nieces and Red. She left out their second conversation. There were a few things she wanted to know before she brought up the email from Tex.

Naked, Roark snatched her for a quick kiss and then headed for the shower. "I meant to ask, when we are leaving for the wedding? Blaine asked me today and I didn't know."

Her eyebrows furrowed in confusion. "You told me your travel agent would handle it when I offered to make the reservations." Arms akimbo, she studied his profile in the shower before speaking. "I wanted to do it, but you told me no. We don't have a way to get to the wedding?"

A minute or two later, he stepped out. Hands up in a placating gesture, Roark walked to the dresser and picked up his phone. After punching in a number, he waited a beat before speaking. Brenda half-listened while he spoke to someone about their reservations. It'd pissed her off when he'd refused to allow her to handle their travel arrangements. At the time, she'd thought he didn't want her to use his credit card, but he'd given it to her so many times since then, she knew that wasn't true.

Clicking off, he leaned into her as he replaced his phone on the dresser in front of her. "I'm sorry about that. Forgive me?" He created a playful pout. Brenda laughed and swatted his hand from her breasts.

Wrinkling her nose, she looked at him. "Go finish your shower."

Chuckling, he returned to the bathroom and closed the door. She looked at his cell. A niggling thought wormed its way into her mind. She wondered if any of his ex-girlfriends called him during the day. Eyes shut, she inhaled deep and long, hating the uncertainty chipping away at her peace of mind. That's what happened when you shared information with other people, their demons mixed with yours and a whole bunch of shit that never bothered you before, starts kicking your ass.

Resolutely, she turned from the small device and focused on her hair. Occasionally, her eyes strayed to the Smartphone. But she remained firm in her resolve and breathed a sigh of relief when Roark emerged from the bath. He walked to his closet and pulled out a suit that was one of her favorites. It looked good next to his complexion and made his dark eyes appear mysterious. It didn't take him long to dress. She wondered at his good mood, the man was humming.

"You're humming." She turned and crossed her arms, watching him buckle his belt. "What's up?"

"Huh?" He glanced at her before sitting on the olive-colored stuffed chair in the corner. Picking up his socks, he returned her stare. "What?"

"I said you're humming," she repeated, her tone ripe with curiosity.

He smiled. "I am?"

She nodded. "Why? What's going on in that smart mind of yours?"

He bent forward and put on his shoes. "Nothing much. It's just a song I heard on the way home and I can't get it out of my head, that's all." He stood, fully dressed.

Her eyes traveled over him jealously. How did men do it? How could he look so polished and yummy in less than thirty minutes?

"You ready?" he asked, meeting her eyes in the mirror as he finger combed his damp hair.

"Yeah. Where are we going?"

"There's this rib joint not too far from here, I thought...."

She whirled, her jaw lax. "What? I don't want to wear this...."

He grabbed her wrist and pulled her back to him. "I'm just playing baby, we're doing Italian tonight. Is that better?" He tilted her chin upward and claimed her attention as he devoured her mouth.

Rational thought careened to a halt as his tongue conquered hers. His moan was the sweetest sound, setting off a tremor of need through her. The possibility of him and another woman sent a chill through her, followed by a bout of shivering. His large palms stroked her back, offering warmth and comfort. Pushing away slightly, she glanced up at him. His skin was flushed, those firm lips now a little puffy, his sherry-colored eyes had darkened to a cognac brown. He flexed his hips, grinding his crotch into hers.

"We need to go if we're going," she whispered, her lips inches from his chin. She watched the struggle cross his face and wondered if they'd be eating in. Moments later, Roark stepped back and cleared his throat. Jaw clenched, he closed his eyes as he moved further away, grabbing her hand.

"Yeah, let's do this." His words sounded strangled. After clearing his throat again, he glanced at her. She smiled and glanced at the large lump in the front of his pants.

"Comfy?" She teased.

"Not even." He picked up his keys, wallet and phone before striding out of the bedroom.

****

Brenda was glad she'd spent the extra time dressing for the upscale restaurant; there wasn't a pair of jeans in the place. The extensive menu held little appeal, especially since Roark had stepped away from her to take a call. Her stomach clenched in a vise of indecision as she tried to figure out how to bring up the topic of ex-lovers.

"You see anything you like?" His voice broke through her musings and set her heart fluttering.

She glanced at him, thinking he was alluding to something else, but his eyes were glued to the menu. "I think I'll have the house special, lasagna."

He nodded. "That's always a good choice. I think I had that the last time, think I'll try the steak medallions tonight." He closed his menu and sipped the complimentary wine the waiter had poured for them after they'd sat down.

"Yeah? When was the last time you came here?" Her voice sounded strained to her own ears, she needed to pull it together before she botched this.

The smile on his face tightened a fraction before he relaxed and shrugged. "I don't remember. Why?"

Her heart dropped, surrounded by sadness. Was she destined to be one of those women who always wondered if she were the only one? After living through that with Tex, she couldn't do that to herself again. "Just wondered." She took a sip of water, avoiding his gaze. "How were things at work today?" She pumped a shot of gaiety in her voice and inwardly cringed at the false note.

The heat of his gaze singed her. "Fine. I went to lunch with Blaine and Donald. I got a lot of things cleared off my desk so I can have some free time later."

She nodded. "That's good. How're your brothers?" Her mind raced. Thoughts of Roark and other women dotted the horizon of her mind. Various scenarios surfaced, weird parallels between her past and present threatened to collide.

"Um, they're good. You okay?" He touched her hand. She started, surprised to see his hand on top of hers.

"What?" She hadn't meant to snap, and offered a smile to lessen the sting.

"You okay?" He leaned back as the waiter placed their salads and rolls on the table. Nodding his thanks, Roark gazed at her. "What's wrong?"

Brenda sighed. She wasn't wired like Denise and a whole lot of other women. Giving fifty or seventy-five percent wasn't her thing. "Do your ex-girlfriends still call you?"

His eyes widened. Sitting back in his chair, fork poised over his salad, he continued to watch her.

Her experience with Tex had taught her to read these silences. Right now, Roark was wondering where her question was coming from. Had he done something to tip her off? Or what answer would keep him out of the doghouse and in her panties? Perhaps he'd flip the script and have her on the defensive, that one had been Tex's favorite response.

Without looking at her salad, she picked up her fork and speared a piece of lettuce. "Gonna answer me?"

"Yeah." He speared a tomato and popped it into his mouth.

She watched him chew and his throat work as he swallowed. "Yeah, you're gonna answer me or yeah, they still call you?"

"Both." His tone had changed, the word sounded sharper with a defensive edge.

"Okay." Brenda focused on her salad and shut down the argument taking place in her mind. No good would come out of pursuing this thread of questions. Maybe they'd talk about it later, in six months or something. *Real smooth ostrich move.*

"Why'd you ask?"

"Just curious." She ignored his stare and silently begged him to leave it alone.

Roark snapped his fingers to the side. "You talked to Denise. She must've told you about some of the women I dated in the past."

She shrugged noncommittally, frustrated that she'd opened this door of discussion. He was eating his salad enthusiastically, while her stomach balked at the idea of anything coming down the tube. God, she was pathetic. Already this relationship had the power to affect her health and emotional well-being. Hadn't she promised not to give anyone that type of power over her again? Angrily, she stabbed the tomato and popped it in her mouth. With deliberate movements, she ate the vegetable and commanded it to stay down.

"Whoa, what'd that red thing ever do to you?" Roark pointed at her other tomato and chuckled. Unsmiling, she continued to chew, her mouth and stomach in a test of wills.

"I admit, I dated some whacked women, and some still call to say hello. Just as friends," he added hastily.

"So you talk to your ex-girlfriends, who you are now just friends with. How does that work?" Her brow knitted in contemplation. If Roark walked away from her tonight, they could never be just friends. She would always reflect back to the intimate moments they shared and it would rip away any façade of friendship. Maybe if someone replaced him in her affections, but even then, she didn't think they could be friends.

"When we broke things off, there were no hard feelings. It was a matter of moving on." He shrugged and pushed away his empty salad plate.

"Moving on?"

He nodded.

"Hmmm." Maybe she should give Denise's words more consideration. He hadn't verbally committed to her. Nevertheless, she'd assumed he operated on the same principles she did. Perhaps that was a mistake.

"What about you?" he asked.

"No."

"No?" He relaxed in his chair, folding his hands on top of each other.

"I don't have many ex-boyfriends and the ones I had, I don't talk to them any longer. Not even as friends."

Neither of them spoke into the silence. After the waiter set down their entrées, they continued eating in silence. What had she expected? Roark was a rich, handsome, single man. Women wouldn't disappear just because he had a houseguest. Inwardly she flinched at her own downgrade.

"How is it?" He pointed to her dish.

Nodding, her mouth full, she spoke around the scrumptious dish. "Good."

He smiled and continued eating his meal and taking small sips of wine from his glass. It came as no surprise when he threw his napkin on his empty plate. He always finished before her. "That was good."

"Yes, it is. Thanks for dinner." She winked at him.

He laughed. "Will you be my dessert?"

Shrugging, she answered. "We'll see." She pushed her plate to the side, the waiter appeared as if he had read her mind and offered to box her leftovers. She thanked him.

Roark grabbed her hand while gazing at her. Their fingers intertwined as they stared each other. "I've had some bad relationships in the past. I don't like to talk about them. Some people are crazy and don't handle rejection well."

Her face heated at his description.

He nodded. "It's true. I can tell you some stories."

"I hope you will." *Is it worse than what I went through? What I did when I was crazy in love?* She needed to know.

He seemed surprised and pulled back a little. "It all happened before we met. That's my past," he said, his tone abrupt.

"But you've been talking to them since I've been here. How's that your past?"

His jaw tightened fractionally and his eyes darkened. "It's just a quick hello, how are you kind of thing. Nothing serious. I don't see them or spend time with anyone other than you." His matter-of-fact tone said to drop it. But she couldn't, not yet.

"Do you get emails and stuff?" Her tone mildly curious, nonchalant even, as if her heart wasn't thumping against her chest.

"Dee told you about that?" He groaned and covered his face with one hand. Good thing, since he missed the shocked expression on her face. She didn't answer.

Red-faced, he glanced at her and then back at the table. His fingers picked up the tiny pieces of lint from the tablecloth. "It was a long time ago. The girl was a stalker. I don't think she was all there upstairs, you feel me?"

Brenda nodded. *She definitely understood.*

"I don't think we need to talk about people from our past. It's not relevant to what we're doing now." This time, his tone had turned surly, adamant.

Does he really believe his behaviors today have nothing to do with his past relationships? Brenda wondered.

"I hear you. To be clear, you're saying you don't want to discuss people we used to date. It's okay to talk or email these people as long as they're firmly in the friend category. Is that right?"

"Are you in love with anyone from your past?" he asked instead of answering her.

"No." she said without thinking. The only man she was in love with was staring at her. Telling her it was okay for him to have female friends. That talking to them or writing e-mails wasn't an issue. Denise had been right.

He leaned forward a cheesy grin on his face. "Do you want to be with anyone you used to date?"

Her eyes searched his for a trace of any bullshit. Finding nothing but sincerity, she breathed her next answer on a husky note. "No."

"Then I say forget them. I don't want to know about it. As long as they're no threat to what we have going on, I'm cool." He tapped her clasped hands. "What about you? Does it bother you that I've talked to people I used to date?"

She shrugged as she thought how to answer honestly. "I'm working on it not being an issue. As a woman, I know how women think. I figure all those women simply moved from the active relationships column into the friends with benefits column. And as long as their benefits are denied, I can deal with it."

Roark coughed, his fist hastily covered his mouth. "You most definitely have been talking to Denise."

Erosa Knowles

Page 44

Brenda's frown deepened across her forehead. "I'm my own person."

"I know, Baby." He reached into his coat pocket and slid an envelope across the table to her. "Open it," he said as she stared at her name on the front.

"What're you up to?" Her stomach flipped as she lifted the parchment. She hadn't quite decided if the feeling was from happiness or dread. Mentally she applauded him for having a back-up plan to recover the earlier mood. The first thing she saw was a colorful brochure. Pulling it out, her heart soared as she realized it was a romantic island get-away. Then she saw the itinerary with her name and Roark's.

"Wanna go?" he murmured, his lip curled at the corner.

Squealing, she covered her mouth with her hand and repeatedly said, "Yes, yes, yes."

He took her other hand, bent over and kissed her palm.

A smattering of applause shattered her euphoric bubble. Dazed she looked at the smiling faces around them, and then at the waiter who'd returned with her bag of leftovers.

"Congratulations," he said with a slight frown.

"Yeah, we're going to the Cayman Islands." Her smile hurt, it was so big.

Red-faced, the waiter nodded and backed away, taking away the dishes. Brenda gazed at Roark, happy and content.

"They thought you were happy about something else." His eyes filled with mirth at her response.

"Huh?" Her mind was on the beautiful places in the brochure, and it took a minute to realize Roark had spoken. "What?"

He signed the credit card slip and stood.

Making sure to gather her precious items, she stood and smoothed her dress in the front. Roark's palm met the small of her back as they walked out the restaurant. Brenda's smile faltered as people stared at them and whispered. She hadn't thought the people were prejudiced when she came in, but now she wondered at their obvious murmuring.

While the valet went to retrieve their car, she mentioned it to Roark.

"I was trying to tell you when we were inside, but you didn't catch on." He placed his arm around her waist and pulled her close. Leaning down, he nibbled on her neck.

"Tell me what?" She closed her eyes and leaned into him, enjoying the feel of his solid strength behind her.

"When you squealed in excitement over your surprise, people thought it was a proposal."

"Proposal?" She still didn't get it.

"Yeah. Marriage proposal. That happens a lot in there, and most women don't respond like you did over a simple romantic getaway."

Oh God! She smacked him on the arm and stuck out her tongue before walking to the car. The valet smiled as he held open her door. She noticed Roark didn't look horrified at the idea of a marriage proposal and a giddy feeling rose up inside demolishing every doubt she'd had about their relationship. This was no fairy tale, it was real and her heart was definitely engaged.

Once the car doors were closed and they'd pulled away from the curb, she took his hand and softly kissed his knuckles. "It means a lot to me that you'd think to surprise me with a romantic getaway. To me, there's nothing simple about that."

Chapter 5

Pulling up as close as possible in Lola's beat-up Toyota, Anna's eyes widened at the sight of her home burning like a contained forest fire. Her duplex blazed bright red and orange in front of her, the crackle and pop of wood from the roof, a mocking sound in the dark night. The smell of burnt materials singed her nostrils as a mélange of fear, rage and frustration battled for supremacy within her mind. She struggled to remain upright, to contain the hysteria bubbling beneath the surface. Her ability to speak deserted her as tears filled her eyes. Everything she'd collected over the years, everything she owned gone in a puff of smoke. No, not smoke, fire.

Taking a few steps toward the line of onlookers, her jaw slackened as she watched her unit burn without restraint while the other unit smoldered. Powerless to do anything other than watch, she pushed her way to the front. A police officer waved her back. A large knot of fear was sitting heavy in her gut and she had trouble keeping her vision clear. Pushing past the pain, she pointed toward her unit and shouted. "That's my home! I live here."

The officer frowned as he glanced at her and then at the burning building. "I'm sorry for your loss, Ma'am. But I can't allow you to get any closer." His eyes searched the crowd while keeping an eye on her. "If you can stand by for just a minute, I'll have someone help you." He waved and another officer came over.

Their voices dropped to background sounds as the pounding in her head escalated. Fear, real and rancid, rose within her. A new shipment of crack had come in today and she'd stashed the bags inside her bedroom closet. She'd been in a rush to meet with the owners of the warehouse and hadn't had enough time to pass it on to her people on the street. Tears flowed in earnest at her predicament.

"Miss?" The officer stood nearby, his voice hesitantly polite. If she gave a shit, she'd be concerned about his thoughts of her dressed in jeans a size too small, a black corset, and a lightweight jean jacket on a cold night like tonight. Eyes straight ahead, she ignored the prick and tried to figure out how she was going to pay for the lost drugs. By now, someone had surely told Ritchie about the fire. She wouldn't be surprised if one of his goons weren't already standing somewhere in the crowd, watching. A wave of fear washed over her. She stiffened, refusing to turn and search for a familiar face.

"Miss?" The officer repeated, this time his voice was curt.

In slow motion, she turned and gazed at him. "What?" she asked angrily, her face hard.

"If you'll come with me, I have a few questions I need to ask." He paused, glancing away from her to his pad. "Do you have somewhere to stay? Someone to call?"

"Umm..." Her voice was low, antagonized. Dazed, she stared straight ahead. A small touch on her hand startled her. Frowning she glanced back and saw Lola. Anna's face relaxed, she'd forgotten her friend was here and she wasn't alone in this madness. "Yes, yes I do." Her voice strengthened as her fingers intertwined with Lola's.

The officer's brow rose as he watched the byplay, but he refrained from making any comments. "Good. Please step over here, I'll get your statement, and then you can leave."

The three of them walked to the police car. Lola stiffened against her side. Anna frowned, until Lola tipped her chin in the opposite direction. Looking to where Lola had motioned, her eyes collided with one of Ritchie's hood-rats. Instantly her heart dropped. He nodded at her, hopped on his bicycle, and rode off into the night. Grabbing her neck, she was breathing so hard and erratic, dots floated in front of her eyes.

"What happened?" the officer yelled as he helped lay her on the ground. Rocks, debris, and glass chips embedded themselves into her flesh, reminding her that passing out did not relieve her of her capacity to feel pain. As she struggled to sit up to relieve the pain, a firm palm to her midriff stopped her movement.

"Stay still, someone's coming." The no-nonsense tone of his voice proved comforting. With her eyes closed, she lay back down and welcomed the darkness this time.

****

The unmistakable sounds of a hospital greeted Anna as she regained her senses. Inhaling the strong antiseptic smell, she wondered why Lola had allowed them to bring her here; the woman knew she hated these places. Gingerly, she opened her eyes, saw the pulled curtains around her bed, heard the nearby voices, and realized she was in the emergency room. Good, they hadn't admitted her. Still a bit groggy, she fell back on the bed when she tried to sit up. Her arm and head competed for the pain-in-the-ass award.

Lola walked in, a tall Hispanic man right behind her. They spoke quietly for a minute, then approached her bed.

"How you feeling?" Lola smiled, taking her hand. The calluses on the palm of Lola's hand told the story of a young woman who'd worked hard all her life at the whim of men who never appreciated her. A woman who'd been beaten and abused by those who'd claimed to love and care for her. The last time, her drunken husband had gone too far, and in a rage, Lola had stabbed him. Fortune had smiled on her, the hospital had a record of her ex's abuse; x-rays of broken legs, arms, nose, jaw, ribs. Lola got off with self-defense. He'd been no better than an animal.

Anna's jaw tightened. "Pissed." Her voice was strained.

Lola nodded and waved toward her. The man began disconnecting her from the IV. "We'll get you out of here," she said, moving to gather Anna's clothes from the plastic bags.

As soon as she was dressed, she slid from the bed and walked through the curtain. The nurses were all busy with other patients who needed their attention more than she did, and they barely glanced in her direction as she left.

Once they were outside, Lola thanked the man and then assisted Anna into her small car.

Seated, Anna breathed deeply to clear her mind. Drugs and emotional upheavals did not mix. She needed to be careful how much she inhaled, tonight could've been worse.

Lola started the car and pulled out of the parking lot.

Relinquishing thoughts of drug overdosing, she changed gears. She had bigger problems. "First thing I have to do is come up with Ritchie's money." She gnawed at her fingertips, knowing he'd kill her if she didn't pay him.

"I can help with that, Chica."

Anna's head whipped around so fast, she gasped at the pain in her head. It was still sore. "Yeah?"

"Yeah. I got you on this. You will pay me back later." Anna winced at the ultra confident tone in Lola's voice. Sometimes she forgot beneath Lola's sweetness lay a steel core. Only fools took the small woman's kindness as a sign of weakness. Anna was no fool.

Rubbing her forehead, Anna willed the tension away. She needed to focus, there was something niggling at the back of her mind, but she couldn't grasp it. Frustrated, she sunk into the seat and let out a heated breath. Lola turned into the driveway of the home she'd shared with her ex. They rarely came here, it creeped Anna out to be in the same house where Lola had murdered her husband. When she'd asked the woman how she tolerated it, Lola shrugged and said the house was a peaceful place now that the jackass was gone.

Opening her car door, Anna stepped out and headed for the porch. A hand on her arm stopped her.

Lola gazed up at her. "I am glad you are all right. It hurt my heart to see you suffer." She picked up Anna's hand and laid it on her cheek for a second.

Anna smiled softly at her. Her eyelids grew heavy as tears stung.

"You may stay here as long as you need." Lola kissed the center of Anna's palm and walked ahead to unlock the door without releasing her hand.

"Thanks," Anna whispered, feeling loved and cherished for the first time in years as she followed her lady inside.

****

The report of the fire and Anna's trip to the emergency room sent a shaft of pleasure through Tex. He had a platter full of nasty surprises for her in the upcoming weeks. He planned to ruin her before authorizing her demise. Death was too easy. The bitch needed to suffer like Brenda had and he'd expended a lot of money to make sure that happened.

Humming, he sat at his desk checking the quality of a new release DVD he'd just copied. It'd been a long time since he'd watched a movie for pleasure, but this comedy had solid punch lines and he found himself smiling, and at times laughing aloud. His enjoyment was such, he didn't hear the door open, and only the scraping of a chair caused him to realize Rafe sat in front of his desk.

Rafe was dressed immaculately in a European-cut suit and silk shirt, sans tie. Some days it seemed his Puerto Rican ancestry dominated his Norwegian genes. Thick, dark hair, expertly cut, every strand in place, framed a face that was smooth and unlined. Rafe always appeared composed and ready for a photo shoot. He'd insisted Tex learn to dress and be well groomed at all times. At first, he'd balked, to no avail. To work for Rafe, you had to represent his sense of style. It no longer bothered Tex to get blood on a five thousand dollar suit when he hunted down those who crossed his boss. In fact, not much bothered him. Rafe would tease him, saying he had no heart, nothing mattered to him. For the most part, Rafe was right. Nothing mattered to him except the thrill of the job. The high that came from winning against the odds, of being respected in his own world on his own terms.

Tex turned off the DVD player and set the master copy aside. Later, he'd take it to the studio to have the copies made. He glanced at Rafe, then noticed the door was closed and wondered why. "What's up?" he asked briskly, the smile leaving his eyes. A strange glint flashed through Rafe's eyes, so fast Tex almost missed it.

"I have news for you." Rafe glanced around the room before settling his dark gaze on Tex again. "First off, well done on the job you handled last week. Your level-headed thinking has caused several ripples that, so far, seem to be working well on our behalf."

Tex exhaled. The tension in his back eased. Conversations with Rafe didn't happen often and he never knew what to expect. One thing he knew, the man wouldn't rush. "Like what?"

Rafe tented his blunt fingertips beneath his chin, his brow rose as he stared at Tex. "For one thing, if you'd destroyed that warehouse, we'd all be dead."

Tex blinked as the words struck his chest and sent adrenaline rushing through his body. "Why?" he croaked, as the room shift slightly. *Dead?* Panic spread across his chest, tightening it in its grip.

Rafe sighed and uncrossed his legs. "It belonged to a small group, backed by a much larger group; in essence, it's organized." He waited a beat before continuing. "They liked how we, or should I say, you, handled the situation. We had a meeting this morning and they want us to work with them." His voice sounded tight.

"Are you fucking kidding…" Tex bit back, nearly choking on the words. He was comfortable with their arrangement, they made good money, he had his investments and in a few years he'd be able to retire. Even if they were caught, the penalty for pirating CDs and DVDs was much more lenient than selling drugs, prostitution and shit like that. He was young and smart enough to want to enjoy his life with his own woman, not be married to the mob with no hope of a divorce.

He laughed bitterly, rubbing his chin. "So, because we behaved ourselves, took back our shit and left theirs alone, now they want to take over our shit? Is that what you're telling me?"

Rafe stared at him for a moment and nodded. "In a manner of speaking, but I'm not sure you understand." Rafe leaned forward, his hands dangling between his legs. "They want you."

A cold sweat broke out across Tex's forehead. He blinked repeatedly as a chill inched down his spine. "Me?" he snapped, unwilling to grasp the message of those three words. His eyes searched Rafe's, wondering if the man was serious. Pity and something else, envy perhaps, was clearly readable in the other man's eyes and made his stomach clinch with dread. A myriad of thoughts flew through his head. Why him? Why now? Nothing made any sense.

"Why?" His eyes ripped into Rafe. Had the man sold him out, bartered him for more money? Rafe had expensive tastes and spent a lot of money on his toys, as he called the fancy cars, jewelry and boats. Tex stood, turned and walked to the other side of the room. His ability to talk fled. They'd worked together three years; Rafe knew of his plans to get Brenda back. He'd even been the one to advise him to back off from, what he termed, stalking her and wait, to save his money so he had something to offer her, and now this. Tex had worked himself up to become the second man in their organization. What was really going on?

Rafe stood as well and watched him. "You're young, smart, disciplined and organized. No matter what you do, you make money. To top all that off, you're loyal. Hector and those guys follow your orders implicitly. I'm not the only one they talked to before they made their decision today." He paused, lips twisted. "Trust me, talking to me was only a courtesy, similar to a reference check before the actual interview. They want *you* to work for them."

Tex's mind raced as he faced the wall again. This was too much, too fast. "And if I refuse?"

Rafe shrugged. "I promised to tell you they want to talk to you. After that I'm out of it."

Tex spun around, glaring at Rafe. "What about all our work? What about everybody working here?" The chill down his back had wound its way to his heart. Tiny pricks rose on his arms as he watched Rafe's shuttered expression, he knew he wasn't going to like his mentor's response.

"They made me an offer for the operation. I couldn't refuse it."

Tex growled, it rumbled deep in his chest. His jaw clenched and his fist balled tight at his side in resentment.

Rafe held both hands out, in a placating gesture. His face and voice were strained. "Seriously, I couldn't refuse. I have a family to think about."

For the first time, Tex noticed glimmer of fear and pain in the man's eyes. The tension in him eased a little, but his shoulders were still squared. "What did they offer you?" His sounded bitter and he didn't care. This was his fucking life, not some DVD, sold to the highest bidder.

"They paid for the business, gave everyone a bonus and an offer of employment if they want it."

"But not you?"

"No. They didn't offer me a job." The man glanced at him, his face stricken with embarrassment.

Tex frowned. "How much of a bonus do I get?"

Rafe swallowed hard. "They'll discuss that when you meet with them."

Gritting his teeth, he tried to understand Rafe's position. Eyes closed he ground out. "When?"

"They're waiting for you downstairs."

Tex's eyes flew open in surprise. For a moment, the room was silent. There were so many things that could be said that weren't. In the end, it didn't matter. Just when things in his life seemed to be falling in place, it went to shit. He gritted his teeth, worried this might cause a delay in reconciling with Brenda. *Hell, no.* He'd waited long enough. One way or another, he and Brenda would be together again. Tex grabbed his coat and stormed out.

****

Without removing her dark glasses, Anna walked to the front desk of the nursing home where two harried women fielded phone calls and talked with other guests.

"Excuse me," Anna said when she felt she'd waited a decent amount of time, in reality it'd been less than a minute.

Frustration seeped from the woman as she glanced up from the phone and held up a finger, silently asking Anna to wait.

Glad she still wore her sunglasses, Anna rolled her eyes and looked around the foyer. There were so many old people walking around with canes or walkers. Many of them talked to themselves as they shuffled up and down the halls. Chill bumps spread down her arms. She rubbed them and returned to look at the receptionist. The woman had just hung up the phone and offered her a plastic smile.

"I'm here to see my aunt, Robin Glazier."

The woman nodded and typed something into the computer.

"Ms. Glazer is in room 301. I need to see some ID and have you sign in here." She shoved the clipboard at Anna and took the fake identification from her to make a copy. A moment later, she handed it back to Anna. "Here you are Ms. Washington, your aunt will be happy for some company."

Anna smiled slyly at the harangued woman. "Please, my name's Brenda. I'm happy you guys are taking such good care of my aunt. I've been away for a while and haven't been here; but now that I'm back, I plan to come see her more often."

The woman's ruddy face brightened. "That's great, Brenda. I'm sure she'll be glad to see you." She waved Anna off and turned to the next guest.

Smiling, Anna strode down the hall, determination in every step. It hadn't taken a genius to figure out who was behind all of her recent misfortunes. That damn Tex. First, he'd had her place torched; she'd had to pay Richie an ungodly amount for the drugs she'd lost. Then Lola's car was stolen. One night after work, somebody attacked her. It was three days before she was able to return to work, only to discover she'd lost her job. The final straw came when the bastard had somehow set it up for Lola to find her in bed with another woman. She had no memory of the event and woke up to find Lola fighting with someone in her bedroom. Groggy, she'd watched the woman beat Lola unconscious before she left them both alone in the room. Later that night, Lola asked her about some phone calls she'd supposedly made, and showed Anna some pictures she'd found. Confused, she'd babbled her innocence. Lola hadn't believed her and kicked her out.

Homeless and with no job, she'd spent the night on her mother's couch in a condo she claimed some man bought for her. Her mama had made it clear they wouldn't be roommates and that night was a onetime deal. It'd been a stroke of luck when she remembered her aunt's house stood vacant on the other side of town. After a little finagling, her cousin gave her permission to stay at the house. With time on her hand, she began plotting a way to get Tex off her back. Brenda was the key. He'd do anything to get the bitch back. Problem was, she had no idea where Brenda was. The only person she knew who might have a clue was that bitch Denise, and she couldn't stand her. The feeling was definitely mutual.

Walking into the dim room, she scrunched her nose at the fetid odor and the sounds of all the medical equipment. Her stomach clenched in anxiety, she didn't want to be here. Stiffening her chin, she strode to the bed and looked into the face of her mother's older sister. The woman's sallow flesh lay loose on her medium frame. Knobby joints appeared dislocated and out of place. Anna made the mistake of inhaling and immediately regretted it as her stomach lurched. Eyes watering, she took a step back as her mouth opened and then snapped close. Words failed her. For a moment, she smelled failure.

Then her aunt opened her eyes. A slit at first, then she widened them further, freezing Anna like a deer caught in headlights.

"Who are you?" The raspy voice and cloudy dark eyes freed Anna from her paralysis. Remembering her purpose, she straightened, smiled and prepared for the performance of her life.

"I'm Brenda, Aunt Robin. I'm sorry I haven't been here to see you in a while," she said, bending forward to kiss the old woman on the forehead. "But I've been out of town and just returned. I wanted to come see how you're doing." She backed up while the old woman turned sideways to get a better look at her. Anna waited nervously trying to think what Brenda would do.

"Where've you been?" The old woman's voice picked up strength as she stared in her direction. Anna wasn't worried the woman would recognize her face, her aunt couldn't see past her nose without her glasses. It was her voice she tried to disguise, and she planned to say as little as possible.

"I met a guy out of town and have been staying with him." She busied herself pushing the old woman's blanket around her legs. "Can I get you something?" Anna asked from the foot of the bed.

Her aunt sighed. "Yes." She pointed to the big black book on her nightstand. "Read me something from my Bible, it always calms me."

Startled, Anna looked up. Her eyes widened as her face caught fire. "What?" she squeaked, backing away from the black book that looked like a cobra waiting to strike.

"Read me some scriptures, I said." She glanced in Anna's direction. "Whatcha doin over there?"

Tripping over her feet, Anna walked toward the doorway. "I left my glasses at home, sorry." Pausing at the door, she looked at the confused expression on the older woman's face. "I'm going to get something to drink, I'll be right back." She pushed herself through the doorway and hustled down the hall until she made it outside. The sights, the smells and sounds of this place made her stomach roll. But she couldn't think of another way to get Brenda back in town to get Tex off her back. Looking up at the darkening sky, she shook her head at the unfairness of it all. *Rain.* Now she'd get soaked trying to catch the bus later on. Grimacing, she stalked back inside, ready to earn an academy award for imitating the woman she hated most, her sister.

Chapter 6

Sitting at his desk, Roark reflected on how different his life had become since he and Brenda had become a couple. A grin split his cheek as he remembered how excited she'd been last night when she opened the envelope with the tickets to the Cayman Islands. Then he frowned, remembering the conversation they'd had before he'd sprung his surprise; he again saw the flash of doubt followed closely by suspicion on her face. Her curious stare had pierced him deeply and he'd felt embarrassed over something she imagined him doing.

For a moment, the thought of confessing a few of his dark escapades had crossed his mind. Paula, Karen, and Mali, were three of the biggest mistakes he'd dated. Fear of her seeing him as the whorish playboy he'd been shut him down. He didn't want to destroy the image of decency he suspected she had of him. He'd been wild, using women for sex, not caring about their feelings. That wasn't the way he wanted Brenda to see him; but he didn't trust his mouth, it might say things he couldn't explain. Asking her about another man was out of the question. An incomprehensible pang of jealousy pierced his chest with the knowledge that there had been someone else. Why would any man want to discuss his woman and some other dude? He had to shoot that idea down before he broke out in a sweat. Brenda was his baby, but he couldn't handle true confessions along those lines.

His cock stirred as he remembered his wake-up call this morning. Brenda had been a hellcat, insatiable. He glanced at his watch, wondering if it was too early to go home for lunch. His office phone rang and his cell beeped at the same time. Irritated at the interruption of his morning fantasy, he picked up both phones, glanced at the caller ID on his cell and groaned.

"Hold on a minute, Ma." Rolling his shoulders, he spoke in an abrupt tone into the other phone. "Roark."

"Mr. O'Connor, sorry to disturb you, but a Ms. Paula Samuels is on her way up to your office."

Roark groaned. Had he thought her up? His stomach soured at the news. "Thanks, Big Guy," he said to the security officer on the front desk. After hanging up, he gazed at his cell for a moment, and realized this conversation with his mother was past due.

"Hi, Mom." His voice warm and inviting in spite of the heaviness in his gut.

"Hey, Baby Boy. I haven't heard from you in a while, figured I'd ring you up." She paused and when he didn't say anything, she continued. "I'm hoping we can all get together for a family outing while we're in Michigan. The twins have rented a large place for us, so where do you plan to stay?"

The woman was digging and they both knew it. If he wasn't on edge with the expectation of Paula's madness, he'd enjoy teasing her. However, any minute one of his biggest mistakes would be coming through his door. Feelings of guilt always assaulted him in her presence, even though he had no reason to feel that way. Though she'd never said it directly, he'd always felt she blamed him for her situation. Whenever she visited, it always messed up his day because he didn't know how to deal with the bad feelings she dredged up. Then he'd feel worse for feeling bad, since he had no reason to take on the guilt.

"Roark!? Roark?" His mama called.

Eyes closed, he rubbed the bridge of his nose trying to release the tension building up in anticipation of their impending altercation. "I'm sorry, Ma. Paula's on her way up here and I...I just don't feel up to her today." That was an understatement of the highest order. He wanted to go home and lose himself in his woman, not face a fling from his past. Besides, after they'd had sex the second time, he'd believed Paula was unstable. That was before her accident. After that, he'd avoided her until she finally tracked him down that night at the restaurant and had the gall to send his ride home. *Damn.*

The sigh through the phone was long and loaded with disgust. His mama wasn't shy about her feelings. A person knew exactly where they stood with her. "Why do you allow her to do this to you?" she snapped. "The accident was not your fault, that heifer was driving under the influence, hitting you with her fist, I might add, and not watching the road." When his mom discovered the girl had been high and driving with him in the car, she'd lost it. It was a sensitive subject that he rarely brought up.

"Yeah, but she saw some things which upset her...."

"Upset? Just because she was hurt didn't mean she had to get high and drive. I told you she wasn't right when I met her."

He chuckled. "She was a *right then* person in my life. It was a casual thing." The light knocking on his door knotted his shoulders. "She's here. I'll call you later, Ma." There was silence on the phone. "Ma?" he called out.

"I hear you. I don't like this. Just as you're coming into your common sense and finding a measure of happiness, she shows up. Hmpf, be careful of that one."

Roark had reached the door, and opened it with a smile frozen on his face as he looked down at Paula in her wheelchair. "Okay, Ma. Will do. I'll call you later this afternoon." After placing his cell in his pocket, he spoke. "Hey Paula, this is a surprise." He pulled the door open wider so she could roll her mechanical chair in. She moved to a spot near his desk. After smoothing the frown from his face, he followed.

"I know," she said, watching him as he walked to his chair and sat across from her. She'd grown her hair out a little longer, tight ringlets framed her face and fell down her shoulders. He'd always thought her dusky complexion, a testament of her Indian heritage, was sexy. No question, Paula was still an attractive woman. He just wasn't interested.

"What's up?" he asked when she continued to stare without speaking.

After a small cough, her hazel eyes met his, sadness and some other emotion he couldn't define in their depths. "I was driving by your place the other week and saw a black chick walking inside with some bags."

His eyebrows furrowed deep, his chest tightened as her words found fertile ground. "You were driving by my house?" he asked, his voice deepening, giving way to a slow boil of anger.

"Well, yes. My cousin has a place not far from you." Her voice was void of emotion as she stared at him.

"Two miles from me in the opposite direction if I remember correctly." His tone was cutting. His mother's warning rose to the surface as Paula's eyes filled with tears. He hated when she did that.

"I'm sorry, I didn't mean for you to get mad." She sniffed, rooting around in her purse.

Roark snapped his eyes shut to block out the image of her face in pain. His stomach dropped to his feet. He knew she was manipulating him, using her paralyzed condition to get him to do what she wanted. If only he didn't feel so damn guilty.

"Does she live with you?" Her tiny voice broke through his mental gymnastics.

"Yes." He opened his eyes, startled to feel a bizarre mix of relief and sympathy flow through him with that one word confession.

Her lips pursed tight, no longer attempting to hide her anger. "You plan to marry her?" The tears had dried up. The small voice was packed away. The scowl on her darkening face an indication of her escalating rage.

"Why?" The guilt fled when her attitude changed. Maybe because he was seeing her again as she truly was. A viperous woman. He straightened in his chair, his thoughts brightening at the idea of her leaving him alone permanently.

"Why?" she screeched. Her hand flew in the air and then dropped. "Because of you, I'm in this damn chair. Why should you have a life when I don't?" Her voice took on a strident tone. Thin fingers curled around the arms of the chair as she attempted to leave her seat.

Silence thrummed through the room. He watched as she tried to rewrap her cloak of misery around her thin shoulders. Her eyes dropped beneath his quiet scrutiny. She'd kept this side hidden since the accident; he'd forgotten how volatile she could be.

"You were high on drugs that night. I offered to drive. You refused." He continued looking at her through lowered lids.

She pointed at him. Spittle flew from her lips as she lashed out against him. "I caught you with her. You were fucking around on me, don't deny it."

He shrugged. "I don't deny I fucked other women while I fucked you. Is that what you mean? We weren't in a relationship. It was casual; I told you I didn't want a commitment when we met. You agreed."

Her lips curled and he wondered why he'd never noticed before how natural that cruel look fit her persona.

"It was never casual to me," she snapped, her voice hitching as she finished her sentence.

"That's not my fault." He paused, undeterred this time by her theatrics. His voice deepened with anger at her blaming him for her own foolishness. "Neither was the accident. You were high and too busy fighting to drive. You ran into that pole."

"Why didn't you get hurt, then? Huh? Why me?" Her outburst should not have surprised him. Paula had always been selfish, even as a lover.

That's why he'd only bedded her twice and that was two times too many.

"Why, Paula," he snickered as realization set in, "you were trying to kill me, weren't you?"

Her head swung toward his, her eyes widened as if she hadn't expected the question. "Whaaat? No…no, you're being silly." She scoffed, although the truth stood out bright as day on her face.

The bitch had tried to kill him, and all this time he'd felt guilty about her condition. She'd planned for it to be the other way around. He'd be in the wheelchair and she'd be what? His nurse? Not likely, not with his family.

"What'd you expect? That I'd be dead or in a wheelchair or something else?" he whispered, picking at his fingernails.

"You're talking crazy. I did not try to kill you. I just hate my life and you're rolling forward with yours. That makes me angry. It's unfair. We were together that night and nothing happened to you." She sniffed and wiped her eyes.

Inwardly, Roark chuckled. This display of waterworks had no affect on him whatsoever. At last, he was free of her and the debilitating guilt of the accident. "You should get counseling, I think you need to talk to someone about what you're feeling, see if you can resolve some of your issues." He pushed back from his desk and stood. "This anger you're harboring isn't good for you." He strode to the door, feeling her eyes on his back. He glanced at his watch; he had just enough time to make it home to Brenda, and maybe lunch.

"So, you're throwing me out of your office now?" She wheeled around to face him, a sad expression on her face. "I thought we were friends and could be honest with each other."

Roark stared at his feet while he choked back a laugh. The woman had tried to kill him and she thought they could be friends? "Paula, let me say this with the utmost sincerity. We are not and have never been friends. This is the last time you'll visit my office. And never visit my home or anywhere you think to find me. As far as I'm concerned, your revelations about the accident severed anything remotely close to friendship."

She rolled her eyes and threw up her hands in surrender. "I didn't try to kill you," she shouted.

"I'm damn glad to hear that," a deep voice said from the hall. Donald stepped into the office and shut the door. Roark bit back a smart remark, his mother had probably called his brother as soon as they hung up. He glanced at the ceiling, wondering if he could leave these two alone while he headed home to his woman.

"Whaat?" Paula's hand flew to her throat as she stared up at his brother.

Donald stepped toward her, his face set in stern lines. "I'm Roark's attorney and I'm sure you don't want him to press charges." He let the threat hang for a moment; it didn't take her long to respond.

"But...but," her head swiveled between both men. "It's not true! I didn't try to kill him." Tears streamed down her face, she was inhaling so fast and hard he thought she'd pass out.

Donald looked at him. He shrugged, just wanting the whole thing over with.

"Then why did you run into the pole that night?" Donald toned down his aggression. His voice became suggestive, reasonable.

"I was high, god dammit." Her voice raised in pitch. "I'd taken a couple of hits because I was so angry that he didn't want me." She looked at Roark. "Why? Just tell me why her and not me?"

"Her?" Donald looked at him.

Roark shook his head. He did not intend to reveal Brenda's name to this vindictive witch. "None of that matters, it's not your business. What matters is you leave and never come back. There's nothing for you here." He stepped back and opened the door. An amazing number of people stood nearby in small groups, no doubt wondering about all the shouting. He patted his pocket for his keys and phone. His wallet was in the glove compartment of his car. He nodded to his brother, who stood beside Paula's chair while she wiped her face.

"I'm gone. Lock up for me, okay?"

Donald nodded.

Roark took one look at Paula's pinched face and walked out.

****

Ten minutes later, Roark opened the door to his home and stepped inside. Inhaling deeply, he released the tension that'd gripped him at the office. A peaceful calm settled on his shoulders. Anxious to touch his woman, he placed his keys on the side table, and took the stairs two at a time, rushing into the bedroom. His heart slammed against his chest as he struggled to breathe at the delicious vision in front of him. No, not a vision, but solid female perfection. Since he'd started dating in high school, he'd always preferred women of color. The variety of skin tones, the various hair textures, the bountiful asses, oh yeah. His woman wasn't the first chocolate drop he'd dated, but something in his gut told him she'd be the last. From the moment he'd laid eyes on Brenda, her lustrous chocolate skin had made his mouth water. He'd offered her sanctuary in his home without giving it much thought.

Bent over, her ass in the air, Brenda turned and smiled at him while she continued to rub lotion into her damp skin. "Hey, Baby." She winked saucily and bit the corner of her bottom lip.

He groaned, words deserting him. His cock twitched in salute. Moving forward, he pulled her against him, enjoying the feeling of her in his arms. He savored the lushness of her body.

"I missed you," he whispered against her ear. His hardness pressed against her naked ass. She wiggled against his dick, eliciting a moan from between his lips. "Woman," he growled, tightening his grip. "Look what you're doing to me." A circular wet spot graced the front of his trousers. She turned in his arms, her eyes soft and heavy lidded as she offered her lips to him.

Long, toned arms wrapped around his neck as he nuzzled her throat. Impatient, his cock jerked in recognition of her natural fragrance. A long sigh left her mouth just before he took her lips. His body pressed against hers, their hips matching perfectly as his still-clothed erection rubbed sensuously along her sex. He took her mouth again and again, their tongues stroking the flames of pleasure. They broke apart, gasping for air as if they'd run a marathon.

Eyes wild, she imperiously waved at his clothes. "Off, take them off."

Fascinated with her eagerness, he watched her nipples tighten to chocolate peaks, and absorbed the shudders that wracked her body.

Impatient, she smacked his chest, regaining his attention, and then unbuttoned his shirt while he pulled off his belt.

"Miss me?" He grinned when she pushed his shirt off his shoulders. Her eyes blazed with a scorching sexual heat that set him aflame and rendered him mute at the same time. Beneath the blatant hunger, there was something more. Something beautiful that ignited his smoldering feelings and humbled his heart.

He wondered at the magnitude of his feelings for her. Some would say this had happened too fast, but he knew better. The timing was perfect. He was ready to take their relationship to another level, to make the ultimate commitment. His thumb stroked her soft cheek. A tiny smile emerged as her eyes fluttered closed. Bending forward he brushed a kiss against her warm flesh. His chest tightened as she melted against him, her head resting on his chest. For a moment, he simply enjoyed the feeling of holding her in his arms.

"Yes, I missed you," Brenda whispered.

He felt the words on his skin, followed by the swipe of her tongue on his nipple. A groan rose from his belly and slid through his mouth at the sensations her tongue created. In a gentle how-do-you-do manner, she kissed his nipple. Then her stiffened tongue flicked it, mercilessly setting off a firestorm inside. He pressed her mouth closer to his hard nub. Potent heat unfurled in his stomach, threatening to consume him. His belly tightened. This is what he'd needed all day, where his mind had been. Right here, in this room with her.

Pliant in his arms, Roark picked her up and walked the few steps to the bed. He frowned as she scampered to push the comforter aside before laying on the cool cotton sheets. Opening her legs in invitation, she sent him a seductive grin. Then she threw her arms above her head and gyrated her hips while watching him stare. One arm snaked down between her legs toward her glistening lips, the other twirled her hair in a seductive pose. His heart hammered in his chest as she weaved her siren's spell on him. A million words caught and lodged in his throat. Words of love, honor, commitment, but her candid need and desire for him rendered him mute.

"Baby, please," she moaned, her hand beckoning him, her hips moving in a seductive dance as old as time.

What man was strong enough to turn away from the woman who held his heart? Certainly, not him. He'd thought he'd be able to go slow, take his time, and love her down right. Something feral rose and overtook him. The need to brand her, claim her, and lay it down on her so good she'd never look elsewhere for satisfaction. That satiated look in her eye would belong to him alone. Moving forward, he knelt on the bed, his breaths short as he hovered over her, searching her face for a sign that she too felt this incredible connection demanding that he make her, his. Not just for tonight, but until he no longer breathed, because he couldn't imagine being without her.

Sobering, he licked his lips, and for a moment thought to tell her what was in his heart. Her fingertip touched his lip and slid into his mouth. He tasted her essence and realized how starved he was for her.

"Love me," she breathed, pulling him forward.

"I do," he said, heart in his mouth as he eased into her tight velvet grip. Sighing at the pleasure of their joining, they stared at each other, speaking the silent language of love with their eyes. She tightened her walls. He pulled back and rammed his whole length into her, causing them both to scream in ecstasy. She gasped and pulled him closer. Brenda's ankles crossed his back while he flexed his hips to go deeper. It amazed him how tight she was. Their grunts, the slapping of flesh, the slight creaking of the bed springs as he pounded into her, created exceptional background music. Grabbing her hips tight, he moved in and out of her, faster and faster.

Her back arched. Her pussy tightened like fingers milking him. Her nails dug into his shoulders, pulling him closer, as though she could pull him into her skin. She screamed her release, her body tensing and then releasing her grip.

Roark bucked faster, harder. He was so close; one last thrust had him grunting his release. He came so hard, his body was hit with wave after wave of ecstasy that was almost unbearable. Back arched, toes curled, and his heart climbed into his throat. *Damn that was good.*

After rolling over, he pulled her tight to his side and kissed the top of her head. Taking a deep breath, his nostrils filled with the honeysuckle lotion she wore and the unmistakable smell of sex. Something eased within him. Her hand rested on his chest, he covered it and held it close to his heart.

"What happened?" she asked, her voice slurred, sleepy.

"Hmm?"

"You're home in the middle of the day." She yawned, turned and curled into his side. His hand rested on the small of her back.

"You blew me out this morning and I couldn't focus." The palm of his hand smacked against her round globes and then rubbed the spot to ease the sting.

She pushed at him. He tightened his grip, smiling as she tucked in closer to him. "I'm glad you did." Her breath tickled the hairs on his chest.

"Me too." His lids grew heavy and moments later he fell asleep.

****

Relaxed, and refreshed, Roark stepped outside and headed for his car, invigorated. There were a few things to handle at the office and then he'd return home. A smile eased across his face, as he thought of Brenda upstairs asleep. His chest expanded in pride. A glint of metal caught his eye. He glanced across the street and froze. Icy dread formed in his chest at the sight of Paula sitting across the street in her van, watching him. He blinked, knowing his mind had to be playing tricks on him. Pivoting, he strode in the direction of her van, his hand pulling out his cell on the way.

"What are you doing here?" he ground out, searching her face for a clue of something, anything to help him deal with this crazy woman.

She shrugged. "Free country."

So it's like that. He flipped open his phone, punched in a few numbers. His brother answered on the second ring.

"Start the proceedings for the lawsuit." He spoke succinctly, watching as a frown gathered on her brow and her lips tightened. "Also, see about getting a restraining order. I just walked outside and the crazy bitch is parked across the street from my house." Anger churned in his gut at her nerve. Why couldn't she just move on and leave him alone?

"Fuck you, Roark," she snapped.

He looked at her abstinent glare and dialed 9-1-1. "There's a woman stalking me." He continued in spite of her angry gasp. "She's parked in front of my house." He paused as she cranked the van, her face set in tense lines.

"No, I don't know what she wants."

She flipped him the bird and leaned out the window. "Big Roark, calling the police for a small woman in a wheelchair." She spit at him, but it landed a few feet shy of his shoes.

His eyes narrowed at her in disgust. "Get the fuck out of here, the cops are on their way."

She rolled her eyes at him. "What the hell they gonna do? I'm in a fucking wheelchair. They won't touch me," she sneered. With those last words, she drove off, leaving him in a plume of exhaust.

Roark stared at the van, a feeling of trepidation rolled through him. Paula hadn't given up. His earlier feeling of euphoria vanished like a puff of smoke, leaving tendrils of gloom behind. He turned and headed back to the house to warn his woman about this crazy bitch from his past. An acrid taste formed on the back of his tongue at the thought of what he'd say. He prayed that she'd still look at him with that look of love and pride in her eyes when he finished.

The house was quiet. He hated disturbing her rest, but knew it was necessary. Paula may be in a wheelchair, but she knew people who knew people, and he didn't want his baby caught unaware. His eyes swept the first floor of his home, wondering if the security system was up to par. He'd have someone check it out, maybe add some cameras or something. They'd be leaving for the islands soon; he could hire someone to watch the house while he was at work. Thoughts of providing for her safety clogged his mind as he walked into the bedroom. His eyes rested on her sleeping form. Bending forward, he placed his hand on her shoulder and shook her awake.

Sleepy eyes blinked at him, a flash of pleasure, and then she rolled away groaning, squeezing her legs together.

"No, Baby. I can't. Too sore."

He smiled as she scooted from under his hand, wrapping the sheet tight around her waist, and turning her back on him in dismissal. His smile quickly dropped away as he realized he was about to disturb her rest with his news. Inhaling the mingled scents of their recent lovemaking, he sat on the edge of the bed.

"That's not why I'm here. I need to tell you something." He wasn't sure if it was the grimness of his voice, or the fact that he wasn't touching her, that caused her to open her eyes.

She stared at him from beneath the sheets for a moment and then sat up. Leaning on one elbow, she started to speak.

He held his hand up to stop her. "I need to tell you something."

She nodded, confusion stamped her face, then slowly cleared as he told her what'd just happened outside. As her eyes chilled, pain lanced through his chest. He was losing her.

Chapter 7

Brenda glanced through the mini blinds and saw the gray van parked across the street, a few doors down. A few days had passed since Roark first explained about the woman who now sat outside his home. Brenda wasn't sure how she felt about the accident yet. A part of her felt bad for Paula, while another felt anger that she'd driven while under the influence of drugs, especially with someone else in the car. Roark had allowed her to read the accident report. The fact that he walked away with just a few scratches surprised her. In the picture, the car had been twisted beyond repair.

The police came yesterday and spoke to Paula about the restraining order Roark had petitioned for. In Brenda's opinion, it only seemed to make the woman angrier and more determined to annoy him like a bee buzzing around his face. Legally, there wasn't much else he could do, but something told her his brothers didn't care much for legalities.

Donald had come and talked to the recalcitrant woman earlier that morning, and she'd sped off in a huff. He'd knocked on the door, re-introduced himself, and then assured her the matter would be handled soon. Brenda wasn't sure what that meant, and nodded without asking any questions. He left shortly thereafter. Idly, she wondered if she should alert Roark that the van was back.

Deciding against it, she twirled, feeling giddy as she released a happy sigh. Ten more days before they left for the Cayman Islands and put this Paula-drama behind. She tidied up the bedroom, and then headed downstairs to start pulling the ingredients together for dinner. Her cell went off. After glancing at the caller ID, she smiled.

"Hey, girl," she cooed, happy to hear from Denise.

"Hey. You good?"

"Yep, still in my happily ever after part of the story," Brenda quipped, chuckling when Denise burst out laughing.

"So, you got the fairy-tale, huh?" Denise said between chortles of laughter.

Brenda nodded, proud of the way she explained how she felt with Roark. "Yeah, I got it."

Denise's voice sobered, alerting her something was off. "Lord knows you've already had the evil stepsister, bitch of a mother, and hard-ass villain. Roark did rescue you and take you away from all that. You deserve all the happiness in ever after land."

"Thanks." She hated to ask, but knew it was necessary. "What's wrong?"

"Got a call from Celia."

Brenda frowned. "Celia, my cousin?" They hadn't talked since she was a teenager.

"That's what she said. I vaguely remember you telling me your mom had a sister who had a couple of kids."

Brenda remembered the conversation all too well. Denise had asked why she didn't leave Tex and go home. Her friend had been appalled after she explained. Brenda's mom didn't have her own place, and her aunt was in a nursing home. Brenda had offered to care for her aunt, but the offer went ignored. Her aunt's children lived out of town, refused to move their mother in with them, and were too embarrassed to allow other family members to move into their mom's home and assist the older woman. It'd been years since Brenda had seen her aunt.

"Yeah, Celia and Clint. What'd she say?" A coil of tension rolled in her belly fostered by guilt. It pierced her, she hadn't thought about her aunt in years. *Please don't let her be dead.*

"Her mom's dying and has been calling out your name. She wants to see you. Your cousin claims she refuses to talk to her or anyone else."

Shock gripped Brenda's throat. "What?...Me? I wonder why?"

"I don't know. I told her I'd try to reach you and relay the message."

Brenda dropped into the chair, her mind racing at the implications. "When'd she call?"

"About ten minutes ago. She left a number for you to call. You got a pen?"

She looked around the room, scattering papers until she found a pen that worked. "Yeah, give it to me." She wrote down the number as Denise called it out.

"How'd she get your number?" Brenda asked, looking at the numbers on the paper in front of her. She didn't recognize the area code.

"Good question." Denise paused. Brenda could hear the mental wheels turning. "She called the house line, so maybe she went through the construction company and they gave her the number. I'll look into it."

"You don't have to do that," Denise said in a rush. "I was just curious." She waited a beat. "How're the girls? Red?"

"You don't change subjects worth a damn. I'mma have to teach you the art of finesse." Brenda laughed until Denise continued. "Everybody's good. The girls wanted to wear their flower-girl dresses to school so everyone could see how pretty they looked. Red was going to let them do it until I explained a few things to his big ass, like sleeping in separate rooms until we say our vows."

Brenda gasped. "You didn't."

"Hell yeah, I did. Their dresses are about the only thing I chose in my whole wedding, I was not about to allow them to mess them up playing dress up. He needs to learn to tell them no, and I'mma help him with that."

Brenda chuckled at Denise's self-righteous tone. A beep came across the line.

"I gotta go, that's my babies' daddy on the other line," Denise sassed.

"No problem. I'll give Celia a call, find out what's up." They disconnected and Brenda stared at the numbers a second or two longer. She had no explanation why she didn't want to talk to her cousin, but a wave of anxiety washed over her at the thought of reconnecting with her family. Things had been great in her world and she didn't want to let in anything from the outside to jinx it.

"God gives you family, you chose your friends." Growing up, her mama's godmother had told her that on numerous occasions when her mother wouldn't return to pick her up for days. As a child, the disappointments stamped on the old woman's face had been hard to understand. After her godmother's death, she'd lived with her mother full time and finally understood. Mable Dupree was not cut out to be a mother. She'd voiced that opinion many times herself and followed it up with her actions, leaving her younger daughter in the care of anyone who'd take her, until Brenda became old enough to fend for herself.

Aunt Robin had tried to intervene, and Brenda had spent a lot of time in her home. Celia and Clint were much older and lived out of town with their own families. Many days, her aunt had been the only person standing between Brenda and foster care. Guilt suffused her as she remembered the gruff older woman who'd made sure she had enough to eat, warm clothes to wear, and a place to sleep. Her aunt wasn't an affectionate or demonstrative woman, but Brenda knew the old grump loved her in her own way. Stiffening her resolve, she dialed the number.

****

Roark watched Brenda pack a small carry-on bag for her flight. A part of him was happy she'd be away from his stalker. Paula had gotten bolder and was sending him ridiculous emails about Brenda. The last thing he wanted was that psychopath fixated on his woman. Maybe her spending the next day or so with her aunt wasn't a bad idea, he reasoned.

"You okay?" Brenda asked, watching him.

"Yeah, just thinking," he answered, rubbing his chin.

After closing the suitcase, she walked over to him and wrapped her arms around his waist. "It's just for a couple of days, you'll have me all to yourself when I get back."

He'd gone completely still when she wrapped her arms around him, enjoying the feel of her cheek rubbing against his sweater, snuggling closer. "I know, but I'll still miss you." His voice had dropped an octave. Her hand made small circular rotations on his back, soothing him.

Roark let go of her then, grabbed her face between his hand, and stared her in the eye. "I don't want you to leave me, not today, not tomorrow, never. You got that?" His heart melted at the change in her face. Water filled her eyes as she nodded. "But, I understand you need to do this. Hell, I want you to do this, just not without me." He grumbled the real reason for his discomfort.

Gentle hands wiped his brow, sending spirals of satisfaction down his spine. His eyes locked on hers as he tightened his hands around her waist.

"I know. But you can't take time off now and then again for our trip later. And if I had to choose between you going with me to see my aunt in a nursing home and taking me to the Cayman Islands…" Brenda let the words trail off. Her face clearly stated her choice.

He chuckled and tapped her nose. "Regardless, I should go with you. I haven't forgotten those assholes who were after you a few months ago."

"Red said they've been taken care of," she said hesitantly as worry lines furrowed her brow.

He grunted, still pissed about her leaving him behind, but unwilling to scare her. "Yeah, he did, but I'd feel better if I were there."

"So would I." She pecked his lips, a small sample of her taste. It wasn't enough, not nearly enough. "But, you have to work, finish up a project, and make sure things run smoothly when you take me away." Her voice had risen with excitement with each word she'd spoken.

Exhaling, he recognized unreasonableness when he saw it, so he relented and put her luggage on the floor. "How much time before your flight leaves?" Although he knew the exact moment she'd be leaving him behind, he wanted her to tell him.

Glancing at the clock on the nightstand and then swinging back at him, she smiled coyly. They stared at each other shamelessly with an undeniable hunger. He pulled off his sweater and threw it to the floor. Her eyes lazily tracked his movements as if mesmerized. An awkward silence fell as they continued to stare at each other. He motioned to her dress. Slowly, as if he were her puppet-master, she unzipped the dress, and stepped out of it. Shy smiles played on both their mouths as they gravitated to one another.

"I have time to take care of you," she whispered, her darkening eyes never leaving his.

"That's where you're wrong." He offered a ghost of a smile struggling to swallow as he brought a hand to her cheek. His eyes roamed over her face, her neck, everything they could touch for memory. "Right now, I'm going to take damn good care of you."

He pulled her close, his hand landing on her chest, squeezing and kneading her breast as they kissed passionately. Breathing was the last thing on his mind. Infused with her scent, his cock hardened to the point of pain. His hand snaked lower to find his treasure. He smiled, pleased she was dripping wet. One finger eased inside her, her breath warm on his chest. She sighed at his entry. He hooked the finger and exited. Her fingernails bit into his back as she moaned and twisted against him. He inserted another finger, her walls flexed and tightened. Releasing his breath, he worked her pussy with his fingers, loving the feel of her riding his hand.

Brenda's forehead hit his chest. Her body stiffened, pressed harder into him, and then she shook with the force of her release. A yell tore from her throat. She held him firmly around the waist until the final shiver stopped.

He removed his fingers slowly and brought them to his mouth. Her sex-glazed eyes watched him suck the fingers that had been inside her. She moaned as he led her to the bed.

"Like I said, I plan to take care of you." He gripped her hips, pulled her close, and proceeded to do just that.

****

Brenda pulled her luggage down the airport corridor and flipped open her phone. After pressing Roark's speed dial number, she waited a beat for him to pick-up.

"Hey, you there already?"

She smiled at the huskiness in his voice. She'd laid it on him before she left; he'd been so tired, she had to drive them to the airport. It came as no surprise he'd gone home and went to sleep. Worry over her aunt had kept her awake during most of the flight. Now that she was in Detroit, she was in a hurry to see the woman.

"Yeah, I'm heading to the baggage area. My cousin is sending her nephew to pick me up or something. They'll take me to see my aunt, and then to Denise's house." She walked at a determined clip toward the exit.

"Sounds good. I hope she's okay." He yawned. "Sorry, 'bout that. Give me a call tonight from Red's so I can put you to bed."

She snickered at the image. "Riiiight, get your rest, Boo. I'll talk to you soon." She clicked off, seeing a short Latina holding a sign with her name. *I thought she said her nephew.* Brenda walked up to the woman, a hesitant smile on her face.

"I'm Brenda Washington," she said, holding out her hand. The woman's eyes flicked to her outstretched appendage and then back at her face. Brenda could've sworn a look of surprise crossed the woman's face; it blanked so fast, Brenda wondered if she'd imagined the reaction. Turning, the woman tilted her chin toward the exit. "We're parked out here."

Brenda nodded and followed. She didn't know any of her cousins' children, but she hoped they weren't all this rude. In the parking area they stopped at a car that looked new. Brenda stored her luggage in the back seat.

"How's Aunt Robin doing?" she asked, her mind returning to the purpose of her visit.

The woman shrugged and started the car. "Don't know." Her terse words made it clear she had no interest in having a discussion.

Okay, gotcha. Heifer didn't even introduce herself. Brenda leaned back and watched the changing landscape as they left the city. After an hour of silence, her imagination had created enough scenarios of her aunt's condition that finally she had to shut it down. Her limited knowledge of everything made guessing a stressful pastime.

"How much longer?" Brenda asked, noticing the sparseness of the area. Homes were few and far between; abandoned factories, stores, shops were everywhere. It seemed out of the way for a nursing home, but maybe that was the idea, to keep these people far away from everything they knew before.

"Not much." After another twenty minutes, they stopped at an old gas station. The woman got out and went inside, leaving Brenda in the car. She decided to call Denise, let her know she'd be late. All she got was voice mail, so she left a message.

"Hey girl, seems like we're running later than I thought, we've been driving for over an hour and still haven't reached Aunt Robin's. This place must be far out, cause ain't much round here but old factories. We've stopped for gas. At least I think that's what she's getting in there. Anyway, I'll call you once I'm on my way to your house, after I see my aunt." She hung up and thought to call Roark to pass the time, until she remembered he was asleep. "I'll call him later," she murmured, and replaced her phone in her coat jacket while leaning against the headrest. She closed her eyes, fighting sleep.

A minute or two later, the driver's side and the rear passenger doors opened simultaneously. Before she could say a word or open her eyes, someone placed a cloth over her mouth and nose. Desperately needing air, she inhaled; her world darkened and went black.

Chapter 8

Denise jumped from the bed to grab her phone while glancing at the clock. "You'd better be glad you're my girl, it's late as hell and I'm still waiting up for you. Where the hell you at?"

Silence met her outburst. "Bren?"

She looked at the caller ID. "Roark?"

"Yeah, and my guess is Brenda isn't there with you."

Her heart dropped at the hopefulness in his voice. "No, she's not here yet." Another glance at the clock, thirty minutes after midnight. "She left a message six or seven hours ago, saying she was running late and she'd call me when she was on her way here. I assumed you were her." Her voice ended in a whisper as fear raced through her. Brenda might blow her off, but not Roark. "Did she call you?"

"Earlier, when her flight arrived. Her cousin sent someone to pick her up and she left with him or her. That was the last time I talked to her." She could hear the frustration and concern in his voice. "Where is she? Any ideas. This isn't like her to not contact anyone."

From behind, Red wrapped his arms around her, offering comfort. "Roark," she whispered, letting Red know who was on the other end. His arms tightened at his brother's name.

Clearing her throat, she spoke. "There's no one here, other than me, who she still dealt with. I know she wouldn't contact her sister or mother." Her heart broke at the thought of something happening to her girl. Brenda had been through so much. "I'mma make some calls, and get back with you."

"Please call me back tonight."

"Brenda?" Red asked, releasing her as she walked to her desk and retrieved her note pad.

"Yeah, she got in this afternoon, and was supposed to go see her aunt at the retirement home. She called while we were at the caterers earlier, but I had the phone muted." She flipped through the page until she found Celia's number.

"She didn't leave a message?" He stood and pulled out his cell.

"Um hmm, said she was running late and would call when she left the nursing home. I have it on my phone." She lifted the device and dialed the number on the pad. It answered on the second ring.

"Either she'll be here tomorrow or Roark will," Red muttered, dialing Smoke and Ross on a three-way call.

Denise agreed. The shit was going to hit the fan as soon as the sun rose, and they needed to be prepared for damage control.

****

After Roark hung up from Denise, he tried to make the room stop spinning. *Brenda was missing.* He couldn't stop the repetitions in his mind, each time it got louder and louder. Overwhelmed, his chest heaved. Struggling to inhale, his breath lodged in his throat. *Brenda was missing.* The words became a roar. He tried to shut them out, to escape the guilt. His legs failed him. He crumpled to the carpet. His heart felt solid and cold, like a block of ice, as his forehead touched the floor.

Brenda was missing; his baby was somewhere out there. He'd known something was wrong. How could he have slept so long? She might've tried to reach him. His heart broke at the thought of her at the hands of those men who attacked her in the restaurant months ago. Why hadn't he insisted she wait for him? Better yet, why hadn't he dropped everything and taken her? The mess with Paula seemed miniscule in light of his woman missing. *Go find her*. The thought rose in his chest, lifting him to his knees with the strength of its demand. Sitting on the chair, he scrounged around for his cell and made a call.

Roark was packed before the call from Denise came. His uncle had given him access to his private plane, but the pilot couldn't make it before four in the morning. He planned to hang out at the hangar in case the man came in earlier. When the phone rang, he saw his future sister-in-law's name and girded up. He needed to be strong no matter what she said.

"Hey?" He infused some hope into his voice.

"Hey." The wobbliness of her voice told him she didn't know more this time than before. "I…I talked to her cousin. She said her nephew must've missed Brenda at the airport; he waited and didn't see her. Then I called the nursing home and they said she came and left around six this evening."

Roark frowned. "No. Something's off with that. She was excited about seeing you and the girls. She would have shown up." His cheek ticked as he thought of the ramifications of her at the nursing home. Did someone take her after she left her aunt? Who picked her up? Unanswered questions flew around his mind. He caught Denise's yawn and remembered the time. Red was going to kick his ass for keeping his woman up this late.

"Get some rest, I'll see you in a few."

Denise chuckled. "Red said you were on your way."

"Damn straight." His tone was serious. He planned to find her and make sure this bullshit never happened again.

****

Twenty-four hours later and he still didn't have a clue. Roark's mind whirled with all the possibilities, chilling him to his bones. Brenda seemed to have vanished. He sat in the stuffed chair in Red's family room, elbows on his knees, hands pressed together at his forehead as if in prayer, eyes closed. A quiet hush hovered in the air, even his nieces gave him his space to grieve. Impotent, he choked back his anguish and despair. *Where are you? I need you*, his mind whispered.

"Roark?" The deep voice sounded familiar.

He blinked and stared up at the outline of his oldest brother. Unsure he was seeing correctly, afraid it was a figment of his imagination. "Frank?" His throat was sore, his voice raspy.

Roark's eyes roved over Frank's face as he stooped down to greet him. A giddy feeling bubbled up from Roark's gut. His big brother was here. Being much younger, Roark's father had been lenient with him and Red, to the point they had little supervision while they grew up. Frank had stepped in and filled the gaps, becoming a surrogate of sorts, making sure Roark and Red had solid foundations. It was Frank who steered them away from gangs. Frank who visited colleges with him. Frank who gave him summer jobs to learn the value of being his own man. It wasn't that his father didn't love him, Roark knew the old man did.

Without thinking, he reached out and clasped the hand extended toward him. Tears welled in his eyes as he searched for reassurance in Frank's. His brother had never failed him. Please God, he prayed, help me find Brenda. With each passing minute, fear paralyzed more of Roark's mind, leaving him unable to move or function.

"Listen, we need to go over everything again." Frank paused and tried to stand.

Roark tensed and squeezed his hand tighter, afraid to let go. Afraid his tether to reality would snap under the strain of his loss.

"It's okay, I'm not going anywhere." Frank's soothing words relaxed him, although he still didn't release his brother's hand.

"I can't find her," Roark whispered, his throat tightening around the words. "I looked everywhere and I can't find her." His eyes locked with Frank's as he tried to communicate his pain with those limited words. Could Frank understand the grayness of his world now that she wasn't here, the agony in his heart, the emptiness in his arms. It all tore at him, ripping him apart. "I need her." He had to make Frank understand he was dying every second he was without her. He needed his brother to know how important she was to him, how he felt. Unashamed, he released the tears as he stared at Frank, knowing he'd understand and not think less of him. "I love her."

Frank nodded and squeezed his hand. "I know, man. We've got you on this. I need you to talk to me, walk me through what you've already done."

Roark stared, watching his brother's lips move. The words became distant, groggy. His eyelids drooped. Dots formed in front of him.

"Roark!"

The loud voice tugged at him, he needed to do something. He couldn't think. The sounds were far away.

"Roark! Come on man, stay with me."

Something cold hit his face, it felt good.

"Whaaat?" He tried to focus. He saw his brother, and then another one. They were in front of him, frowns on their faces. "What's wrong?" He wondered why they were mad.

"Nothing. When did you last eat?" Red asked.

"Have you gotten any sleep since you've been here?" Frank interrupted.

He shrugged. All of his energies were targeted at finding Brenda. Neither food nor rest had entered his mind.

"Damn." Red stood a ways behind Frank.

"Come on, you need to rest a minute, and then we'll talk." Frank eased him up. Roark's legs felt rubbery, but his brother kept a firm grip on his arm as he walked him to the downstairs bedroom. A fuzzy calm washed over him. Frank was here. They'd find Brenda and he'd kill anyone who'd tried to hurt her. That was a good plan. The darkness in the room welcomed him and his morbid thoughts as he lay on the bed. Yeah, the fucker that messed with his woman wouldn't see the light of day after he found him.

Frank walked back into the family room where Red waited. He'd never seen Roark so out of it before. Vaguely he remembered the girl his brother had rescued from the restaurant months ago. Obviously, things had changed tremendously since then. Roark was in love with the girl. He watched Red pace, and exhaled.

"I came home as soon as Denise called me, about an hour ago. She was worried because he was just sitting here and wouldn't respond to anyone. I'm surprised he recognized you." Red shook his head as he looked at Frank. "I almost called mama."

Frank chuckled, imagining his mom's reaction to any of her sons being in a comatose state. It wouldn't be pretty. "We may have to eventually, but let's wait. I want to hear the message Brenda left Denise, and I need the address to the nursing home."

Red nodded and left.

Frank pulled out his phone and punched in a few numbers. Veronique answered on the first ring. He smiled.

"How is he?" she asked before he offered a greeting.

"Pretty bad. I just put him to bed, he hasn't eaten or rested since he's been here."

"I'm sorry. I wish I could help."

"You can. I'm going to the nursing home and I need something legal to access their records. Can you hook me up with something that'll get me in the door?"

"Frank, are you asking me to do something illegal?" The smile in her voice cued him in that she was teasing him.

"The only illegal things I want you to do are with me, in a closed room, with the lights on. I need to see every inch of you." He chuckled at her small gasp.

"Remember where you are. Now's not the time to talk dirty. Focus on your brother," she chided.

"Whenever I talk to you is the right time to talk of my fantasies. As for my brother, I can multi-task."

"Tsk, tsk. Give me the name and information on the home along with Brenda's aunt's name. I'll fax over something to get you into her files. But

I'd start with the visitor logs if I were you."

"Okay, tell me what I'm looking for." He took the seat Roark had been in and listened carefully.

"Denise told me the phone call to come see her aunt came out of the blue. Apparently her aunt was having dreams or visions, and wanted to see Brenda before she died. If that's all there is, you need to know that."

"But you think there's more."

"Yeah. According to Denise, Brenda hasn't seen the woman in years. So why now? I think the cousin is telling the truth as far as she knows. But there's probably a reason for this sudden need to get Brenda back in Michigan."

"Damn, Baby. I hadn't thought about it from that angle. Somebody wanted Brenda here, alone. But who? Who would've gone through all that trouble? Those assholes that fucked with the company are either dead or locked up."

"Maybe they have friends or family. Wouldn't you want retribution against someone who messed over one of your brothers? Or sister?"

"Most definitely." He thought for a moment. "Okay, just get me access to the visitor's logs so I can see who's been visiting the aunt. I think you may be on to something. Red's getting the tape from when Brenda called Denise yesterday afternoon, I'm going to draw a map in several directions to discover which direction she may have taken based on the time she called Denise."

"That's good. Let me know if you find anything."

"When does your flight get in?" Frank missed her terribly. He didn't know what he'd do if this was Veronique and not Brenda. He'd waited so long to find love and now that it had kicked him on his ass, he held it tight with both hands.

"Tomorrow night. I'm renting a car and heading to Cherise's."

"No!" Frank stiffened. Anger pulsed through him. There was no way he'd allow her to be in the same town and not stay with him.

"Yes," she said in a calm tone contradicting him. "I want to see my daughter and grandchild. You'll probably have me so busy I might not get a chance later. Don't be selfish."

Tension flowed out of him at her words. Another thought hit him. "I haven't been introduced to Cherise as your man. Do you want me to meet you there before we go to the hotel?"

Veronique took a moment too long to answer.

His stomach dropped. "Unless you don't want to. I guess you want time alone with her. I understand. Call me when you get here." He spoke fast, backtracking his offer.

"No, it's just, you're right. I hadn't thought about it that way. Come to think of it, I haven't been introduced to your family as your woman either." She sighed. "I'm so used to having you to myself; I never think to include anybody else. I figured we had 'til the wedding at least. I guess we have to let everyone know we're a couple this trip, otherwise they'll think you're stalking me."

"As if," he snorted, taking her jibe good-naturedly, although it did remind him of another problem his brother had back at home. Roark was definitely going through some challenges right now.

"I'll call you from Cherise's, and we can have dinner together with them," Veronique said.

Excitement raced through him, she wasn't brushing him off. His chest lightened. "That sounds good, Baby," he purred, his eyes lowered to the ground. "I miss you."

"Same here. Probably more, but I'm not going to argue about it." She laughed when he grunted. "I'll see you tomorrow." She clicked off.

He continued staring at the floor, a grin on his face.

"So it's like that, huh?" Red asked, handing him their home phone.

Frank's face heated as he took the device. "Must be something in the water." He smirked, and turned on the phone. Seconds later, Brenda's message came across the line. When it was over, Frank sat thinking about possible locations.

"So who is she?"

Startled, Frank looked at Red. Was it possible his brother really didn't know? He was sure Denise and Cherise talked. And Cherise knew he and Veronique were dating. Testing the waters, he glanced at Red. "Who are you talking about?"

Red rolled his eyes. "Who's the woman who put that silly ass grin on your face?"

The smirk turned into a full-blown grin. He wasn't ashamed and took the ribbing in stride. "Veronique." He laughed at the confusion on his brother's face.

"Veronique?" Red paused, and then his eyes widened in enlightenment. "Cherise's mom? The lawyer?"

Frank nodded slowly, his head tilted in a proud angle. "Yeah, we met in Philly a little while back and things just clicked. She'll be here tomorrow." He glanced at Red. "Close your mouth."

Red's mouth snapped shut. "Congratulations, big dog. She's one fiery, feisty lady. You'll need to watch your step."

Frank shrugged. "I like her fire just fine." He winked at his brother and looked for his car keys. "I'm going to head to the nursing home and have a look around. Watch Roark and make sure he eats. Have him call me after he eats. Tell him I will not speak to him until he's eaten a full meal."

Red nodded, a large grin appeared on his face. It was obvious he relished teasing his brother. "He's going to be mad."

"Yeah, but he's going to need his strength to find Brenda." Both men sobered. Frank looked at Red. "We all are. This stinks and right now, we don't have a clue where she is. I hope I find something at the nursing home that Roark overlooked. Veronique gave me some fresh ideas I plan to pursue.

"As it is, Blaine and Donald are rearranging their schedules to get here in the next day or so. Mom is harassing dad's probation officer to let him come early before the wedding, and Uncle Nate is calling in favors. Roark's situation is weighing heavy on mama and dad."

"I know." Red paused. "Should I postpone the wedding?"

Frank snorted. "No. Mama would have a fit even if Denise agreed. We'll find her in plenty of time before the wedding." Even if it's just her remains, went unsaid. He thrust away the morbid thought, afraid of what it might do to Roark's psyche if Brenda were dead. His brother was in the grips of his first true love, losing her might crush him.

Chapter 9

Taut nerves and a lack of appetite left Roark feeding off reserve energy. They still hadn't located his Brenda. She could be anywhere. Frank had gone to the nursing home yesterday and was denied access to the records he wanted to see. Veronique worked her legal magic, and he and Frank were allowed to view the visitors logs at the nursing home today. Either the log was a fake, or somebody was a fake, because the log was wrong and he let everyone know, loudly. The administrators of the home called the police and there was an investigation pending. He prayed it wasn't too late. Things were moving much too slow for him.

He and Frank then headed to Ross and Cherise's for an early dinner. Red and Denise drove in the car ahead of them, and he didn't doubt Smoke and his new woman would be there as well. *Food and strategy*. He could do without the first; he wanted to move on to the second. His baby could be anywhere; he wondered if she had food. The temperatures had dropped; he prayed she was warm. She hadn't packed much. Clenching his jaw, his eyes closed tight against the mental image of Brenda hurt and alone somewhere. *I'm coming, Baby*. He sent warmth and love with *Jedi* messaging in the hope that maybe, just maybe, she'd know his heart and mind were with her.

A hand fell on his shoulder. "We're going to find her. I know it's hard, but we will find her." Frank's gruff voice filled the void of silence in the car. Too upset to speak, Roark nodded and continued to stare out the window. They soon approached the gated community where Ross and Cherise lived.

"First we'll grab a bite, then put our heads together, see where the holes are and plug'em," Frank said, his tone certain, leaving Roark alone with his thoughts.

Roark felt his brother's concern. They all watched him when they thought he wasn't looking. What they didn't understand was he could feel the weight of their stares on his back, there was no need for subterfuge. Staring at the passing landscape, he fantasized that this was all a bad dream, that he'd wake up and find Brenda in their bedroom waiting for him with her sexy grin. He loved the way her eyes lit up as he strolled into the room. Or, she'd be in the kitchen fussing at him for stealing something from a pot. A grin tilted the corner of his mouth in memory. The woman was ferocious when it came to her kitchen; she kept it spotless and made the best dishes out of things he'd never liked before. He didn't think he'd ever look at liver quite the same again. His baby had a way of turning one of his least favorite meats into a gourmet dish. He closed his eyes in anguish. *Brenda,* his heart cried out, missing her, scared for her, most of all loving her. He should've told her he loved her. That he wanted to marry her, spend his life with her. In light of everything going on, waiting to propose on the Cayman Islands seemed stupid. There was so much he needed to say to her, he prayed he'd get a chance.

"We're here." Frank opened his door and stepped out.

Roark hadn't realized they'd stopped. He got out of the car and immediately noticed the brisk evening air felt good against his warm flesh. Inhaling, he allowed the cool breeze to clear his mind. He needed to be sharp, focused. One step in front of the other, he moved toward the front step, determined to get through another painful night.

"Hey guys," Cherise said as he and Frank reached the porch steps. Roark could hear the twins, his nieces Shantel and Shannon, greeting Ross's daughter, Lenora. There were some other voices in the background as well. He offered a smile, gave a nod in greeting, and shook hands with robotic precision.

"Come here," Frank growled, pulling a grinning Veronique to his chest. Roark's eyes widened as his brother threw down a lip-lock on Cherise's mom. The kiss seemed to go on for days. Even the twins took notice.

"Look at Unca Frank. He kissin." Shannon pointed out the obvious.

"That's my Nana he kissin." Lenora pointed at the pair with a hand on her hip and a disapproving glare.

The couple broke apart, laughing.

"Mama, Unca Frank kissing Nora's Nana." The twins ran out the room, yelling.

Roark smiled at the scene. His brother looked happy holding his woman. He left the two lovebirds. It hurt to watch, so he walked toward the family room.

"Hey, Roark." Ross strode forward, gave him a fist pound and then slapped him on the back. "Good to see you, got some food and drinks in the back. You want anything?"

"Nah, I'm good. Thanks though." He waved down the offer.

Ross nodded and headed in the opposite direction. Roark walked into the family room, and noticed Smoke with a very sexy Latina on his lap. They disengaged as soon as they noticed him. The woman's cheeks pinkened and Roark could imagine what he'd interrupted.

"Whassup?" Smoke greeted him, tapped his fist, and stood back, watching him closely.

"Nothing much." Roark nodded and looked at the woman standing next to Smoke.

"This is my lady, Vianca, private investigator extraordinaire." Smoke pulled the voluptuous beauty close and kissed her forehead.

She punched Smoke's shoulder. "Asshole. Just a simple investigator. Nice to meet you."

"Same here." Roark's chest ignited. An investigator? Things were looking up. A flare of hope blossomed. Between all of them, they should be able to find his baby.

"Look man," Smoke said, watching him narrowly, "I know you don't feel like doing much of eating or talking right now. Fuck, if she was missing," he tilted his head toward Vianca, "I'd be losing my damn mind. I just want you to know that every man here gets where the hell you're coming from, and anything you need or want to do, we got your back."

Vianca pushed away from Smoke and glared up at him. "Don't be encouraging him with your vigilante thinking. We'll get Brenda, but then we need to turn things over to the authorities." She turned and looked at Roark. "You don't want blood on your hands from this."

Roark stared at her. As far as he was concerned, if someone took his woman, they were dead. If she was lost or in an accident, he'd find her and take care of her. Period.

"I told you, Vee, this is a man thing. Muthafuckers can't mess with a man's woman, that shit just don't fly." He stared at Roark and an understanding passed between them. If this was an abduction, the bastard would pay with his life.

Vianca groaned, threw up her arms, and headed out the doorway. "Men and their damn egos."

Roark sat in one of the oversized leather chairs. Smoke took another chair; it was obvious he had something to say, so Roark waited.

"I have some friends that can do some amazing shit. I haven't contacted the main guy because I wanted to talk to you first." Smoke looked at him, his face set in stern lines.

"I'm listening." Roark sat forward, his arms on his elbows. Right about now, he was game for anything. He wanted, no needed, to do something.

"He's…let's say connected. If I call him, he'll get the information we need, but you can't control the outcome. In other words, he'll handle things the way he sees best. His moral compass ain't all that, you feel me?" Smoke tilted his head toward the picture of a cross on the wall and chuckled.

Roark nodded, thinking quickly. "Brenda won't be hurt?" He could give a shit about the rest, he simply wanted his woman safe and well.

"Nah. You have to tell me what to tell him and he'll find her. If someone took her, there will be a body count." He held up his hands to stall Roark's comments. "Think first about what I'm saying. It's one thing to think about taking someone out. It's another to be responsible for it. And make no mistake, if I talk to him about this on your behalf and blood is spilled, it's on all of our hands." Smoke paused, his face a calm mask. "Now, I've been on this road before, so the shit don't bother me. But you'll need to be ready to deal with your own conscience. Ain't no fucking do overs."

Roark only waited a second, his mind already made up. He met Smoke's eyes and locked down. "If it turns out someone took her, I want to be the one who puts the bullet in the fucker's head. Will that be possible?" He asked in the same tone he'd use to discuss the weather. Obviously, Smoke didn't know the real history of his family. His dad and his uncles had their own gang, their own brand of justice and had passed it on to their sons. You hit one, each sibling was affected and they retaliated as one axe to obliterate the problem. For someone to accost anyone the O'Connor men considered under their protection was tantamount to suicide. Over the years, blood had been shed, bodies disappeared. Despite the professional faces he and his brothers wore, they had no problem getting dirty.

Smoke coughed and choked at his unyielding request. "Damn. Guess I mistook the situation." Their eyes met again. "You serious?"

"Most definitely." Roark said in the next breath. "If your friend finds her with someone, I'd like the pleasure of a conversation with the dead bitch." The pitch of his voice didn't alter. His face remained impassive. Inside, rage boiled and bubbled at the thought that someone held Brenda against her will. Scenarios rolled and faded in his mind as to how he'd deal with the son-of-a-bitch.

"Okay, I'll talk to him." Smoke looked at him again for a long moment and then leaned back in his chair.

"You don't think this is related to the problems the company had a few months back?" Roark asked.

Smoke thought through the question. Of all the partners, Smoke was the most street savvy and would have a better feel if this was connected somehow.

"Not unless the dead can walk."

"Huh?" Roark tried to follow Smoke's cryptic remark.

"He's dead."

"Did he have any friends?"

"Maybe, but Brenda wasn't involved with anyone working with the company. From what Veronique was saying earlier, it looks as though someone lured her here and away from you." Smoke shook his head. "It just don't make sense to be part of that bullshit."

Roark exhaled, head bent, eyes closed. He wondered for the hundredth time, what had happened to Brenda.

"There you are." Veronique breezed into the room and handed him a cold drink. "Frank's bringing you a plate." She turned and winked at Smoke. "Hi, handsome."

Smoke saluted her with a nod and smile. "Hi, gorgeous."

"Stop flirting with my woman," Frank said as he handed Roark a plate piled with meat and veggies. He pointed at Roark. "You need to eat, keep up your strength."

Veronique sat next to Roark and took his hand in her much smaller one. Surprised, he met her eyes for a few seconds before she spoke. "I know you don't want to be here, you want to be out there." She tipped her head toward the window. "I don't blame you. But if you give us a few minutes, listen to everything we've all come up with, then you'll be able take off in a better direction. Is that fair? Can you give us an hour of your total attention? I wouldn't ask if I didn't think we could help. The last thing anyone wants is to waste your time, especially now." Her eyes reflected how serious this matter was for him. Of all the people in the room, he felt she connected and saw his vulnerabilities.

Exhaling, he nodded. "Yeah, I can do that. What do you have for me?"

She nodded. "Okay. You know someone has been using a fake ID at the nursing home, claiming to be Brenda."

Roark nodded, he and Frank had discovered that today. He'd exploded, and was summarily thrown out of the building.

Veronique continued. "I checked her aunt's financials, and there isn't much money. The little leftover after her care goes to her two children. So we can check that off as a motive. I talked to the police officer and he said a detective has been assigned the case." Collective groans went up in the room.

"No…no, that's not bad," Veronique said, holding her palms up in a placating gesture.

"They drag things out," Red said, sitting next to Denise on the sofa, on the other side of the room.

"They always suspect the person closest to the victim," Denise said, nodding at Roark.

"Well, he was out of town when she disappeared, so they'll have to find someone else to blame," Red said, his voice heated.

"The detectives will do their job and we'll do what we do." Frank looked at Roark and nodded.

Vianca walked into the room carrying two plates. She handed one to Smoke and sat beside him. Looking over at Roark, she asked him a question. "Who would want to take your lady?"

Roark jerked back from the jolt her words sent through him.

Vianca shook her head. "That didn't come out right. What I mean is this, someone claimed to be Brenda Washington. According to the logs at the nursing home, they visited the aunt every other day. When this fake Brenda misses a few days, the aunt goes through withdrawal-like symptoms, wailing and screaming for Brenda. This prompts a call to Brenda to come see her aunt. She comes to Michigan, bent on seeing her aunt, and disappears enroute." Vianca paused into the silent room. Roark watched expressions chase across her face as she put the pieces of the puzzle together.

She frowned, worry-lines spreading across her forehead. "A stranger didn't do this. This was someone who knew how everyone would respond under those conditions. What I'm asking is, who would that person be?"

Roark sat frozen, unable to answer the question. Her analysis of the situation sounded like a badly written movie. A simple and complex plan. So much could've gone wrong. How'd they know he wouldn't come? How'd they know he wouldn't have insisted she rent her own car? Was it possible they didn't know about him? Maybe he never figured into the equation. Brenda didn't talk much about her family. As far as he knew, she didn't have many friends.

"She has a sister, but they don't get along," Roark said, feeling his way.

"No. She and that bitch don't speak. Bren wouldn't have dealt with her at all. I don't think they've spoken to each other in three years," Denise said, her voice tight with anger or sorrow, Roark couldn't tell which.

"Why?" Veronique asked. Although she looked at Roark, she directed her question to Denise.

"Anna, that's Bren's sister, had a lot to do with her break—, oh shit!"Denise jumped up and walked in a small circle. "Oh, shit."

Red stood and rubbed her back to calm her down. "What?"

Denise looked around the room, her eyes wide when they fell on Roark. "Tex," she whispered.

Roark shrugged. The name meant nothing to him. Obviously, he was someone important to Denise.

"Brenda's ex-boyfriend. Tex. They lived together for a few years." She turned to Red. "You remember, the four of us went out together at first."

A thread of apprehension slid through Roark's chest. *Ex-boyfriend*? What the fuck? "Finish about her ex." He hadn't meant to snap, and ignored Red's frown.

Denise rubbed her forehead and re-took her seat. Red followed and placed his arm around her shoulders in a protective gesture. "I can't believe I forgot. He contacted her…"

"What?" Roark jumped up. A strong sense of foreboding destroyed his patience. "When? While she was with me?" He shook his head in denial. He refused to believe Brenda had been talking to any other man while they were together.

Denise waved him down. "It was the night you took her to dinner and surprised her with the island trip. Earlier that day, he sent her an email. It said something like, 'Hi, what's up?' I told her to send it to me so I could answer his trifling ass. But she'd deleted it already."

His heart calmed, she hadn't even responded to the asshole. *Why hadn't she told him?*

Brenda continued. "She said if she didn't respond, he'd never know if he reached her, or something like that."

"Good thinking," Veronique said.

"She planned to tell you at dinner that night about it." Denise bit her nail and looked at him askance.

"What, Denise? If there's more, tell me," Roark said, aggravated at her coy act. There wasn't a bashful bone in his future sister-in-law's body.

"I advised her not to tell you unless you told her of your past stuff." She said the sentence in a rush. There wasn't a sound in the room when she finished. Roark wondered if everyone was as surprised by her audacity as he was. That busy-body! Vividly, he now recalled the dinner conversation that night; he'd told Brenda he didn't want to know about her past men. But he'd been covering his own indiscretions, not thinking of hers. What a fool he'd been.

"Wow," Vianca said before popping a meatball in her mouth.

"Okaaay," Veronique said drily into the wall of silence. "Tex, that's a new name in the equation. What do you know about him, Denise?"

Clearing her throat, Denise said, "He was cool at first, they dated while they were in college. Then he started hanging with the wrong people. Things got worse." She met Roark's eyes as they hardened. Inhaling, she continued. "They'd been together a couple of years when he started selling drugs or something low key, I'm not sure what. Bren said he came in one night with Anna, they were both high, and her sister put her hand down Tex's pants. Even though he was high, he pushed Anna off him. Somehow they got to scuffling and Brenda lost the baby."

Baby? Brenda lost a baby. Panic seized Roark's reason. He couldn't speak. He *needed* to speak. It hurt. It hurt that he didn't know this about the woman he loved. That someone else had created life with her. That someone else had harmed her. His heart hammered in his chest. Breathing became a necessary chore. "Go on." His whispery thin voice betrayed his calm façade.

Denise swallowed noisily. Red rubbed her back. "Well, from what I remember, Brenda said she was lying on the floor, bleeding, and Anna ran outside. One of the neighbors called the police. Tex was high, one of his boys came to the door and told him Anna was up to something and he needed to leave before the cops came. He left."

"What?" Vianca exploded jumping up from her seat. "He left her alone bleeding in the middle of a miscarriage?"

Denise nodded, tears falling down her bronzed cheeks. Red rubbed her shoulders and pulled her close.

"That bastardo," Vianca snapped, and pulled out her cell phone. Someone answered and she spoke a spate of Spanish, waving her arms as she walked back and forth near the wall.

Frozen, Roark's heart stopped. It must have, he couldn't feel anything. He struggled to remain calm. His unfocused, dazed eyes stared at the wall. How could anyone have done that to her? To his Brenda? Nausea cramped his stomach as he imagined her lying helpless with his child. A chill ripped through him. Blocking the debilitating thoughts, he tried to focus on finding her, healthy and whole.

Small, warm hands covered his. Tension ebbed from his shoulders as he suppressed a ragged sigh. He didn't look at Veronique, but was grateful for her presence.

When she spoke, he appreciated her even more. "Okay, we put Tex down as a person of interest. But, according to Denise, Brenda hasn't talked to or seen this guy in over two years. Would a man wait that long to do something like this? Was he incarcerated or something?" She looked around the room.

Vianca held up her finger while listening on the phone. A few seconds later she hung up, her lips tight, face grim. "His real name is Bruce Gordon. He served a few months in jail on some petty stuff. No prison. There's not much on him, he's pretty clean. I think he's connected." She glanced at Smoke, who frowned.

Connected? What the hell did that mean? Roark didn't get an opportunity to ask his question.

"So, if he wanted Brenda, he had plenty of time. Why would he do all of this now?" Frank asked, looking around the room. "Denise, did the email sound like he was trying to reconnect with her?"

Denise shook her head slowly, staring at the floor in concentration. "No. Like I said it was one of those, how are you, hope everything's good, kind of things." She raised her head and gazed at Frank. "But she didn't like it. For some reason she was afraid of him. She never explained everything that happened after they broke up, but he scared her, that's a fact."

Roark tensed.

Veronique squeezed his hand in reassurance. "Is this something a man would do?" She looked at each man in the room. "Would you break up with someone and wait two years to kidnap them?"

Silence brushed the room.

Smoke spoke up. "Not if I had the opportunity to see her in the interim. Why wait? She's only been gone a few months, right?" He shrugged as he looked around the room.

"It's not normal, but he may not be normal," Red added.

"Or, he may be one of those guys that leaves his ex alone as long as she is alone. Once a man comes into the picture, it pushes another button," Ross said quietly from the corner where he'd been reclining and listening.

Frank nodded. "Yeah, there are some men like that." He paused, a frown on his forehead. "But that doesn't sit with me." He looked up and caught Roark's gaze. "Dude hasn't been locked up, keeps low, out of trouble. He's got to be making some kind of bank to do that, especially if he started with drugs."

"He probably gave that up," Smoke interjected, sitting forward, hands clasped.

Frank nodded in agreement. "So he has some sort of self-control. Waiting to get himself together, might not have been hard."

"Give her some space, but keep her within his sights while he gets things ready. Then he contacts her, but doesn't hear anything," Red said, filling in more blanks. "Yeah, I can see that. I wouldn't do it, but I can see how it'd work."

"He didn't figure me into the picture," Roark said, stopping all conversation. He continued staring at the intricate patterns on the rug beneath his feet. "What if I'd have come with her? Or insisted she get a rental car, or had Red pick her up? So many variables could've thrown the whole mess off. Not to mention, if I'd taken Brenda to see her aunt, the bullshit would've hit the fan. Brenda and the woman on the ID look nothing alike."

"Wait!" Denise said. "I didn't know there was a picture of the woman. What does she look like?"

Roark shrugged, not remembering the particulars. He'd been so angry to discover someone had been using Brenda's name, he'd lost it. He looked at Frank. "You remember anything?"

"Dark hair, dark eyes, round face, she wasn't smiling or anything. It could have been one of those pictures you get when you buy a picture frame, you get me?" Frank explained.

Denise nodded and dropped back on Red's chest, grabbing his hand.

"So you don't think it'd be this dude?" Smoke asked Roark.

Roark shrugged. Uncertainty weighed him down. "It doesn't feel right. If I wanted a woman I thought was mine, I wouldn't risk her bringing another man into the picture." He looked at Smoke. "I started to come with her. I wanted her to wait a few more days so I could tag along. I know we wouldn't have gotten into a car with someone I didn't know, and this whole scheme would've been blown. There's no way anyone on this end could've known how I would react. I don't think they knew about me." He glanced at Smoke. "But I'd like to talk to Tex, just to be sure." For a moment, he stared into Smoke's eyes. Request made and verified as Smoke nodded.

"I don't blame you." Vianca stroked Smoke's arm, breaking the connection.

"Yeah," Veronique said slowly, squeezing Roark's hand while pursing her mouth in thought. "This guy, Tex, right?" She glanced at Denise who nodded. "He didn't walk into the nursing home pretending to be Brenda. That was a woman."

"True," Smoke said. Vianca nodded.

"Not only was it a woman, but it was someone who was able to get decent ID and fool Brenda's aunt," Ross said. "Even if the old woman couldn't see, she could hear. And at some point the person imitating Brenda had to know something the aunt could relate to. The fact that she requested Brenda means she felt a connection. Whoever pulled that shit off, knew something about Brenda and her aunt."

Roark nodded. He hadn't thought that far. But Ross made a lot of sense. Thinking back on all the conversations he'd had with Brenda over the past months, there was no one, family or friend that he could think of with that type of connection.

"What about the cousin? The one that called Brenda?" Frank asked, glancing in Denise's direction.

"I don't know," Denise said hesitantly. "I doubt her mom would've been fooled into thinking she was Brenda. Besides, why would she do that? From what I understand, she never comes to see her mom, anyway."

"Hmmm, good point," Frank said. "What about Brenda's mom or her sister?"

Denise frowned in concentration. "I wouldn't put it past her mama, if there was money involved. But Aunt Robin is her sister, I don't think she could've tricked her. They didn't have the best relationship, that's why Brenda stayed with her aunt so much while she was growing up. Truthfully, I don't see Bren's mom or sister in this drama. Both women are selfish and look out for themselves. From what I remember, none of them have much to do with each other. Bren's sister was doing drugs while we were in college, but I heard she got herself together and moved away. I don't even think she's in town."

"Okay," Veronique said. "We know there is a woman who has intimate knowledge of Brenda's relationship with her aunt and used it to get close to the woman, and ultimately, to bring Brenda back to Michigan. What we don't know is why? Or who this woman is. And most importantly, where they've taken her."

Veronique turned and looked at Ross. "Can some of your men ask around, get us some answers to those questions?" Some of the men who worked for the construction company had connections to gangs and crime syndicates. Those men had used their contacts earlier that year when the company had come under attack by another prison inmate.

Ross looked at Red and then Smoke.

Smoke spoke up. "I've got that covered. I should have some answers to those questions real soon."

Ross stared at Smoke and nodded.

Red exhaled deeply, rubbing his forehead.

Veronique stared at Smoke a moment longer. "Good."

Roark understood something major had just transpired. Red looked flushed. Ross stared at the wall, and Smoke rubbed Vianca's thigh.

Frank stood and reached for Veronique. She squeezed Roark's hand and stood. Frank stepped forward, wrapped his arm around her waist and dropped a kiss on her forehead.

Cherise walked into the room and glanced around. "Did I miss everything?" Her voice was whiny. Ross pulled her onto his lap. "You've got to tell me everything I missed." He kissed her on her nose and whispered something to her.

Roark stopped watching and listening. Everyone in the room had what he had with Brenda. Please let her be safe, he prayed.

"Roark can ride home with us," Denise said, as Frank pulled Veronique into the hall.

Frank looked at him. "I'll see you in the morning."

Roark strengthened his voice. "Sounds good. Thanks, Veronique, for everything. Much appreciated."

She smiled at him and left with Frank.

Smoke, Red, and Ross looked at each other for a moment.

"Veronique and Frank?" Smoke asked, grinning. "When the hell did that happen?"

"They met at some conference," Red said, a smile lighting his face. "Fire and ice, huh?"

"As long as my mom is the fire, its okay," Cherise said.

"Baby, everybody knows your mom is a pepper. Although, I've seen her freeze people with a look." Ross laughed as Cherise smacked his shoulder. The two tussled, laughing for a few moments.

"Are the girls sleeping?" Vianca asked.

Laughing, Cherise pushed Ross's groping hands away. "Yeah, that's what took me so long. They're knocked out."

Smoke tapped Roark's knee as he stood. "I'm gonna go take care of that now. I'll get back with you as soon as I hear something."

Roark nodded, noticing the silence that fell on the room. Once again, he wondered who or what type of contact did Smoke have that would cause everyone to shut down like that.

Chapter 10

Tex pulled his coat flaps close together to keep out the howling wind. It was another cold, dreary day. Looking upward, gray clouds populated the sky, blocking out the warmth of the sun. He glanced at his watch. Traffic had been abysmal, but he was still on time for his appointment. He hated these calls to visit what he thought of as "the house." The large mansion sat isolated in an upscale subdivision outside of Detroit. One would never know economic blight had befallen the big city by driving down this street. Large estates dotted the landscape with well-manicured lawns and electric fences. Excessive lawn decorations, statues and ponds were the norm. Some people had it like that.

He moved steadily up the stone pavered path to the porch. The door opened before he touched the doorbell. Nodding, he spoke to James; he assumed the older man was a butler or something. "Hey man, I'm here to see Mr. —"

"He's waiting for you in the library, Mr. Gordon." James took his coat and then ushered him to the large room on the other side of the home. Tex always imagined the place had a layout similar to the White House, on a smaller scale of course. His boss used one side strictly for business, like the west wing. The family lived on the other side and rarely ventured to the business side. James knocked on the tall wood paneled door; there was a sound and then Sabatino, his boss, opened the door. Tex schooled his features, refusing to display the surprise he felt seeing another person in the room.

"Good afternoon." Tex nodded to his boss and then waited for the reason for this summoning. Surreptitiously, he looked at the man standing near the window with his back to him.

"Thank you for coming," his boss said graciously, even though they both knew he had no choice but to come when called.

Tex nodded and remained standing.

Sabatino rubbed the back of his neck, faltering with his words.

Tension crawled up Tex's spine, vertebrae by vertebrae, until it choked him by the back of his neck. Mentally, he went over all his numbers. He hadn't been short; in fact, he'd sold more than his projected share of CDs and DVDs. He wasn't aware of any distribution problems. Despite the chill in the air, sweat broke out on his back.

"I have a situation that I hope you can help me with." He looked at Tex.

"If I can, I will," Tex said promptly, returning his stare even though he was keenly aware of the quiet stranger in the corner. Was it the police? No. Who was he? What's going on? Random scenarios ran through his mind, but nothing fit.

"My associate here is searching for a young lady who is missing, and he believes you may have information on her whereabouts."

Tex's head jerked upward, unable to mask his surprise. His mouth opened before he snapped it shut. His brows lowered in a deep frown. "Me? A missing young lady?" he scoffed. He wasn't a monk; there was always a warm, willing body to slake his sexual thirst when the need arose. Seldom, if ever did he take any woman to his home, and he never made commitments. He set the rules and if they didn't like them, there was always someone else to take her place, for the night at any rate. Curiosity got the best of him. "Who?"

The male turned from the window and stared at him. The dark piercing eyes that drilled into him took Tex aback. For a moment, neither moved.

"Brenda Washington."

Tex's jaw dropped. The two words, though spoken softly, screamed at him. Inexplicably, his heart slammed in his chest and then stuttered, making it difficult to breathe or think. It couldn't be, she'd been on his mind lately. "Did you…" He coughed and then swallowed to clear his throat. "Did you say Brenda Washington?" Surely, this stranger didn't know his Brenda.

"Yes."

The cryptic answer said more about the stranger than Tex was willing to think. So he didn't. The rest of Sabatino's word crashed into him. "Brenda's missing? How? From where?" Confusion muddled his thinking; he lost control of his features. Worry and concern laced his voice. "I mean, how can she be missing? Where was she at?" He stepped closer to his boss, looking from one man to the other.

Neither man spoke.

"Talk to me!" He snapped. "What happened to her?"

"You know this woman?" Sabatino asked, watching him closely.

"Yes. We dated a few years ago. I haven't seen her in a couple of years. But she is special to me. I don't want anything to happen to her. So if there's something going down and she's somehow involved, I want to know about it." He turned to the silent stranger who'd been watching him. "Tell me. What's going on?" Swallowing his pride, he prepared to beg for information about the one person who'd pierced his thuggish shell and touched his heart.

"A friend has asked me to assist him in finding her. It seems she flew into town two days ago and hasn't been seen since," the man said, watching him just as close as his boss had. Tex didn't care.

"Damn, she's been missing for two days?" He paced, wondering why he was just finding out. He needed to get word out on the street to look for her. Rubbing his forehead, he thought aloud and said, "Okay. Where would she go? Not to her mama's, that's for damn sure. Who else?" Tex snapped his finger and looked at the stranger. "She has a best friend, Denise. She's dating Irish. Has anyone contacted her? Brenda would've called her."

"We have talked to Irish's woman." The man spoke with a slight accent.

Tex nodded, looked up at the ceiling wracking his brain. "Damn, it's been so long. I don't know what she's been up too. I sent her an email a couple of weeks or more ago I think, she never responded. I don't know if she even got it." *Where would Brenda go?* Was she looking for him? Nah? She'd made it clear the last time they saw each other how she felt. He'd meant to give her a little space, a couple of months at the most. Things snowballed and it turned into years. But he'd always meant to get back with her. Always.

"Why did you send her a note?" The man asked, his tone soft, curious.

"It was right before I came on here." He tipped his head to his boss. "I saw her sister, and started thinking about her."

"And you haven't seen her in two years?"

"No." Tex stared at the man and wondered how much he should share. The thing with Brenda haunted him. He wanted another shot with her.

"You would like to see her?"

"Yeah, of course. But, I did not take her and I don't know where she is…yet. I'm going to find her. If she's in Michigan, I'll find her." He looked at the stranger and then his boss.

"And what will you do with her when you find her?"

Tex tried to smile, but it was no more than the tilting of his lips, his memories saddened him. "Ask her to forgive me for being such a stupid ass before and see if she'll give me another chance."

"You will make this woman yours?" Sabatino asked, moving closer, standing between him and the stranger.

"Yes, if she will have me." In his mind it was a given, Brenda had always been his. He'd been her first. They had a history, volatile no question, but there were a lot of good times.

"This Brenda, she is special to you?" Sabatino pushed.

Tex sighed. "Yeah. She's *the one* and like a fool, I let her get away. There's never been anyone else." He glanced at the stranger before looking at his boss. Tex knew Sabatino would understand, they'd had numerous conversations about family and preparing for a future.

His boss nodded. "Does anyone else know she is special to you?"

Frowning, Tex looked at Sabatino. His boss had complained that Tex was too closed off, never opened up about himself, why would he ask him that. "No, I don't talk about her." Or much else was implied.

Sabatino nodded and glanced at his silent guest. "Is it possible this is about him?"

The man shrugged, as if he were unconcerned.

"Is there anything else?" Tex asked, his mind focused on the contacts he needed to tap to find Brenda. He missed his boss' question. "I'm sorry, what'd you say?"

"I asked about her sister. You know her?"

Aggravated by the delay, Tex inhaled. "I know her."

Sabatino frowned at his short answer. "Tell me about this sister," he said, his voice curt.

Tex knew he'd crossed a line. "She lives in Detroit, used to work at the warehouse on Fifth. I fired her, and burned her house down. I've been doing things to make her life hell." His chin notched up a bit. Unashamed, he returned his boss' stare. Anna deserved everything he did and more. He wasn't finished with her yet. Not by a long shot.

Sabatino frowned. "Why?"

"A few years back, she set me up. Placed something in my drink. I didn't know what was going on until I got to the apartment I shared with

Brenda." He stared at his boss, his anger flaring at the memory. "Brenda's sister, Anna, planned to have sex with me right in front of Brenda, who was pregnant at the time. Brenda started yelling; she pushed the bitch off me and tripped over something. I don't remember what. Lying on the floor, she started bleeding. I sobered fast at the sight of all that fucking blood. I was scared she would die and leave me. Holding her hand, I told her to hold on, promised her everything would be okay. She cursed me and her sister. All she thought about was the baby. My son." Tex looked at Sabatino, his eyes hardened at the memory. Still he continued, filling the room with his putrid memories. When he finished, he closed his eyes in shame. Remembering this bullshit never got any easier. He'd fucked up big time by acting out of fear.

"I jumped in my car and left." He stared at his boss, too ashamed to glance at the stranger. "I left my woman on the floor in the middle of miscarrying my child to save my ass." He shook his head. "I went to the hospital the next day to see her, to apologize, grovel, beg, anything to get her to give me another shot. All she said was I killed her son and any chance we ever had. That was the last night I did drugs or touched liquor, but it was too late. A foolish mistake set up by that bitch."

Nodding, Sabatino said, "I see."

Tex felt numb. Reflecting on his actions that night four years ago had drained him. Granted, he was a different man then, but he'd paid a high price. He'd lost the only woman who truly loved him.

"Would Anna abduct her sister?"

Tex turned toward the stranger, thinking on the question he'd asked. "She might. She hates Brenda, but why would she do it now? What would she get out of it?" Would Anna do something so bold, brash? Chills raced across his flesh at the thought of his gentle Brenda at the hands of her street-wise sister. He should've killed her weeks ago instead of dragging it out. He'd correct his mistake as soon as he left here.

"Do not kill her," the stranger said. "I think she is the key to this puzzle and we will need her to locate Brenda."

Tex looked at Sabatino, not appreciating that this stranger was giving him orders.

"He is right, we will need the sister. If all goes well, you may yet have your vengeance."

Tex's jaw clenched in anger, he *would* have his vengeance. Consequences be damned. A hand touched his shoulder and then rested heavily on it. Sabatino claimed his attention. Tex stared down at the man. "As long as I've known you, I never knew you had this one soft spot. I hope she is not a pawn in a vicious game. It is good to know you have the capacity to care so deeply. I was concerned. This is good, makes you human not robot. But you must wait, there are things beyond our control at work here."

Tex tensed. A towering rage ramped up inside him at his boss's words. Didn't the man hear him say how much she meant to him? How could he expect him to know she was lost and not do anything? Too much time had passed already. She could be lying somewhere hurt. The thought pierced his heart, pain radiated abysmally in his chest.

Sabatino squeezed his shoulder, regaining his attention. "You are one of my best. I ask you to trust me." They stared at one another. The older man's light gray eyes had darkened to a turbulent black. His cheeks had reddened to a rosy blush. Something was off about this whole deal.

"What are you asking me to do?" Tex asked. His stomach dropped to his feet in trepidation. He'd been loyal, followed directions, and never asked questions. He'd become a rich man, but what good was all that if he couldn't follow his heart this once.

"I am asking you to allow my associate and his people to locate your woman."

Tex pushed his boss' hand off his shoulder and stepped back. His face blazed. A frown marred his forehead as he shook it back and forth in slow motion. "What? Not look for her?" he sputtered, disbelief riddling his tone. "She could be anywhere, lost, alone. I have to look for her. She needs me." The flat of his palm slapped his chest giving credence to his belief. "This time she needs me!"

Sabatino and the stranger stared at him. Tex refused to waiver at the pity and disdain he read in each man's eyes, respectively.

"I can't *not* help. I have to do it right this time. I have to." Tex's voice rose with the force of his convictions. This was his opportunity to show her how much she meant to him. To show her he'd always be there for her.

"If you go against me in this, I cannot protect you. There may be danger," Sabatino reasoned.

Tex stared at Sabatino and then the stranger. "There's more to this than you've said." He slapped his forehead and backed up. "Hell, you haven't told me anything, I've told you everything." He looked between both men, the deep sense of betrayal bit deep. "After all this time…" he let the sentence drop off and then looked at his boss. The man who'd recruited him with offers of money and a better way of life. Well, it'd worked for a season, but now when he needed the man to back him up with this one thing, he caved. He'd thought Sabatino was different, he was wrong. *Fuck it.*

"I understand." Tex backed up, heading toward the door, his voice tight with anger and even more baffling to him, pain.

"You do *not* understand," Sabatino said, his voice troubled. "Wait!"

Tex wasn't sure why he stopped. In his mind, these fuckers stuck together screwing everyone else, there was no loyalty for others. Perhaps it was the note of desperation he'd never heard before in his boss' voice that grabbed his attention, but he stopped.

"Give me something," Sabatino growled to the stranger.

The man smiled. It made him appear much younger as he spoke to Tex. "If you will allow me to handle this, I will bring her to you. You will have a few hours to state your case, if she chooses you...." He shrugged as if it were no small matter.

Tex moved toward the man. "I'll need more than a few hours. Give me a day with her." The man paused, as if he were considering his words. Tex pushed his case like a high paid corporate attorney, "I've waited a long time to apologize, to tell her how much she means to me. We have a lot of baggage to sort through. I'll need time to state my case. A day out of her life isn't that much."

"If she is unwell?" The man asked silkily.

"Take her to the hospital, stat. Her health comes first." Tex glared at the man for even asking such a question. No matter how much he wanted his baby in his arms and bed, he wanted her healthy.

"What if she does not wish to see you?"

The question sent a flash of pain through him. It was a distinct possibility Brenda would spit on him and scream at him to get away from her. Biting the corner of his lip, he spoke the only words his heart allowed. "I still want to see and talk to her."

"To be clear, so there are no misunderstandings, you will not kill off the sister or search for Brenda Washington. Once located, I agree that you'll have up to twelve hours to make your case. Not a minute more." The man's voice hardened. "At that time she'll make a decision. If she wants you, she stays. If she doesn't want you, she leaves and you forget her. Never attempt to contact her again. For all intents and purposes, she'll be dead to you. Understood?" he asked, his tone low and dangerous.

Tex's heart thumped so hard he was sure they could hear it across the room. *Never see Brenda again?* The room shifted slightly as he stared ahead, seeing nothing. His world turned dark. Somehow, he had to convince her they belonged together.

"If you do not answer me, tell me you understand, I will kill you now." Although the words were spoken softly, the menacing steel beneath couldn't be discounted.

"Tex?" Sabatino called out, worried.

"I…I'm trying to think of a world without her. It's taking me a minute." He looked at the stranger. For some reason the man's anonymity made it easier to utter the heartfelt words Tex had kept hidden so long. "She hasn't picked me since we lost the baby. But in the back of my mind, there was always this hope, this belief that one day she'd forgive me and we'd be together again. Get married, have another kid. She's the best thing that ever happened to me. You're taking that sliver of dream from me."

The man nodded. "Yes, I am. And it's important that you understand what I'm offering, it's a one shot deal. If for any reason you violate this, you will die, and so will Sabatino." At that remark, both Tex and his boss started. This day was full of surprises. Tex wondered what the hell would happen next.

"Why?" Tex asked, confused.

Sabatino answered, his shoulders sagging, his voice resigned. "Because I asked him to give me something. The twelve hours with your woman is what he is giving me for you." Sabatino nodded in agreement to the other man before turning to Tex. "Earlier, you thought I betrayed you. I read it in your eyes; I could not allow you to leave believing that. You are worth much more than that to me. I must help you."

Tex's chest tightened. He reached back, his hand groping and finding a chair, and sat hard. Taking large gulps of air, he tried to settle the butterflies in his stomach. Sabatino's life was in his hands. *Ohmigod.* He had to give up Brenda. Only if she doesn't want you, his mind argued. But why would she want you, you killed her baby. It was an accident. *Ohmigod.* They'd kill him and Sabatino if he tried to talk to her after she refused him. You have no choice. *But, she was the only one to ever love me.* They'll kill you.

"Not even hello if I see her on the street?" he whispered, his voice threadbare. It hurt to think of a world without her.

"No. One does not talk to the dead. And she will be dead to you."

"What if she speaks to me?" Knowing Brenda, she would say hi. The thought gave him hope, made his world less gray.

"You will ignore her. She'll think you're an asshole and will eventually ignore you as well."

"So I have to fight her off if she approaches me?" He looked up, disgusted at the corner he'd been backed into.

"If you want to live."

Tex grew tired of the cryptic answers. He really didn't have a choice, he wasn't ready to die, and he didn't want to be responsible for his boss' death either. He nodded. "I understand and agree to everything. I only ask, when you bring her to me that there is some privacy." Catching Sabatino's eyes, he chuckled with no humor. "It's hard to beg, I mean, talk, in a restaurant or club."

Chapter 11

Brenda moved sluggishly. Her head and throat hurt. She blinked against the moonlight filtering through the window. Tiredness pushed against her chest as she tried to move again. *Thirsty*. Instinctively, her hand flailed outwardly, searching for something to wet her parched throat. Finding nothing, she stilled. Random thoughts skittered across her frazzled mind. Frantic, she forcibly tried to line up her thoughts. She needed something to drink. Focusing, she redirected her energies. Why was she lying on a mattress on the floor?

It hurt to think, but she pressed forward. The dots slowly connected; she'd been on her way somewhere with somebody. Everything went black after that. Who was she going to see? The answer slipped from her mental grasp. She had to pee. Not here! Then she saw the open door. Her mind screamed as she rolled to her side and realized there was rope around her ankles. It took her a while, but she finally untied her feet.

She pushed herself up on her elbow. Either the room or her head was spinning in the midst of a whirlwind. Her stomach lurched as she went up on her knees. Panic set in; what if she couldn't make it to the bathroom? Pushing hard, she raised up on one leg while the other remained on the ground. Her leg wobbled and she fell to the floor. Pain radiated through her body. Chest heaving, she bent over for a few moments to prevent herself from vomiting all over the floor. Once her stomach settled, she crawled in the direction of the open door, praying all the while that it was the bathroom.

The cool tile, so different from the coarse carpet, eased her fears. Moments later, after flushing, she returned to the room with slow and precise short steps, eying the room with distaste. The cobalt blue walls made the small space appear smaller. The mattress was the only thing in the room. No chairs, dressers, or mirrors. Halfway across the room, she froze and tilted her head to the side, listening. *Strange*. It's quiet. Each time she'd previously woken from whatever sleep she'd been in, she remembered there was always noise. Searching her memory, once there'd been arguing, another time music or television, another, grunts and other animalistic sounds that made her skin crawl thinking about them. Glancing around the room, she noticed the absence of food and drink. Someone had always been in the room to feed her and take her to the bathroom. How could she have missed that when she first opened her eyes?

Brenda's heart clamored as she stepped to the door and tried the knob. It turned. Euphoria chased the remaining cobwebs from her mind. Had the door been unlocked all this time? She had no idea about anything. Opening the door a bit, she cringed as the hinges creaked, and prayed it wouldn't give her away. Ear pressed to the crack between the door and the frame, she heard nothing. Emboldened, she opened it fully and stepped into a small hallway. A stinking odor knocked the breath out of her. Something foul had been in this place and she didn't want to know what it was. Covering her nose, she tiptoed in the direction that appeared to lead outside. Small measured steps led her past a kitchen. There were a few bottles of water on the counter-top. She snatched two as she passed. When she reached the corner leading into the dark living room, she stopped. Beams of moonlight filtered through the curtains and fell on what looked like her carry-on luggage in a corner. It was then she noticed how cold it was in the house. Goosebumps rose across her skin. She shivered as she moved toward her luggage, intent on grabbing something warm before braving the cold outside. Her toe hit the corner of the table, and she covered her mouth to smother the shout of pain. Wiggling her bare feet, she looked about for something to wear.

Mentally, she screamed at the delays as she rifled through her luggage. For a brief moment she thought about taking it with her, but decided it was too much. She still had no clue where she was or how she'd gotten here. But she planned to leave, pronto. She stuffed a pair of socks and underwear into the pockets of a coat she found beneath her bag. It wasn't hers, but it fit. Now outfitted with boots and hat, she headed for the door and braced for the cold. But before she shut the door, she dashed back inside, and picked up the water bottles. She glanced hungrily at the kitchen, but decided not to press her luck. Instead, she retraced her steps and walked into the night.

The brisk wind and biting cold cleared her head. A quick look in both directions told her she was in a poor area of town. *Damn.* She hadn't navigated these streets since she'd been a child, living off and on with her mother. Moving in the direction toward what she hoped was a main road; she pulled one of the bottles out of her pocket and almost emptied it in one pull. She tossed the empty container into a dumpster. There were quite a few people on the street, and for the most part they only watched as she trekked steadily toward the main road.

Sweat beaded on her upper lip as she grew hot. It didn't take a genius to realize someone had put something into the water. Determination etched her steps; the faster she moved, the further away the bright lights of the main road appeared. Someone walked behind her, talking. She couldn't make out the words and stumbled. A hand jerked her up. Her mind swirled. Her stomach clenched. Overwhelmed, her stomach heaved and she let it rip.

"Hey!" someone yelled as she puked up her guts. "Bitch almost got me."

When there was nothing else, she turned. In her mind, she could still make it to the corner. There was a part inside her that pushed her to get up. Her body rebelled. Her legs shook under her weight; every time she straightened, her knees gave out.

"Ow!" She yelped against the pain. Had she escaped one hellhole for abuse on the streets or worse? Someone snatched her hat from her head and pulled her hair, craning her neck upward.

"Stop," she yelled as they laughed, circling her like sharks smelling her vulnerability, preparing for the kill. Brenda fought to stay awake, to keep them away. Her mind darkened. It wouldn't be long before she'd be out of it.

Just as her lids drooped, a deep voice sounded from a distance, "Back up, that's Tex' woman. He'll destroy you if you don't back the fuck up."

"Tex?" she murmured, and passed out.

****

Tex and Sabatino sat in the office watching a football game. He understood the older man didn't want to let him out of his sight; after all, both of their lives were on the line. No introductions between him and the stranger were made. Tex knew better than to ask questions. Twelve hours had passed since they'd come to their forced agreement. Despite his calm appearance, he worried. Brenda could be anywhere. Someone could violate her a hundred ways before they found her. Or worse, she could be on the side of the road, hurt, broken. His hands balled into fists so tight, the knuckles made cracking noises, drawing his boss' attention. Their eyes met. There were no words, so they remained silent.

A funky rap song rang out, mixing with the cheers of the crowd on television. The home team had made a touchdown. Cheering was the last thing on his mind. After glancing at the caller ID, he answered.

"Tex." He wondered why Blue, someone he hadn't heard from in years, was calling him.

"This Blue, man. Pug told me to contact you at this number and tell you he had that package the two of y'all talked about in the club a ways back."

Tex took a quick breath. He raked a hand over his chest to calm himself. The main thing he'd talked to Pug about was Brenda. A glance at Sabatino told him the man was paying attention to his call. "Where's the package?" At his question, his boss turned and stared at him.

"On the corner of Fifth Street, he said you knew where." The man clicked off. Tex wondered how Pug was able to commandeer the hot head to do his bidding. It didn't matter. His mind raced. He hadn't gone looking for Brenda, but what if she fell into his lap? Was that violating the agreement?

"I do not like that look on your face. Tell me what has happened?" Sabatino snapped, facing him.

Tex hesitated. "That call was from a stool. He claims an associate of mine collected a package that he and I talked about at a club."

"Package?"

"I think he has Brenda. She was the main thing I remember us talking about. It's what got me to thinking about her again." He shrugged and stood, watching his boss. "Tell me, what should I do?" He waited while Sabatino frowned in concentration.

In the end, he picked up his phone and punched in a few numbers before handing the phone to Tex. "Tell him what you know, and then we'll decide."

Tex wouldn't take it.

"It's your life. Trust me when I say, they will kill you."

He took the phone and spoke. "This is Tex, I just got a call." It bothered him to turn this over to someone who didn't even know his woman. At least his time with her would begin soon.

Chapter 12

Roark shot up from the bed, confused. Sharp pains lanced his chest. He couldn't see. He gasped for air. A bizarre thirst choked him. His dry mouth tasted bitter. His heart beat at a staccato pace. Caught up in his nightmare, strange sensations assailed his body. His knees ached, his scalp pulsed in pain, the palms of his hands burned, and he was cold. Teeth chattering, he shivered in the warm room. It was as if his body refused the heat offered and gravitated to every chilled particle of air. In a desperate search for warmth, he slid beneath the blankets. Heat evaded him even as his lids grew heavy; the cold pierced his senses, reminding him that he was helpless, vulnerable against greater forces. He was terrified and lay shaking as darkness overtook him.

The next morning marked day three in the search for Brenda. Snatches of Roark's restless night plagued him. He'd passed by a mirror and noticed the dark circles beneath his eyes, his skin looked sallow, and his lips were dry, cracked. He'd tossed on the same sweater and jeans he wore yesterday when Frank had knocked on his door, demanding he come into the family room. His mind rebelled, he didn't want to make polite conversation. He wanted to pound on doors or heads, it didn't matter to him, until he found Brenda. Frank continued knocking until he promised to get up and join the rest of the world.

Exhausted, Roark sat on the sofa as Veronique and Frank talked to the detectives, and fielded questions from their mom and dad over the phone. The police wanted to go public with Brenda's disappearance and ask the public for information. Frank wanted to wait one more day to give Smoke's contact the best shot at delivering Brenda safely. Everybody, except the police, was of the opinion Smoke's contact was the best bet to locate her. So far, the police were waiting based on some technicality Veronique cooked up.

Staring at the picture of Red, Denise, and the twins on the wall, Roark got to thinking. The wedding was in three weeks, his trip to the Cayman Islands in a week, and Brenda was still missing. Could he walk down the aisle escorting another woman? His heart screamed, *No!* There was no way he was going to the Cayman Islands alone; he'd planned that trip specifically to propose to her. At a loss, he sat and went over the facts again in his head, reviewing every scrap of information of this disaster, and still came up blank. He had no idea where Brenda could be. He refused to believe she'd left him intentionally, although the thought slid across his mind from time to time. Also, he refused to believe she was with another man. No matter how much his mind argued he didn't know everything about her, his heart knew hers, and he sided with his heart over his cynical mind.

Frank strode into the room and handed him his phone. "Blaine has been trying to reach you; your phone keeps going to voice mail. Where is it?" he asked, his voice testy.

"It's right here." Roark patted his pant pocket for the small device and pulled it out. A sheepish grin crossed his face as he looked at it. "It's dead." He walked back to his room to plug it in.

"I know." Frank swiped at him, missing by a large margin. "Call Blaine, he says it's important."

"I'm on it," Roark said to Frank's retreating back, glad to have a task to take his mind off his gloomy thoughts. A moment later, there was enough juice on his phone to make a call. After punching in his brother's number, he waited, wondering what could be so important.

"Charge your phone," Blaine snapped instead of offering a greeting when he answered on the first ring.

"Hello to you, too," Roark snapped in return.

"Yeah, yeah. You okay?"

"No, but that's not what you called about. What's up?" Roark hoped Smoke would get back with him today.

"Somebody broke into your place."

"What?" Roark yelled. His mind abruptly abandoned its wandering as he stood. Frank raced into the room, followed closely by Veronique and Cherise. Roark waved down their questions as Blaine continued to speak.

"Last night or early this morning, we think. The alarm didn't go off, but your neighbor noticed the front door was wide open and called it in. I got the call a few hours ago. I've been trying to reach you, but…"

"I know, I know." Roark closed his eyes, counted to five and exhaled. "Damn! One minute." He covered the mouthpiece and told everyone what'd happened.

"Hell," Cherise moaned.

"Shit," Veronique chimed in, squeezing his arm in a show of solidarity.

Frank watched and waited for more information.

"What did the cops say?" Roark asked as a wave of tiredness washed over him.

"Not much. They have no idea if anything was stolen. I was no help with that. I'll have my security guy come and look around, see if the system's been tampered with."

"Thanks, I appreciate that." He released a sigh of relief, glad his brother was there to handle this mini-crisis. The tension in his neck eased at once.

"I'm thinking you should ramp things up around here." Blaine continued.

Roark had lost interest. "Whatever you think is best, I appreciate it."

Blaine spoke to someone in the background. "The cops are clearing out here. That girl's van is across the street and they're talking to her."

Roark snorted, unable to find the energy to care about Paula. "She probably paid someone to break in, wouldn't put it past her. She's crazy."

"Donald told me about it. Listen, if you need us, we'll be there on the next thing smoking. Frank has kept us in the loop, so we know what's going down. We figured we'd keep an eye on Frank's business and your place so you don't have to worry about the home front. But if you need an extra pair of hands, just holler."

"I know, and I appreciate you watching my place. I'm going to need it tight when I bring my woman home. Just handle the security for me. I wanna know if they find out anything, okay?"

"Got it, and take care of yourself. You need to be healthy to take care of her," Blaine said before clicking off.

Frank moved a step closer. "What's going on?"

Veronique and Cherise left quietly.

Roark repeated what Blaine had said.

Frank grimaced when he heard about Paula. "She still hanging around you?"

"I have a restraining order on her, but she's gone batty, man. She came to my office and said some wild shit." Roark then told Frank about his last conversation with Paula.

Frank whistled. "Be careful with that one. People think that just because a person has a disability, they aren't vicious and calculating. Plus, she's a woman who didn't get the man she wanted. I think there's a bullseye on your forehead with that one." He slapped Roark on the shoulder and walked out the room.

Roark's cell rang again. Thinking it was Blaine, he answered without looking at the caller ID. "What'd you forget?"

"Where are you?"

His back went ramrod stiff when he heard her voice. "How'd you get my number?" he growled through gritted teeth.

"Answer my question first. The police are at your house. Are you having problems keeping your girlfriend safe?" Paula asked in a singsong voice.

A chill slid down his spine. At that moment, he'd gladly beat the shit out of her without regret. She'd passed the nuisance stage. Why did she ask about Brenda? "You had someone break into my house. What did you have them take, a pair of my drawers? Clean or dirty?"

She gasped at his crudity. "No. I don't need anything from you."

Leaning forward, his elbow rested on his knees. "Yeah, if you don't need anything from me, why are you stalking me? I think you had someone go inside and take a look around. That's how you got this number. What else did you get?" His gut told him she was behind the break-in.

"Hey, don't blame me if you're going through a spell of bad luck. I told you Karma was a bitch."

"You're the only bitch around. Stop fucking around my shit, Paula. I'm trying to be cool, but if you send someone to my house again, or go in yourself, shit's gonna fly." He squared his shoulders in preparation for the forthcoming verbal battle.

"Shit's been flying since the fucking accident. You think you can turn me into a cripple and then live a happy life." She paused. "Fuck you, that's not going to happen. Every day I wake up, I'm reminded of every fucking thing I lost, because of you. It's all because of you." Gasps for air punctuated her words.

Roark steeled himself against her angst and the pity that welled up inside him. "We only went on two fucking dates. How can you blame your life on me?"

"You used me, acted like I mattered to you. I fell for you, but you used me."

"We had sex twice, that's all. We weren't in a relationship. You agreed it was just sex."

"If I hadn't agreed, you wouldn't have gone out with me."

Duh. "Right. I wouldn't have. What does that tell you?" It dawned on Roark they'd never had this type of conversation dealing with her motives before.

"You're an asshole. You knew I wanted more."

"I swear I didn't. What I don't understand is why me? How did you fall so fast for me?" Silence met his earnest question. Maybe he'd understand her obsession better if she explained a few things.

"You were nice at first," she said, her voice soft like a child's. "My heritage didn't matter to you. It'd been a while since I met someone halfway intelligent without biases. I thought it was a sign."

Inwardly, Roark groaned. *A sign*? He'd just wanted some pussy, that's all. Paula was nuts, but at least they were talking instead of yelling and exchanging insults.

Roark tempered his words with kindness, not wanting her to go off. "I think I should say thanks for the backward compliment. When we met, I wasn't ready to settle with one woman. You took everything personal, but there was no one special person in my life back then. I was very careful to be honest about what I wanted. I expected the same from you. You're telling me you lied to be with me and that's wrong. You're blaming me because you didn't get what you wanted."

"I knew and accepted that. But now you're ready for a relationship and I'm so fucked up, you won't even look at me," she said, her voice low and tight.

"Ah, Paula." Understanding flashed like a neon light in his mind. "It's not that you're in a wheelchair. It had nothing to do with you and everything to do with her. I met her on a trip and it was sudden, hit me like a sledgehammer. Love is weird like that, unplanned."

"I know, that happened to me."

"Then you know it's hard to control. I was fortunate she felt the same for me. It was like a wild fire." He felt they were making headway, having an adult conversation.

"You're right. It's hard to control, but you expect me to control it."

Her words slapped him. His mouth opened and then snapped close. He needed to say something, but rational thought escaped him. Was she saying she loved him? Her love for him made her act the way she did? His stomach dropped as nausea rumbled in his belly. "Paula," he whispered, his voice laced with pity and sorrow. He'd never been interested in her like that. Granted, he knew she liked him, and hated him. But *love*? He couldn't grasp she'd felt that for him.

"I'm glad we had this convo, Roark. Now you have an idea of what I'm going through. What if this woman you love, was in love with someone else and you saw them together. You knew they were together doing things you'd done with her before. How would you handle it?"

Speechless, he couldn't respond. A debilitating pang smacked his chest at her words. That was the bullseye Frank talked about. He didn't believe she knew about Brenda missing, but her questions hit his vulnerable spot dead on. "I don't know, I haven't thought about it," he lied.

"Well, whenever you're cussing me out in your mind, remember what you said. Love is unplanned, hard to control." She paused. "Oh yeah. There's a thin line between love and hate." She chuckled, sounding crazy again. "I believe there's a song about it."

"Paula, stop. This isn't helping." He tried to reach the reasonable part of her he'd been talking to a minute ago, but he doubted she'd resurface.

"Helping? Is that what you think this is about? I'm not here to help, no, no, no. Not at all." She laughed, a hoarse braying sound. He cringed and held the phone away from his ear. "We're not friends, isn't that what you said?"

"I didn't...."

"Yes, you did mean it asshole, stop lying. At any rate, I have one question. The woman you chose over me is missing. What are you going to do now?" She hung up. The dial tone loud in his ear.

Roark stared at the phone, incredulous. If he didn't know any better, he'd swear Paula was somehow involved with Brenda's disappearance. Someone *had* been impersonating Brenda while they were in Pennsylvania. Could she have set all of this up? He'd swear Paula didn't know who Brenda was, even though she'd seen her walk outside. Nothing made any sense. When his cell beeped again several minutes later, he almost didn't answer, but thought it might be Smoke. It was.

"Smoke?" Roark answered, his heart in his throat.

"He found her."

Roark yelled and threw his fist into the air. After the weird talk with Paula, this was the news he needed. His heart raced as he dashed the tears from his eyes. Frank and Veronique came into the room, hope in their eyes.

"They found her, they found her," Roark repeated before talking to Smoke. "Where is she? Is she okay? Give me the directions."

"There's more. I told you my friend does things his own way. There's going to be a delay before he turns her over."

"What?" Roark shook his head in denial. "Why? What do you mean a delay? What's going on?" Roark couldn't hear past the roaring in his ears. He attempted several times to swallow. "I don't understand."

"If everything goes right, she'll be with you in twelve hours."

"What the fuck do you mean, she'll be here in twelve hours? What's wrong? Tell me. What's that muthafucka's gonna be doing with my woman all that time?" He yelled into the cell.

"Calm down, tell me what's going on." Frank pulled the phone from Roark and spoke quickly. "What happened? What'd you say to cause my brother to fall to his damn knees?"

Roark knelt on the floor in a state of disbelief. The man was holding Brenda for twelve hours? And didn't think he needed to explain why? What kind of shit was going on here? A spurt of panic squeezed his chest. He frowned in confusion as the hurt wrapped itself around him.

Frank pulled him up by his arm and sat him on the bed. Veronique sat on one side, Cherise on the other. Frank kneeled in front of him. "Brenda is safe, a little disoriented, but safe. Smoke wasn't told where she'd been found or where she is now. They informed him that she would be returned to Smoke or a place of his choosing in twelve hours. He doesn't know anything more than that." Frank placed his hand on Roark's shoulder, drawing his attention. "I need you to stay strong, it won't be much longer." Frank squeezed him and stood.

"You need to eat something," Cherise said, rubbing his arm.

"Maybe later, I'm not hungry right now," Roark said. She nodded and left.

He and Veronique sat quietly next to one another for a few minutes.

"You think she's okay?" He asked in a quiet voice, afraid to voice any more of his fears. *What if she ran off to be with someone else?* With ruthless abandon, he squashed that heinous thought.

"Yes, she's okay. Smoke's friend would've said if she wasn't." She paused, thinking. "Smoke's friend is honorable. His code is unorthodox, but he does have one. Although we don't understand his reasoning about the delay, there always is one."

"So he plays God with other people's lives?" He asked bitterly. Her answer scared and surprised him.

"Sometimes." She patted his hand and walked out.

Chapter 13

Brenda woke in slow degrees. The pain in her head competed with the tightness in her throat for attention. She tried to swallow, and flinched in agony. Her head was lifted, a straw placed between her lips, and she sucked. Cool water eased down her bruised esophagus. A soft sigh of pleasure escaped. She sipped more until satisfied, and drifted back asleep.

Soft instrumental music was playing in the background the next time she reached consciousness. It sounded familiar. Inwardly, she smiled at Kenny G's rendition of When a Man Loves a Woman. It'd been her favorite. *When*? The question was fleeting, she couldn't remember. It wasn't the only thing. Where was she? She focused, thinking hard, trying to get her bearings. A sharp pain exploded in her head. She squeezed her eyes shut and waited until the pain abated somewhat.

The last thing she remembered was the house. Leaving a house and it was cold. She'd been outside walking, going somewhere when she discovered the water had been drugged. She gasped. Her eyes shot open. Had she done it again? Was the water she'd just drank drugged?

"Oh no," she murmured, and looked up with a start, her eyes widened and her skin flushed. Brenda listened and looked straight ahead at the ceiling. Clean décor. She inhaled the fresh, not stale or stagnant, air. Nothing happened; no one called her out. Curious, she glanced around, taking in the closed curtains, the matching table and chairs, dresser, mirror.

Pushing up, she leaned on one elbow and froze. A man with long legs sprawled out in front of her, sat in the corner in a chair. Although his face stayed hidden by the shadows in the room, she felt his eyes roving over her face, chest, and every bump and hill of hers under the sheets. Nervous, she turned to face him, scooting backward.

"Who are you?" she asked with a thread of desperation.

"Someone who is happy that you're okay. You scared me." The dark cadence of the voice teased her memory, but she couldn't place it right then.

"Was the water drugged?" She asked after a period of silence. Her mind was still sluggish, processing things a few beats slower than she'd like. Even if she wanted to run, she couldn't get through the muck and mire of her thoughts to give coherent instructions to her limbs.

"No." His sharp tone surprised her; she pulled the sheet closer to her neck. "Did someone drug you? Is that what happened?" he asked in a gentler tone.

"I think so." She struggled to swallow and keep the tears back at the same time. "I don't remember a lot." Her stomach growled loud into the quiet.

"Okay. Let's get some food up here. You still like cheeseburgers and onion rings?" He picked up the phone on the table next to the chair.

Surprised, she gazed into the shadows trying to make out his face. He hadn't moved yet. Her stomach growled again. She nodded. "Yes."

"With a ginger ale?"

She grinned at the smile in his voice. It was nice. "Yeah, I'd love to have one right now." Brenda looked around the room as he ordered her food.

"Where am I?" she asked when he hung up the phone. Curious, she gazed around the room. Her inner thoughts tried to line up and failed. The overwhelming fear and desperate urge to run were strangely absent. For a moment, she tried to process those feelings and stopped when her head started pounding, signifying the onset of additional hurt if she continued traveling that avenue.

"Embassy Suites in the city. Do you remember what happened to you before now?"

She sensed he was paying close attention to her every movement."Who are you? You sound familiar, but I can't place your voice. Have we met before?" Silence sliced through the room. Brenda stood, pleased her legs supported her, and turned in his direction.

Finally, he answered her. "I'm an old friend. When I heard there was a problem, I immediately came to help. I'm glad you aren't hurt. The part of town you were found in is dangerous in the daytime. You were walking around at night, why'd you do that? Was it the drugs?"

She shrugged, itching from the sand or dirt on her arms, but she didn't dare take a bath with a stranger in the room, although something told her it'd be okay. He'd protect her. She couldn't shake the feeling that she knew him.

"I don't know. I just needed to get out of that house." Wrapping her arms around her waist, she paced in a tight circle, her mind whirling. So many thoughts, nothing settling. Maybe after she got some food in her system, she'd be able to pin down a thought that made sense.

"Is that where you got those marks around your neck and arm? You were in a house? You walked away?"

She turned at the excitement in his voice. It was misplaced, and her glare conveyed her displeasure. "Why are you so happy I walked away from a house?"

"I want to know who took you there, who hurt you and now I know where to start looking for clues. Trust me, I will find them."

Her mouth opened and then closed shut as his words penetrated her befuddled mind. An awkward quiet fell as her eyes slid to the opposite side of the room. "Ummm." She stuttered, unsure what to say. No wonder her throat had hurt so bad when she woke, she tried swallowing again, the pain wasn't as bad.

"Did you get a look at anyone who took you to the house or who kept you there?" He asked.

Now that she knew why he was asking these questions, she relaxed. They both wanted the same thing. Catch the people who had drugged her. Her brow creased deep in concentration. His chuckle broke her flow of thought.

"What's funny?"

"The face you made while you were thinking, it was cute. It reminded me of something, that's all."

"Glad I could be of service," she deadpanned, moving toward the chair on the opposite side. "I don't remember anyone," she said, frustrated. Her mind still wouldn't cooperate. She had no idea how long she'd been in this room, and was going to ask when he spoke up.

"It's all good. It'll come back to you. Maybe you just need to eat and relax. The food will be here in a minute." He turned up the music as she reclined in the chair, eyes closed. The jazz instrumental relaxed her; she jumped when the knock hit the door.

"Go on, answer it. I'm here. No one's gonna mess with you." She looked back at him, and then headed for the door. The delectable scents of hot cooked food brought moisture to her mouth. After scribbling her name on the ticket, she opened the dishes and took a bite of her burger. No one spoke until she'd consumed her entire plate of food and drank her ginger ale. Another can of her favorite drink sat next to her glass for later.

Brenda stood, feeling full and sleepy. "Thanks, that was good." She patted her stomach, and released the top button on her jeans. She yawned. "I don't mean to be rude, but I'm really tired and need a quick nap. Must be the drugs. If you leave your number, I'll call you when I get up." She walked over to the bed and then glanced at him. He hadn't moved.

"I can't leave you unprotected. Go ahead, rest. We have plenty of time to catch up." There was a raw note of sadness in his voice that confused her. As soon as she regained her strength, she'd solve the puzzle of where she was and why.

****

Brenda woke, feeling more refreshed than she'd felt in days. Arms over her head, she stretched long and hard. Mouth dry, she glanced at the table next to the bed, and smiled at the glass of ice and unopened can of ginger ale. Scooting to the side of the bed, she popped open the can and poured a generous helping into the tall glass. Her mouth watered as she watched the bubbles. She took the glass of the refreshing liquid and sighed her pleasure, and continued drinking until there was nothing left but the ice.

"Aw, that was good," she murmured, placing the glass back on the table. She stood and walked into the bathroom to relieve herself.

She jumped in surprise when she walked back out and saw the man sitting in the same chair in the corner. "What are you doing here?" she snapped, grabbing her chest. Her heart raced, not in fear, but shock that someone else had been in the room the entire time and she hadn't noticed. "I asked you to leave."

"I told you I couldn't leave you alone." His calm reply irritated her for some reason.

Brenda rubbed her forehead, commanding the discomfort to stay back while she pulled herself together. "Right, that's right, you did say that." She looked in his direction, sheepishly. "Sorry about that." She took a mental tally of her body; everything seemed okay. He hadn't taken advantage of the situation. Inhaling, she stalked to the chair on the opposite side of the room and sat.

"Who are you? Why are *you* watching over me? Do I know you? Why am I here? How long will I be here?" She spat out the questions in rapid succession, without giving him a chance to speak until she finished.

A long sigh whistled through the room. It sounded so familiar, a thought, an image that played loosely just out of reach.

"I told you, I'm an old friend. I'm watching over you because I care about you more than my own life, and would die before I allowed anyone to hurt you. Yes, you know me. You're here because you were hurt and needed care. You should be able to leave in about," he looked at his watch, "two and a half hours." The hurt in his voice touched her.

"It bothers you that I'll be leaving?"

"Yeah."

"Why?"

"Because I won't ever see or talk to you again."

"Why?" He sounded so sad, it disturbed her on a visceral level. For some reason, his pain bothered her.

"It's complicated, but it's true."

"I know you, right?"

"Yeah."

"Were we friends?"

"At one time, we were really close." His voice dropped to a low whisper and she had to lean in to hear him.

"Close?" She tried to think of a good friend from her past and couldn't remember.

"I thought so."

She shook her head, intrigued. "My mind's not operating on all cylinders. Tell me who you are and when were we friends."

"Brenda, you hate me."

"I don't hate anybody!" She pulled back, her eyes wide trying to see. "Stand up! Come into the light, stop the games. Let me see who you are."

"Can I please tell you what I need to say before you see me? I have so many things to tell you and not a lot of time."

"No." His intensity scared her. There was something about him that called out to her and pushed back at the same time. It was confusing.

"Please, Brenda. Just let me talk, and then you can talk. I won't ever ask anything of you again. Like I said, when we leave, we won't ever see each other again. I need this time with you to fix things. To set the record straight." She couldn't ignore the pleading in his voice or the pain.

"Okay, go ahead." Arms crossed, she stared at the shadow in the corner. For some inexplicable reason her heart beat erratically in her chest, as if she'd run a marathon. No matter how she tried to remain calm, her mind insisted she step back, blot out his voice, and guard her heart. That startled her. Why her heart?

"First off let me say I'm sorry."

"Why? What'd you do?" She jumped up with fists balled and walked toward him.

He stood as well.

She stopped, surprised by how tall he was.

He stared down at her as she moved closer. "Please, Bren."

An odd chill rippled across her skin. She shook her head and took a step back. "No, no." She stared disbelieving. "Tex?" she breathed, rubbing her face in shock.

"Please, just this one time, let me explain. I promise this is the last time," he pleaded, stepping forward into the light.

She was too incensed to speak, her breath came out as short snorts from her nostrils. Her heart slammed against her chest, her fists clenched in and out of tight knots. "No fucking way," she growled, stopping a few feet from him. She pointed. "Stay the hell away from me!"

"I have. I haven't come near you in over two years." That stopped her tirade. She looked up at him again, searching his eyes for traces of his normal bullshit. All she saw was hurt and desperation.

Tilting up her chin, she motioned to him. "What's going on? How'd you wind up here?"

He rubbed his eyes and looked back at her, his face pained.

She'd seen him in a rage. She'd seen him running games, fighting like a man possessed. She'd seen him at his sexiest best, but she'd never seen this look of desolation on his face. It was as if his world was over and he had to go make restitution to everyone he'd fucked over.

"I…can I just start from the top? I promise I'll get to that point." He stared at her, his eyes suspiciously glassy. *No fucking way*. Her heart hurt for him. Whatever was going on with him, it rode him hard. She nodded, returned to her seat, and crossed her hands over her lap.

He wet his lips, glanced at her and then looked at the floor. "Like I said, I'm sorry I was such a shit-head when we were together. I was young and tired of being poor." His head shot up and his palm went out. "But that's no excuse." He rubbed his head.

Brenda remembered he did that when he was nervous. The thought of him being uneasy around her, calmed her.

She took a moment to look at him as he moved around. Tex had always been tall, with a solid build and exotic features from his Asian-Puerto Rican-African American roots. Thick, dark wavy hair brushed his shoulders, long eyelashes over slanted eyes, and a straight nose in a square face, all so familiar. He'd filled out and buffed up some, but overall he looked the same, too handsome for his own good.

"Nobody ever thought I was smart. Remember when we first met on campus?" He stuffed his hands in his pocket, watching her.

She nodded, unsure if he wanted her participation.

"You were so…so beautiful. Walking across campus, these guys, smart and rich guys, were checking you out. I didn't think I had a shot and it made me mad. When we bumped into each other at the student union, at first I was surprised, then I got angry. I was about to say something stupid, but you smiled." He scratched his chin, shaking his head. "At me. You gave me this big ass real smile that knocked me on my ass. I couldn't say much cause I felt like shit, but I knew right then that I had to get to know you. And you started hanging with me." He swallowed hard. "When I lost my financial aid and dropped out after that second semester, I never said, but it hurt. It hurt more than I wanted to admit. People didn't know I'd lost my aid and said some stupid stuff. They wrote me off as just another black man who failed." His eyes drilled into her.

Her heart sped up, not in fear, but in anticipation of the punch line. Was he another Donald Trump or something?

"You were the only person who looked beyond all my bullshit and saw me as a man with potential. I never felt dumb or stupid around you, even when I did stupid shit. And I did a lot of that." He glanced at her. "Stupid shit, I mean. I put you in a fucked up situation, you missed classes, got behind in school. I know apologizing doesn't change the past, but I am very sorry for that craziness."

Nodding in acceptance, her eyes welled with water as she joined him on this painful journey. They'd never taken it before. All along, she'd known how badly she felt, but had never guessed how deeply everything had affected him.

"The night, that last night." He inhaled.

Brenda shook with emotion as he delved into one of the most painful events in her life. She hadn't realized the wound still festered until her eyes narrowed and she jumped up. "You and Anna killed my baby," she spat, her eyes throwing daggers at him.

"No. That's where you're wrong, Bren. I killed *my* son. And knowing that has left me bleeding all these years." He was breathing hard, his eyes filling with tears. "You kept forgetting I lost my son that night. I fucking died that night, and I was alone. The only person I knew who'd get what I felt was you, but I'd ruined that as well." He turned from her, but not before she saw the tears roll down his cheeks.

All this time, she thought he'd been unaffected by what happened. It was the reason she'd been so careful with men after him. In her mind, she'd miscalculated with him, thinking he was one way, when he was another. The unfamiliar taste of guilt filled her mouth.

"Tex, I—"

"No. I need to get all this out first, remember?" he asked softly, turning to face her. His face was blotchy, but composed.

She nodded, totally out of her depth. This was a Tex she didn't know. Normally, by now they'd be rolling on the bed, playing, or loving. He'd never been big on talking and now…time did change people.

"That was the last night I did drugs."

"What?" She forgot to keep quiet.

He smiled, reminding her of a little boy receiving the highest praise from his teacher. "Yeah. Went cold turkey. Giving up the drugs was a lot easier than giving you up." He frowned and bit the corner of his lip. Another nervous habit he had.

"It was as if I needed you to tell me things were going to be okay, or something. I needed to see you, even though you didn't want to see me. There was this big piece missing, and sometimes things would get real bad and I'd be tempted to go back to my old ways. Those were the days I'd violate the restraining order and see you anyway. I didn't understand how you could hate me after loving me so long. So I pushed and pushed. Until you yelled and told me how you felt." He shook his head, and turned away. "The only reason I didn't go out and do something stupid was because I knew you were alive. Hurt and pissed at me. But alive. My son was dead. I could never make it up to him.

But one day I could prove to you I was the man you always told me I could be. Don't get me wrong, you broke my heart. But I will never get a chance to say this to you again." He turned and looked at her, his eyes bright.

"Brenda Washington, I've loved you from the moment you smiled at me in the student union. If I have any success, it's because at the back of my mind I knew you believed I could do anything I set my mind to. I know I've hurt you and I will kick my own ass for that a thousand times throughout my life. You didn't deserve the first tear you shed over me and my bullshit."

Water ran down her face. Her heart ached for him. This was the first time he'd ever told her he appreciated her. Now, after all these years, he'd confessed how he felt. Her heart leaped with joy. He held his hand toward her. She took it and they held each other as huge sobs wracked her frame.

"I'm sorry about the baby," he murmured, rubbing her back, tears in his voice. "I'm so sorry." He broke down and cried, soaking her shoulder. For several minutes they stood in a comforting embrace, allowing their tears to wash away painful memories, cleanse festering wounds, and free them from emotional entanglements so they could heal.

Brenda inhaled Tex's familiar scent. How could she have not recognized him? He'd been her lover and friend. So much had happened, she'd buried the memories so deep, and many had become twisted. They'd both been young and naive. Neither had stellar role models at home and they'd made things up as they went along. Because of her insecurities, she'd accused him of cheating more than once, only to discover she'd been wrong. She'd been so needy, constantly wanting reassurance of his feelings and commitment to the relationship. Afraid he'd abandon her if she didn't go along with things that she knew weren't right. She'd lost herself in him.

Pushing him away, she turned, and wiped her face with the back of her hand. "How'd you get here?" Her throat was unexpectedly tight all of a sudden. She stepped away to a safe distance. Things between them had always been hills and valleys. That was okay when you were younger, but she couldn't ride that train again.

"Like I said. I always thought…I mean I always hoped you'd give me another chance." He paused.

She didn't turn and face him. Not yet. She couldn't look at him right now, too many emotions were charging through her.

"When I discovered you were missing, I set it up that the moment you were found, I'd be here to talk to you." He stopped when she stared at him.

"Missing? How long have I been missing?" Clicks of memory started tumbling into place.

"From what I understand, you flew into town three days ago." He reached out and caught her before she hit the floor.

Her head spun. *Three days*? "Where have I been? Who? What?" She sputtered, unable to grasp the magnitude of what he was saying. No wonder he'd kept asking her questions earlier.

"I don't know who took you, yet. But my money's on that bitch, Anna."

At the mention of her sister's name, she jerked from him. "Anna? What makes you think that?"

He stuffed his hands in his pocket. "I just do. Do you remember anything?" He glanced at his watch, his face tightened. "Who picked you up from the airport?'

Brenda shrugged, her mind was racing, trying to put everything together. "A Spanish lady. Short, pixie haircut. I thought she was related to my cousin…that's right." She placed her hand across her mouth. "Ohmigod!"

"What?" Tex asked, stepping closer. "You remember something?"

Eyes wide, she looked up at him, nodding. "I flew in to visit my aunt; she was sick and wanted me to come see her. I told Roark." She stopped and pivoted. *Roark.* Her stomach dropped. He'd probably freaked out when she didn't call him.

"I need a phone. I have to make a call." She looked around anxiously, the need to contact Roark overriding everything else.

"Brenda."

"No. I have to make a call. He's probably worried. Lord knows what he's thinking." She picked up the phone and tried to get an outside line and couldn't. "What the fuck?" she yelled, looking at him. "I need to make a damn phone call right now!"

She stared at him, bristling. How could she have forgotten to call Roark the moment she realized she was safe? Her face burned. How could she have been so caught up on memory lane that she didn't think to contact him?

"You can't. Not for another hour. I told you that already."

This time the pain in his voice pissed her off. His time was up. Whatever they hadn't discussed would have to be okay. "Tex." She tamped down her anger. "I have to call my boyfriend. He is probably going crazy right now. Please." She stared at him, ignoring the flash of pain across his face. She held out her hand, asking for his phone.

He raised his hands to the side. "I don't have my phone. Or any way to communicate with anyone outside this room. Someone will be here in another hour and that'll be it."

Anger lit her face. This was her life. "I'm not playing this game with you. I need to contact him." She walked to the door and tried to open it. The handle didn't turn. She kicked the door and yelled. "Open this fucking door. Open it now!" When that didn't work, she pounded on the hard wooden surface until her hand hurt.

Turning, she marched back into the room where Tex sat in his chair again. "What the fuck is going on?" She pointed at him. "Don't give me a bullshit answer either; we're supposed to be coming clean with each other."

"Yeah, you're right," he said, resigned. "I was called into my boss' office and told you were lost. I was pissed because I didn't know you were in town and started to leave right then to start a search. My boss asked me to allow this other guy to do the searching, since they'd already started the process." He held up his hand to stop her questions. "Before you ask, I don't know who the guy is, but my boss was afraid of him. I told them how I felt about you and how I'd always wanted the opportunity to tell you how I felt about losing my son and our relationship in general. He agreed that if I let him find you, he'd give me twelve hours to state my case. And ask for another chance." He glanced at her. "At the end of that time, if you chose to give me another shot, we ride into the sunset together. If not...." He shrugged and turned away.

"If not?" she pressed, knowing she wouldn't like what he had to say.

"If not, I never see or speak to you again under the threat of death, both mine and my boss."

She gasped. Her hand covered her mouth.

"You slept almost ten of the hours, so I've been rushing to tell you as much as I could before my time was up."

Brenda sat in shock staring at him. So many emotions ran through her, she couldn't track them all. First and foremost was Roark. She pictured him somewhere wondering if she was okay. She didn't doubt for a moment he was searching for her. Lord, she loved that man, just thinking about him made her warm inside. He never tried to change her, although she had changed. He never mocked her dreams, although she'd put the unrealistic ones away. He'd always encouraged her to do what made her happy, and loved her through the challenges of following her dreams. Roark held her heart, bruised and battered as it'd been, and coaxed it back to life with love and patience. He'd been her anchor and she missed him.

In addition, here was Tex, her first love, saying all the things she'd dreamed for years he'd say. Her anger over him not caring about their baby dissolved under a stream of tears. In some regards he'd changed. Loyalty had been bred into him; he wouldn't back off a promise. And his lifestyle was a choice he'd made and couldn't change. He'd probably never have a W-2 or file taxes, never work in a legitimate business, and never talk about the things he did on a daily basis. Tex actually preferred his way of life, claimed it was tailor-made for him. She thought it a great waste of potential. Some things hadn't changed, that chapter of her life remained closed.

"Today was the first time you told me you appreciated me." She looked at him.

"Is it?"

"Yeah."

"I showed you every day, though." He chuckled at the lie.

She let it slide. They had more pressing issues. "I should apologize for setting you up for failure."

"What? No, you helped me. You didn't set me up for anything."

Smiling sadly, she walked up to him and rubbed his arm. "Tex. I made you my whole world. I expected a lot from you. No man should be placed on a pedestal like that, especially someone only twenty years old and away from home for the first time."

He hugged her.

She returned his embrace. "We were young."

"But it was good, some of it was good, right?" he asked, his face buried in the crook of her neck.

Stroking his head as she'd done so many times before, she smiled. "Yeah, some of it was good. But, that was then. And I've met someone else." He squeezed her tight, and stepped back. They stared at one another. Brenda marveled at how handsome and fine he was. One day he'd meet someone who'd love him and share his life.

"Does he treat you right?" he asked.

"Of course. I wouldn't settle for anything less."

He smiled. Even though it didn't reach his eyes, she appreciated the effort.

"I want you to be happy. I'll probably always love you; always kick my own ass for my stupidity. But I want you to be happy." He pressed a kiss on her forehead.

She closed her eyes. It was a bittersweet moment. The ties that bound them were broken. He stepped back and chucked her beneath the chin, something he used to do all the time. Standing on tiptoe, she kissed his cheek.

"I want that for you, too. All this time, I was reading a lot of things wrong. I thought you didn't care about the baby. Knowing you did, helps. Thanks for sharing everything with me." She shook her head and looked up at him. "I don't like what they're making you do. You've been a part of my life for so long, the thought of you not being somewhere happy, hurts too much to think about. Can you talk to them and ask them to release you from that?

"No. I can't. It's not just me. But, thanks for saying that. It helps." He looked at his watch and then grinned at her. "We've got another thirty minutes." He held his arms open. "Dance with me?"

Brenda remembered slow dancing had been his favorite thing when they went out. She smiled. They really did have fun back then. She wagged her finger at him. "No bumping and grinding."

He placed his arms around her waist. "You're no fun."

"In that case…" She tried to pull away.

He pulled her back in. "Beggars can't be choosy." They danced to her favorite song, *When a Man Loves a Woman*. How appropriate as their last dance.

Chapter 14

Roark stared at Smoke, his face on fire. "You're shitting me, right?"

Smoke's head shook slowly, his lips pursed. "No. I've been trying to reach him all day. He finally called me back and told me what was going on."

Frank and Red stood on the side. "Are you saying your friend found Brenda for Roark, but decided to allow her ex-boyfriend to make a play at her first?" Frank's tone said what Roark hadn't voiced, that shit was fucked up, and it didn't make sense.

"He said it was necessary for business reasons and to shore up some other things. He said you'd understand and appreciate it later." Smoke shrugged. "I don't understand what's going on, either. I thought Denise said Brenda hated this guy."

Red corrected Smoke. "She said Brenda was afraid of him and didn't like him. Hate might be taking it too far."

Roark stared at Red. "What? What, you think Brenda might be tempted to deal with that muthafucka? Give him another shot?" Shoulders squared, he nearly choked on the words.

"No. That's not what I think. Brenda's a good woman. She don't roll like that." Red stared Roark down.

"I don't get it. Why twelve hours? That's a long time for someone to plead his case. He planning to wear her down or something?" Frank asked, looking at the other men.

Roark looked at his watch. "One hour to go." He exhaled and looked at Smoke, embarrassed by his outburst. "I'm sorry bout jumping on you and shit. Truth be told, if I'd known that shit at the beginning of the twelve, it would have drove me crazy wondering what she was doing all that time. In a short minute, I'll know. Thanks man." He fist bumped Smoke, turned his cheek, and sniffed. He needed a shower. Looking up, three pair of eyes stared at him.

"Yeah, you smell," Frank said, his cheeks ticking as he held back a grin.

Red stepped in front of Roark and pushed him in the direction of his bedroom. "Go wash your stank ass before your woman gets here. If she smelled you now, she might turn and run. And change the damn sheets!"

Ignoring the laughs following him, Roark gave Red the finger, and closed the door. He fell on the bed, curled in a ball and prayed. He prayed she'd choose him.

****

Roark stood behind the glass panels next to the front door of Red's home, listening to each tick of the large clock mounted on the wall behind him. Minutes crawled like Friday's rush hour traffic. Flushed with uncertainty, sweat glistened on his brow in the cool of the foyer. His heart thumped heavily in his chest in dread and anticipation. A metallic taste coated the back of his tongue, the product of his doubts. His breath hitched as a long limo slowed in front of the house and then stopped. Without thinking, he pulled open the door and stepped out onto the porch, watching as the back door of the car opened and the most beautiful sight in the world stepped out. Relief, tsunami-sized, washed over him.

"Brenda." He didn't realize he'd said her name aloud until her head spun in his direction. She dropped the small carry-on luggage and ran toward him, almost tripping into his outstretched arms. Meeting her mid-way, he encircled her tightly, absorbing the tremors as they raced through her body.

Eyes closed, he gave silent thanks to God as he inhaled her uniqueness, and kissed the top of her head. Her tears soaked his cotton shirt and the tee beneath. As she nuzzled his chest with her chin, a habit she'd started with him during their time together, his chest expanded with gratitude. *His baby was back*. He'd never let her go.

He brushed his lips on her forehead, assuring himself this was no hallucination. Brenda stood in his arms on Red's front lawn. Surrounded by a peaceful bubble, he allowed his own tears to fall, silent cleansing tears that acknowledged they had a lifetime to share both their pain and passion. There was a lot to discuss. She needed to know about her aunt and he needed to know about her captivity. But for right now, he basked in the knowledge that she'd chosen him. Joy resonated through him, thrilling his beleaguered soul. His chest burned with all the things he wanted to do; kiss her, hold her, and tell her how much she meant to him.

"Brenda," he whispered the name that had kept him awake the past few days, firing his soul with a fierce determination to find and defend her again. As her man, her safety fell on his shoulders, and he'd failed. Grateful he had another shot to get it right, he tightened his hold on her with a silent vow to make sure this shit never happened again. She was his first priority, the agony he'd experienced the past few days had cemented that truth.

He felt her sobbing against his chest. Gradually, her eyes met his, flooded with tears, reflecting a love made stronger through this raggedy ordeal. He swore his heart stopped at the innate trust shining through her eyes. He'd been afraid of a lot of things, the loss of her trust was the tip of the iceberg. Blessed beyond measure but still needing a taste of her, he gently pressed his lips to hers, unsure if she were ready or not. She moaned and pushed hard into the kiss, offering all that he'd hoped for and more.

Roark squeezed her waist, deepening the kiss, delighting in the taste that was simply her. *His Brenda.* She moaned again. His cock swelled in welcome as her hands slid up and down his back. They broke for air, and her forehead collapsed onto his chest. Breasts still heaving, the flat of her hand reached up to stroke his cheek.

"I…I," She choked, her body taut.

Her distress ripped a hole in his chest. "Shhh," he said gently, placing a finger over her lips. "We'll talk later, right now I need to hold you just to make sure I'm not dreaming."

"My dream just became a reality," she said, staring into his eyes, peeling back the layers of her heart and bringing him to his knees.

A shudder tore through him, rendering him speechless. During the past few days he'd rehearsed in his mind all the sweet, romantic things he'd planned to tell her when he saw her. But now that she was back, safe and sound, all he could do was stare into her hopeful eyes, mute. After a moment, her eyes shuttered, cutting him off from her sentiments. His heart rebelled at the emotional amputation. His mind demanded he reassure her that she wasn't the only one madly, deeply in love and wading in heartrending waters.

"I love you so much, please don't ever leave me again," he blurted, gripping her upper arms in desperation. His face and neck blazed as he concentrated on explaining the churning feelings in his gut. "I…I can't take it. Just, don't leave me."

A myriad of expressions, surprise, relief, and happiness, crossed her face. Her hand cupped his chin as she stared into his eyes. He knew she'd see his soul, because he was wide open for her.

"I love you too, Baby. Don't be sad, I can't take that. I'm sorry to see all the pain this caused you. I wouldn't hurt you for anything. Believe that." She wrapped her arms around his neck and kissed him long and thoroughly.

Everything ceased to exist except the woman in his arms and the world they created. He melted at the feeling of her against him. Then she thrust her hips erotically against his cock. It'd been too long.

He reached behind and cupped Brenda's ass in his hands, lifting her for better contact, better friction. A long sigh slipped appreciatively into his mouth as she tangled her tongue with his, holding his head in place. She wrapped her legs around his waist, grinding on his stiffening erection.

"I need to be inside you, right now. Is that okay, Baby?" he asked, his voice gruff and heavy with need.

"Please," she whispered into his ear. The warmth of her breath sent tingling sensations straight to his needy core.

Impossibly, he hardened further.

"I need you inside me, too. It's been too long. Show me that reality is better than the dream," she said.

He turned, and with long strides entered the house. Brenda tucked her head into the corner of his neck as he nodded to his brother, who stood grinning like a buffoon in the hallway. Another nod to Veronique, who had what appeared to be happy tears in her eyes, and then Red, who held a weeping Denise in a snug embrace.

"Give us a few minutes, we'll be back to talk later," Roark said without breaking his stride toward their bedroom.

Brenda's head lifted and she waved. "Hey Dee, Irish, and everybody. I need to…" The door closed before she could finish her sentence.

Roark held her up against the wall, his cock strained against the rough cloth of his jeans as he pressed into her. He took her mouth, plunging deep with his tongue. Their hips gyrated frantically, seeking satisfaction that would only come when they linked up.

"Clothes off," he muttered against her lips, allowing her to slide down his front. She wiggled on his erection. A hiss of pleasure escaped his lips. Within seconds, he stood naked in front of her. Brenda bent over to take off her boots, her ass high in the air. Roark's breath whooshed out his mouth. He grabbed her from behind, catching her as she tilted sideways toward the floor.

"I missed you so damn much." All the pent-up frustration of the past few days smashed into him as he held her close. Flesh to flesh, he spoke his heart. "I've never been so scared," he whispered, his breath hitching. "I kept thinking of all the things that could go wrong and I'm not gonna lie, I lost it a few times." He shook his head to clear it of the unbearable memories. "The thought of something happening to you…" He couldn't bring himself to say the words. His chest heaved as he struggled to hold in the overwhelming sentiments. Overflows of tears rolled down his cheeks as he held her secure in his arms. She'd stabilized his sanity as soon as she stepped out the limo. He hadn't realized until now how close to the edge he'd been.

Heart full, Brenda turned in his arms and gazed up at him. Her strong, loving, confident man, had bled over what might have been. She brushed away one of his tears and kissed away others, allowing him this time to deal with his personal demons, just as she'd been dealing with hers.

Finally, she took his face between her hands to make sure he understood the depth of her commitment. "I love you, Roark. I'm not going anywhere, Boo." She spoke the words from the depth of her heart, intending for them to soothe his aches and hurts. Reaching around him, she held him tight, stroking his back and nuzzling against his chest. He'd lost some weight, but then again, so had she. The time apart had altered them both in some ways. She kissed his chest. "I love you. Only you." She punctuated her words, sensing he needed more from her.

His arms tightened and then loosened as his fingertip lifted her chin so they were staring into one another's eyes. A reluctant smirk grew into a full-blown grin. His lips brushed across hers as he framed her face between his hands. "Thank you," he said with heart-felt conviction.

Even though she wasn't sure what the thanks was for, she nodded as much as his hands allowed.

He pecked her lips and touched her forehead with his. "Thank you for choosing me."

She stiffened. Roark knew about the deal with Tex? Pushing away, she tripped over her lowered pants and boots. She would've hit the floor had he not caught her. Pulling her upright, he held her loosely; a discomfiting silence fell as they continued to stare at each other. She wet her dry lips with the tip of her tongue, aware his eyes tracked her every movement.

"You knew?"

He nodded. "Just found out an hour ago."

"I slept ten hours of the twelve."

He grinned, a boyish smile that lit his eyes and made her cream. "Good. I'm glad you're rested." His brows wiggled as he leaned forward and took her lips.

Pushing him back, she pointed to her twisted pants. "I need to get these off."

"I'll do it." He knelt and lifted her foot, removing the boot.

Brenda's face warmed in embarrassment remembering the itchiness of her skin earlier, she needed a shower. After he removed the other boot and slipped off her pants and underwear, he held her around the waist, her stomach pillowing his head. For a moment they remained locked together in a comfortable embrace. Her fingertips massaged his scalp. His lips grazed her stomach.

"Come with me," she said, pulling him up by the arms. She took his hand and led him to the shower.

"Shower sex, yeehaw," Roark teased rubbing his cock on her ass while she turned on the water and stepped forward. A second later, he followed and pulled her tight against him, his erection pressed between their bodies.

"Mmm," he moaned, moving back and forth in small rotations, taking her with him. Warm water sluiced down their bodies as she pulled him down for a kiss, starving for more of him. He released her and went onto his knees. His hair slicked across his face as he kissed her pubes.

Tapping his shoulder, she wagged a finger at him. "No face-fucking until *after* you bathe me." She handed him the soap and turned around.

He groaned and grabbed her ass. Batting his hand away, she said, "Work first, play later. I know your mama taught you better manners."

"Don't bring my mama in here," he said. He soaped up the cloth and washed her back, starting at her shoulders, and then worked down the valley of her back and onto the hills of her ass. He took his time teasing every inch of her, lingering on her vee-jay. A warm curl of lust tugged inside her as his touch changed, became more possessive.

"You're mine, Brenda. No one comes between us." He spoke into her ear while tugging her nipple.

"Yes." She hissed at the pleasure shooting through her.

His finger slid gently down her slit, sending zings of delight to her throbbing clit. "This pussy." He patted her vee-jay, staking an unmistakable claim. "This pussy is mine." His voice had deepened into her favorite panty-wetting cadence.

Inside, her walls clenched in agreement. Eyes closed, legs trembling, she nodded. "Yeah, I said yeah." By the time he rinsed her, she trembled on the brink of orgasm. He stood close, so close her nipples brushed against his chest. His fingertip flicked her clit and she lost it. Roark caught her as her legs buckled under the spiraling onslaught. Brenda rested her forehead against the wet tile while he held onto her with one hand. The other rubbed soap haphazardly over his body, their eyes never broke contact. He threw the cloth down, grabbed her and roughly pressed his lips to hers, his tongue prying her mouth open. She moaned at the exquisite sensations of her body igniting and melting into his as they continued to kiss.

"Need you," he muttered right before he lifted her and stepped out the shower. Enfolding her within a thick towel, he patted her dry, taking care to be gentle. Like a precious gift, he unwrapped the towel. Then he leaned forward and stopped just shy of kissing her. Their eyes met in a quick glance before he continued staring at her neck.

"What happened?" The hoarseness of those two words sent her scurrying to the mirror. The panic in his question puzzled her as he touched her neck in a few places. She winced and gazed deeper into the glass. Her jaw went lax at the faint marks around her neck. Gingerly, she touched them. Tex had mentioned something like this but she hadn't paid it any attention.

"It looks like someone choked you."

Although couched as a statement, she knew it was a question for which she didn't have any answers. Now she wondered what *had* happened while she'd passed out. Surely, she would remember if someone choked her, wouldn't she? Concentrating, she tried to remember and couldn't. Tex said she'd get her memory back in time. Brenda caught herself before mentioning her ex's comments and instead said, "It does."

Brenda wrapped her arms around her own waist as a feeling of vulnerability swamped her. She stared at Roark, hating the deep frown marring his handsome face. A need to explain and to comfort tugged at her.

"I was drugged most of the time. I didn't know I'd been missing this long until a few hours ago. I…I wanted to call, but there were no phones. I'm sorry, Roark."

In two long strides, Roark stood in front of her with his hands atop her shoulders holding her steady as his eyes searched hers, telling her without words she had no reason to apologize. In hindsight, the time she'd spent with Tex now seemed wrong and sent a pang of guilt crashing through her.

"You have nothing to be sorry for. Remember that."

He was wrong. She shouldn't have enjoyed her final time with Tex, but she did. It had felt good to talk to him without all the drama that had coated their relationship. She'd always grieve for her unborn son, but knowing she hadn't grieved alone went a long way to putting the past to rest. Perhaps she'd be able to talk to Roark about having kids. He'd joked about the two of them having a basketball team once. It'd been dark in the bedroom, so he hadn't noticed her terror. Pregnancy, with all its emotional and physical pitfalls was a touchy subject for her. Thankfully, the subject had never come up again.

Roark whispered against her forehead as she leaned into his strength. "You didn't do anything wrong. I just hate that someone hurt you, that's all." He touched her neck. "I hate that I wasn't there to protect you." Squeezing her shoulders, his eyes slid to the marks on her neck and his jaw clenched. She could smell the spicy scent of rage pouring off him, taste it even.

Time to change things up. Lowering her hand, she stroked his cock, providing an instant distraction. Widening eyes traced the movement of her hand. A certain part of his anatomy rose in appreciation of her handiwork.

"You were going to prove reality is better than my dreams, remember?" She pouted, releasing him as she backed up, then gave him a saucy wink and walked with a little extra jiggle to the bed. "Unless you changed your mind," she added. Her words were like kerosene on a fire and his eyes flared in response.

Like a puppy on a leash, he followed her down and nipped at her lips before taking control of their kiss. Kneading one breast, he pulled and pinched her nipples with an expert touch. Her man always mixed the right amount of pain and pleasure for her senses. God, she'd missed him.

He dipped his head to take the right one his mouth. A jolt of pleasure shot through her as he suckled and lapped alternately. She cried out as his teeth dragged along the bud of her nipple. Panting in excitement, her hands raked through his hair and then pulled a fistful tight, earning a small bite on her soft flesh. He eased one finger inside her. She moaned in response and spread her legs. Deliberately, he bent his finger so it stroked her spot, and pulled it out. Creating a rhythm, he inserted another finger along with the first, ratcheting up the tension along her back. Her hips rose and fell in a concerted effort to hit her peak. Her walls contracted against his fingers. Everything within her stiffened.

"So tight," Roark hissed, and increased the pace and the pressure of his thrusts. Her back arched taut. A scream of pleasure rumbled up from her belly and out through her throat. She clenched her pussy muscles while pleasure rippled through her body. Roark held her through the aftershocks. When she could see clearly, she smiled at his cocky grin and watched him suck his fingers clean. His lips and tongue took longer than necessary to do the job. She squeezed her thighs together.

"Now that the appetizer is out of the way, ready for the main course?" He rolled over so she straddled him.

"You want me to top you?" Her brow rose as she lined up above him.

"If you think you can, show me." He winked as he reached for her.

She pushed his hand away and tweaked his nipple. "If I think I can? You forgot I got skills." She loved when they played cat and mouse. Tonight she planned to be the cat. "Hands above your head." Roark hesitated at the bite of command in her tone. Her smile challenged him.

"Scared?" she asked, mocking his masculinity, her hand planted firmly on his chest. The next second his hands reached upward and grabbed onto the headboard just as she knew he would. *Men.* Their eyes locked as they stared at each other instead of moving.

"You want me?" He rolled his hips beneath her. She gasped in pleasure as his cock rubbed against her clit.

"Always." She bent forward and took his nipple into her mouth, pleased when a fine tremor ran through him. Light nibbles on the tip of his buds had his back arching from the bed.

"Shit." He groaned as the flat of her tongue rasped over his nipple before power sucking it into her mouth. Roark's legs shook. His arms lifted from the headboard and then clutched back onto it with a grip hard enough to break it when she stroked his hard rod.

"You like that?" She purred, turned on by his reaction to her play. "You like when I touch you like this?"

"Yesss," he hissed, his tongue licking his lips in rapid succession. Brenda stared at his magnificent, thick, veined cock. She hungered for a taste, but needed to feel him inside her more. After taking one quick swipe over the crown with the flat of her tongue, she rose over him. Lined up part A to slide into slot B and lowered onto his slick rod. Her eyes rolled backward at the exquisite homecoming, stretched and filled to the brim. Slowly she rose and fell, forgetting for a moment she wanted to ride lead tonight. His loud moan confirmed they were both reconnecting on a level that surpassed words. An itch burned deep in her core, she moved faster on him to flame the fire. Roark met her every move; pushing up when she came down. Her hips bobbed up and down on his cock seeking satisfaction. Abandoning the headboard, he grabbed her hips, and pistoned in and out of her faster and faster. Brenda screamed and came like lightening. Her toes curled and her back arched before she slumped, totally wiped, onto his chest.

He reversed their positions, flipped her on her back, raised her leg over his arm and slid home. She gasped as he buried his cock until his balls slapped her flesh. Brenda felt the muscles on his lower abdomen flex and bunch, contracting hard every time he thrust. Her head lolled from side to side, every plunge shook her to the core as the pressure built again. A quick move and her legs were higher. He moved his hips, rapidly hitting her walls from another angle. Sweat rolled from his face onto hers, their breaths and grunts filling the room. Roark picked up the speed, pounding his cock into her erratically, Brenda knew he was on the precipice and tightened her walls, sending them both over the edge, screaming.

Chapter 15

Sometime later, Roark and Brenda left the privacy of their bedroom to find food and talk to the family. Everyone had been worried over her disappearance and wanted a chance to talk with her. She understood, but would have preferred to hide away with her man for a few more days, instead of just the hours they'd had. Refreshed after more rounds of sweaty, mind-blowing sex, another shower, and more conversation, she dressed with the assurance that their bond was now stronger than before.

Brenda wore a mock turtleneck sweater to cover the fading bruises and a pair of jeans from her suitcase. She'd been grateful to find it in the limo, but hadn't given it much thought before now. Roark, who looked good in anything or nothing at all, wore a pair of sweats and a tee.

Red and Denise sat in the family room watching TV. Frank lay on the sofa with his head in Veronique's lap, reading some type of manual. Four pair of eyes glued onto them as they headed toward the kitchen, whispering and touching each other like horny teens. Roark opened the refrigerator and searched for something quick to eat. Brenda stood to the side, holding his hand and giggling at his side comments while trying to see what she wanted to eat.

"Hungry?" Red asked in a dry tone, standing in the doorway with Denise under his arm.

Roark glanced at his brother and nodded. "My appetite has returned." He grinned and stole a kiss from Brenda's lips.

"We heard," Red muttered, earning a warning glare from his fiancé as she pushed away from him.

"Bren, you okay?" Denise walked to the island and sat on one of the padded stools.

Brenda turned and smiled. "Yeah, I am now. But I was really out of it for a couple of days. I didn't even know how many days I'd been missing until Tex told me."

At the mention of Tex's name, everyone looked quickly at Roark and then back at her. Roark squeezed her hand, letting her know he was okay with the discussion. After two rounds of marathon sex, her vee-jay couldn't take anymore loving. They'd taken a brief nap, and then spent some time talking about everything she could remember that'd happened since she left

Pennsylvania. Well, she didn't tell him how fine her sexy ex was, or that they held each other close and danced a few times, or that he kissed her a wet one good-bye, that information went into the need to know file.

"You don't remember what happened when you got off the plane?" Frank asked while sitting on one of the stools at the island. Roark placed a sandwich in front of Brenda along with a can of ginger ale.

"Thanks." She smiled at him and took a bite before answering his brother. "Only that a short Hispanic lady picked me up from the airport. I don't think she ever told me her name. We drove a long time; I remember I kept asking how soon before we got to the nursing home."

"Hispanic, hmmm. Hair color?" Veronique asked, writing everything down on a small pad of paper.

"Dark brown I think." Brenda tried to see what she wrote, but couldn't see that far. Glancing at her plate, she was surprised to see it was empty. Specks of mustard dotted her thumb and forefinger.

"Eyes?"

"I don't remember."

"Any tattoos? Or other marks on her body?"

"I think there was a tattoo, I'm not sure." She jumped as Roark sucked the mustard from her fingertips, his tongue circling each digit sent tremors down her spine.

"Tastes good," he said, releasing her hand. They stared at each other, slow grins spreading from ear to ear. Bubbles of happiness burst inside as she walked, uncoached, into his arms. They stood in an easy cuddle, inhaling each other's scent, taking and receiving reassurance for a few seconds.

"Sooo, any idea who took you as a guest for three days?" Denise asked, a deep smile on her face as well.

"Not me," Brenda said, the side of her face plastered on Roark's chest. The steady beat of his heart was a pillow of solace after the storm of the last few days. "Tex thinks it was Anna."

"Most likely," Brenda said, agreeing with Tex in a once in a lifetime event.

"Your sister?" Veronique looked stunned.

Brenda nodded.

Roark rubbed his chin on the top of her head. "Can we move this to the family room?" he asked while turning Brenda in that direction. She grabbed her ginger ale off the counter and left with him.

It was a cozy setting. All three O'Connor men sat next to their women. For a moment, Brenda was tempted to make a comment regarding how weird it was, but realized they had all been worried about her and required answers for their own peace of minds. When this conversation was over, she needed to visit her aunt at the home, talk to Denise about the wedding, and check her messages online for any instructions from her teacher. Life had intruded and she needed to get back on target.

"Is it likely your sister was behind your abduction?" Veronique asked. She was sitting thigh to hip next to Frank, his arm carelessly thrown across her shoulders in an unmistakable claim of partnership. Brenda wondered when those two had gotten together. She stuck a pin in that thought to ask Denise later.

"It's possible. I don't know why she'd do it. But I wouldn't put anything past her," Brenda said, her thoughts settling on the possibility. If Tex thought Anna was responsible, she probably was. He had a keen eye for details and a mind like a trap. He could have done so much more with his life, if only…she blocked out that path and focused on the questions.

"There was a woman posing as you visiting your aunt at the nursing home. One of the nurses said the woman was about five feet five, slim but heavy on top, and she kept her sunglasses on the entire time." Frank waited for her response to his description.

"It's been a few years since I've seen Anna. That could be her." Even though her mind rebelled against believing that her sister would do something that low, she'd long ago accepted that her blood kin had no honor or morals. Anna wouldn't blink if she could make a dime or come up with a way that made things better for her."But where did the Hispanic woman fit in?"

"That's what I want to know," Denise said.

Brenda hadn't realized she'd spoken aloud.

"Is Anna gay?" Red asked.

Brenda looked up, startled. Her jaw dropped at the implication. A spurt of dry laughter flew from her mouth. "It's possible. She believes she's better than the rest of us. Smarter for sure."

"She gets off on teasing guys, making them look bad. Remember,

Bren?" Denise said, her face scrunched in disgust. "Remember that guy from the Red Dragon club a few years back. He bought her drinks and followed her around like a damn puppy. She used him for months and then dumped him for another guy, right there in front of everybody. The two men almost got in a fight while she laughed at the first man. I felt sorry for the old fool."

Brenda nodded as that embarrassing moment resurfaced. The man had been someone her mom had lived with for a year. Then he'd dumped her mom for her sister. When the incident went down that night at the club, she never told Denise how she knew the man and didn't want to get into it now, either.

"Like I said, it's possible." Brenda left Anna's sexuality on the table, refusing to give it another thought. Anna had lived with Mable, their mother, most of her life, and if God gave anyone a pass for being messed up, it'd be Anna. Mable possessed alley-cat morals and wouldn't blink an eye if one of her lovers crossed the line with her daughter. That was the reason Aunt Robin had taken Brenda in. Her mama's boyfriends were getting too friendly. Brenda could only imagine what Anna had lived through.

"Smoke said they got your luggage from a house near Fifth Street on the north side. You remember anything about that?" Veronique asked.

Brenda told them what happened after she woke up in the cold house. Thankfully, no one asked any questions about her time with Tex. But the gleam in Denise's eyes said she wasn't off the hook, they'd discuss that in private. After all the questions were asked, and possible scenarios dissected, Brenda was drained.

Sliding forward to stand, Brenda looked around the room at her friends, and hopefully family in the future. "I want to go see my Aunt at the home. She must be confused by everything that's been going on."

"Bren." The hitch in Denise's voice ticked off a premonition of disaster in Brenda. Her heart accelerated as she searched Denise's face first, then Red's. The look of pity on his face sent an icicle of fear into her gut. She struggled to ask what had happened.

Veronique's glassy eyes matched the look in Red's. Brenda reached back and grabbed Roark's hand. He squeezed hers in a show of unity and asked the questions she couldn't. "What's wrong? What happened?"

"The detective informed us about thirty minutes ago. Your aunt passed this morning at the nursing home." Frank paused. "I'm sorry, Brenda."

Her heart dropped in anguish as she sucked in a painful breath. Roark enfolded her in the warmth and strength of his embrace.

"She's dead?" Brenda whispered, gazing into Roark's eyes, her anchor. Her mind refused to process what she'd just heard. Confused, her brows furrowed. "But I didn't get to see her or talk to her." She swallowed hard as tears filled her eyes. "I didn't tell her how much I appreciated her taking care of me, and saving me from Mable." Her eyes snapped close. Her head swung side to side in denial. "She can't be gone. I need to talk to her, I gotta tell her how much she means to me." Her eyes locked with his teary ones. "Roark," she cried desperately. "She can't be dead. Please, tell me…tell me how to make this right." Her forehead collapsed against his chest, the pain was excruciating as she burrowed into him and cried. Cried for the missed opportunities through the years; she never should've waited this long to come see her aunt. For some reason, she always put it off for tomorrow. Tomorrow was today and now it was too late.

"Baby." Roark touched the side of her face in a light caress before he stood and picked her up. "Give us a few minutes?" He asked of everyone as he carried her away in his arms to grieve in private. She loved him more at that moment than ever before. She'd made the right choice.

****

Brenda knew her aunt had prepaid for her plot and casket, had written her service, and probably the eulogy as well. That's why she couldn't understand why the funeral was five days later. Roark stayed the extra days, never leaving her side. His attendance meant they'd had to reschedule the Cayman Islands trip. But he wouldn't go home without her and she had to stay to see her favorite relative put to rest. So they agreed to take the trip after Red and Denise's wedding.

Just as she suspected, both Cherise and Denise cornered her at lunch one day to grill her about the time she'd spent with Tex. It no longer hurt to think about him. He'd matured. They both overcame high odds. She knew he cared for her, enough to let her choose someone else and walk away. One day she hoped he'd be happy. Their relationship went into her mental file labeled Things to Learn From and Never Repeat. The days flew by quickly and the nights with Roark were incredible. As impossible as it seemed, each day she fell more in love with him.

****

Standing in the family processional prior to entering the church, Roark stood on her right, her hand securely in his. Denise stood on her left, a pit bull in the wildest sense. The woman glared, and possibly growled, at everyone who stared at Brenda and Roark a second longer than *she* felt necessary.

Staring straight ahead, Brenda ignored the looks Mable sent her. The woman's gaze slid to Roark, and then Denise. The one person Brenda wanted to see was not in line. Anna hadn't made an appearance yet. Tex's suspicions had taken root and Brenda wanted to look her sister in the eye for the last time. She planned to ask a few direct questions. Each began with one word. *Why?* Why would she attack her while she lay unable to defend herself? Why did she go to such lengths to torment her? Why did she hate her so much? It was the *whys* that baffled Brenda. And she wanted answers.

The processional started. Denise grabbed her hand and squeezed it as they moved forward. The church was half-full or half-empty, depending on your preference. Her aunt had been a tough woman to take, but she'd been fair. Her cousins, Celia and Clint, their children, and Mable filled the front row. Brenda released a sigh of relief, she wouldn't make it through the next hour if she had to share a row with Mable's fake tears. Roark sat at the corner of the next row, which placed her behind her cousin, Celia.

Brenda prepared for the drama. Celia hadn't been the most loving child, and probably felt three times the guilt weighing Brenda down, for putting her mama in a home in a different state from where she lived. Because Celia lived so far away, she'd rarely visited her mother and had left her care to strangers. Brenda had lost all respect for her much older cousin after that. Celia turned slightly, looking behind her. Her glassy eyes met Brenda's, recognition set in and she smiled. It was one of those, I'm glad you're here, but I wish you weren't kind of things. Brenda offered a slight nod, the only concession she was willing to give. Especially since Celia was the one who had called her and set the whole kidnapping thing in motion.

The funeral took on a surreal feeling. True to form, Celia required constant attention, yelling for her mama, reaching for the casket and all types of theatrics. Denise stared at the cross in the background to keep from saying anything ugly. This was neither the time nor the place to show her feelings.

There were other outbursts throughout the building, but the person who surprised her was Mable. Brenda stole looks at her mother and was stunned to see a woman perfectly groomed. Her thick hair was cut short in a flattering style, highlighting her large eyes. A serene mask covered her face as she stared at her sister's casket, tears rolling down her face. Not once did Mable scream or beg forgiveness. Her grief was private, personal.

As they were leaving the funeral, someone touched Brenda's elbow. Celia stood behind her. Guilt was a hard taskmaster; her cousin looked horrible.

Celia's mouth opened and shut. Roark stepped closer to Brenda's side while Celia pulled herself together. "I…I just want to say thank you for taking such good care of mama. I didn't know you lived out of state when I called. Still you came. I'm sorry about all the stuff you went through. I never told mama about the fake Brenda; she was so happy I didn't want to take that from her." Celia swallowed and touched Brenda's hand. "I shoulda let her stay in the house with you when you asked. I was embarrassed that you were willing to take care of her and I wasn't. I'm sorry about that. I know you loved her and she certainly loved you." She waved away a group of people who called out to her and looked back at Brenda. Her nose twitched. "They think I don't know that they never liked mama, they just go from funeral to funeral to have something to talk about."

Brenda chuckled. A wall had come down between the two women. "I loved my Auntie and I hate what happened. Most of all I hate that I didn't get a chance to see her after I got here. Out of everything that happened, that hurts the most."

Celia nodded, blinking back tears. "I know. I know. She talked about you all the time. It was if I didn't exist. I admit I was jealous and didn't like it. I hope we can let all that go, I'm running out of sane family members," Celia said, her tone dry and brittle as she looked around at the gathering of people.

Brenda sputtered. An awkward laugh flew through her lips as she looked around as well. Celia had a point. Roark squeezed her hand gently.

"Amen to that," Denise muttered.

Celia smiled at her. "How you been Denise? Heard you and Irish about to get married."

"You know what they say about rumors," Denise said in a somber tone.

Celia frowned.

"I'm better now that Bren is safe. Red and I are getting married in a few weeks. The rumors *are* true in that regard," Denise said, enjoying the look of confusion on Celia's face.

"This is Roark, my man. Roark, my cousin, Celia." Brenda waved between the two of them, stopping Denise before she had Celia twisted in a mental pretzel.

Celia gazed at him for a second, smiled and extended her hand. "Hi. You sure you want to be a part of this crazy set of genes we call a family?"

Roark took her hand for a second or two and released it. "I'm sure I want Brenda in my life, and whatever it takes to make that happen, I'm game."

"Ooooh, great answer. Smart and good looking." She winked at Roark before returning to Brenda. "Thanks for having a heart as big as Texas, I appreciate everything you've done." She brushed a kiss on Brenda's cheek, squeezed her arm, and walked away.

"Why'd she turn out all nice and stuff. I enjoyed not liking her." Denise pouted as they headed for their car.

"I know, right?" Brenda said, swinging Roark's hand while grinning at Denise. "I picked up on the whole rumor mill thing, you were about to take her for a ride, weren't you?"

Denise laughed. "She asked for it. It's not cool to tell someone you heard something about them. I planned to school her on the rumor mill, that's all."

Brenda picked up the cunning look that returned to Denise's eyes. "Don't even try it. I know you, remember that."

"True, true." Denise chuckled. "Crazy dog coming in at three o'clock." Denise stepped up, blocking Mable's access to Brenda.

"Still running interference, I see." Mable glared at Denise, not realizing that was exactly what Brenda's best friend wanted.

"I don't call it interference. I call it friendship. A new concept for you I know, but you should read up on it, might work." Denise preened at the dig. Brenda knew her friend had wanted to do that and much more for years. But just as Brenda didn't rip into Denise's unreasonable father, to date Denise had left Mable alone.

"Yeah. Whatever." Mable brushed Denise off as you would a fly and turned to Brenda. "You're leaving without speaking?" she asked, her voice husky from years of smoking all types of things.

Brenda took in her mother's appearance in a quick sweep and had to give it to Mable; she looked good. Her mahogany complexion had cleared and looked healthy. Her hair had a slight sheen, and her dark navy suit appeared expensive.

"Yeah." Brenda threw Mable's answer back at her and moved to step around her.

"I'm Mable, Brenda's mother." She stuck her hand toward Roark and waited for him to acknowledge her.

Roark looked at Brenda, his eyes asking what she wanted him to do. Her chest expanded at his respect for her. She nodded. He took her mother's hand briefly and dropped it without saying a word. Brenda thought the dig was well done.

Mable's lips tightened, marring her previous good looks. "I see you've trained him well."

Brenda bristled.

Denise snorted derisively at Mable's attempt to score put-down points, causing others to turn in their direction.

Mable used words with the same precision as a surgeon. She gloried in putting people in what she considered their place. When Brenda was younger, her mom's taunts had often reduced her to tears. That was a different day, different time, and a different woman.

"Actually, he's trained me," Brenda said as though revealing a secret.

Mable frowned.

"You see I normally wouldn't stand in the street, or in a house, or anywhere and talk to a woman who abandoned her children to follow after every hard cock with a little jingle in his pocket. Or a whore that'd allow a man to fuck around with her own kids because she was too lazy to get a job. Nope, I wouldn't do it." She tipped her chin toward Roark, while watching Mable's mouth open and snap shut. If the woman's jaw got any tighter, it'd break.

"But he's convinced me to be civil to everyone, no matter how low-down and disgusting I think they are. So you see, *Mable*, he's the only reason I'm speaking to your ass."

This time when she went to step around the woman, Mable moved to the side as if Brenda had a contagious disease. Roark and Denise walked alongside her quietly. The moment the car door closed, Denise tapped her shoulder from the back seat. Eyes wide, she had a shit-eating grin spread across her face. Roark and Brenda laughed at the comical expression on Denise's face.

"Damn, my baby's all grown-up," Denise said, wiping non-existent tears from her cheeks.

Chapter 16

Donald O'Connor strode down the linoleum-covered floors toward Tom Diggins, the Chief of Police's office. Face grim, he understood the sensitivity of this visit and if it weren't his brother, he'd let nature take its course. But Roark was his brother and that trumped friendship, it changed things. He and Brenda planned to return home after the funeral, and Donald wanted this matter settled by then.

"Hello, Janice." Donald greeted the older woman whose job it was to screen all those who wanted to talk to her boss. She and Donald had always gotten along, neither one of them taking the other for granted.

"Hi, Mr. O'Connor." She smiled warmly. "Go on in, he's expecting you."

I bet he is. Donald nodded and headed into the room. There was another man sitting in a chair near the desk. He glared at Donald as he walked closer to the desk. Tom stood and offered introductions.

"Hello Don." He extended his hand, which Donald took, pumped a couple of times and released. Turning to the stranger, Donald looked at him expectantly. He had no idea who the man was or why he stared at him as though he'd stolen his pension fund.

Tom waved toward the other man. "This is my brother, Jerry. I thought it was important that he see and hear anything you had to say regarding this situation."

Understanding Tom's position, Donald was unsure exactly how to greet Jerry. He nodded; it wasn't returned. Donald moved to the other chair to sit and change gears. Instead of meeting with a friendly associate, he prepared for a hostile environment. The other two men followed suit.

Donald slipped into legal counsel mode, determined to win this round. "I appreciate this meeting, Tom. But I wanted to give you the first opportunity to see what I have before I file the paperwork. I think you'll agree my client has sufficient grounds."

"If what you hinted on the phone is valid, you may have a point. And I do appreciate you talking to me first." Tom nodded.

Donald glanced around the room, ignoring the water color artwork on the wall, the over-stuffed bookcases and file cabinets. He settled on the TV and DVD player tucked away in the corner. "We can use your DVD player or my laptop, which would you prefer?"

Tom stood. "We'll all be able to better watch what you have on the bigger screen." Within moments, the TV and player flickered on. Donald handed him the DVD and waited. He and Blaine had watched the thing at least ten times. It sickened him to know that someone would violate another person's space to this degree. He watched Jerry, instead of the monitor, as the person became clearer. The man's face grew redder and redder as the scene unfolded. None of the men spoke. By the time the screen blanked, Donald knew two things. One, Jerry Diggins would never be his friend. The man's beet-red face, tight jaw, and heaving chest pronounced his anger and frustration. At who, Donald didn't know or care. Secondly, he knew this case would never make it to trial. Tom's precarious position as top cop wouldn't fare well under the media exposure.

Tom looked at Jerry, a look of awe on his face. "I didn't know she could walk."

"Me neither. I've tried to get her to use those things and she refused." Jerry covered his eyes and rubbed them as if to rid him of a painful memory. Donald waited, forgotten as the two men discussed what they'd just seen.

"But she can't climb stairs," Tom said. "She tried and fell. Wonder why she kept trying to go upstairs?"

Donald could've told them she wanted to make it to his brother's bedroom, perhaps to lie in the same spot he'd laid in. Or to go through his closet. Who knew? Paula was a sick woman and this DVD showed how warped her mind had become.

"No matter," Jerry snapped. "She broke into this house three times that I counted." He paused. "Don't look like she took anything."

"No, she's not going into my client's home to steal. She's violating the restraining order he placed on her last month." Donald slid a copy of the order to Jerry, who stared at it in horror.

"A restraining order?" Jerry looked at Tom, who sat dazed looking at the paper. "You know about this?"

"No." He croaked, cleared his throat and spoke again. "No. I didn't know." He glanced at Donald. "Why'd he place the order on her? This an ongoing problem?"

Donald nodded, preparing to wade shark infested waters. "Yes. She's been stalking him for a while now. They knew each other prior to her accident; in fact he was with her when the car crashed into the pole."

The temperature in the room changed immediately. Rage replaced the shame on Jerry and Tom's faces. Donald wasn't surprised; they now had another target to focus on.

"You representing that scum?" Jerry snarled his eyes hard.

"No, I'm representing the man your daughter is stalking, has been stalking for years. He's tried to be nice, asked her not to call or visit, but she won't leave him alone. She has broken into his home, knowing he's not there, for the sole purpose of being close to his things. Her van is parked on his street for hours daily, the neighbors have complained to the police, it's a matter of record."

Tom's face paled at Donald's words.

Jerry's fist balled tighter. Oh well, she was his daughter. "She wouldn't be in this mess if it weren't for him."

"Paula wouldn't be in a wheelchair if she hadn't snorted cocaine and decided to drive under the influence. Would you like to see the police and hospital reports?" Tom shook his head. "Face it, she was high and wrecked her car. My client is the victim here, she broke into his home."

No one spoke.

Donald inhaled a calming breath. Getting upset might make him sloppy, he couldn't afford to lose ground. This was personal. She'd violated his little brother's space, rolled around on the bed in the downstairs bedroom, laid on his sofa, sat in his chair.

"What do you propose?" Tom asked, resigned.

Jerry's mouth thinned into a thin line.

"What do *you* propose is the question? I have one recourse and that's to press charges against her. That's it." Donald spread his arms in supplication.

Tom's eyes slid to his brother and back at Donald. "Jerry?"

Jerry glanced at his brother. "We'll talk and get back with you," he said to Donald in dismissal.

Tom's eyes widened. "No. We'll settle this now." He glanced at Donald and then glared at his stubborn brother. "Agreed?" he asked Donald.

"If we can find an amicable conclusion to this matter, then I agree.

Otherwise, I'll head across the street and file the paperwork."

Jerry swung around in his seat, his eyes shooting bullets. Donald, not a small man mentally or physically, sat unfazed. He glanced at his watch and gave them thirty more minutes of his time. This short interlude with Paula's father had him leaning toward trial. It might help father and daughter to have their day in court; it would certainly adjust their entitlement attitudes.

"I have another appointment at one o'clock. Tell me what you have in mind," Donald pressed.

"You know what you have to do." Tom looked meaningfully at his brother. Jerry whimpered and turned away, his face tortured.

Donald had no idea what placed that distressing look on the man's face, but Tom did. He reached over and patted his brother's arm. "She's gotten worse. If this goes to court, the judge will demand a psychiatric evaluation; she'll be put away."

"So, what you're saying is I should do it before the courts do? How can I do that to my own child?" He stood and walked to the window. "I can take her away. We can move to somewhere like Montana, on the other side of the country."

"She can drive back," Tom said.

"I'll sell the truck."

"She will make you miserable just like before, and then you'll give her whatever she wants. This is not about you, Jerry. This is about Paula. She's sick and needs professional help. No one breaks into someone's home repeatedly for no reason. If you can't get her the help she needs and make sure she's confined until the doctors say she's better, then this needs to go to trial. She's a real threat in this unstable condition."

Jerry's shoulders slumped as he stood near the window. "Can I have some time to think about it?"

Donald replaced the papers in his satchel and stood. "Yes. I'll file the papers today. Keep the DVD." His chin tipped in the direction of the TV as he placed his business card on the desk. "Have your attorney give me a call if you want to settle this before court."

Tom walked Donald to the door. "Thanks, I know this is difficult for you. I had forgotten your brother was in the accident, and I appreciate you letting me see this first." He patted Donald's shoulder as he held open the door and leaned forward. "If you can wait until the end of day before filing your petition, I believe we'll have an agreement worked out that should satisfy your client."

Roark wanted the crazy woman out of his life and away from him. Short of that nothing would satisfy. Donald nodded and left.

Chapter 17

Tex sat in the hotel room. Word came for him to wait for additional instructions. Crossing his foot at the ankles, hands behind his back, he gazed at the ceiling, his thoughts taking flight. Brenda looked good. Really good. His dick hardened as he re-envisioned her asleep on the bed in front of him. So close and so far. For ten hours he'd watched her breathe. It would have taken a better person than him not to have lain in the bed beside her. He was no saint.

He'd touched her face remembering the mornings they'd lay in bed talking of their dreams. She'd always tried to get him to go a different direction than he had gone. Even then, he enjoyed the rush of outwitting the cops, making large sums of money and the respect in the eyes of his subordinates. He'd never experienced that working those minimum wage jobs he'd done when they were together.

His jaw tightened in remembrance of the bruises around her neck. Someone would pay for choking her, especially while she couldn't defend herself. For hours, he'd inhaled her scent, embedding it in the corner of his mind. Touched her skin and whispered his innermost fears and thoughts to the one person who could cripple him. She was his one weakness.

He sighed. There was a time when he couldn't be around her for ten seconds without touching some part on her body. Her hand, thigh, even her fingertips. They'd had an amazing connection between them. Like a fool, he'd assumed it was rubber, able to bounce back no matter how far he stretched it. But even rubber had a breaking point.

Eyes closed, he allowed the reality of the situation to wash over him. Brenda didn't choose him. It was a long shot, he'd known the odds but he'd had to try. It'd been time to man up and clear the air. For a little while they were able to talk like back in the day. Then he mentioned how long she'd been missing. The look on her face when she realized she'd been gone for three days, and her man would be worried, dashed his hopes of getting her back. Roark, she'd called his name with such heartbreaking need, it decimated him. Each word, every action she took to contact this man sent shafts of pain through him. In that moment, it became crystal clear he'd lost Brenda's heart to someone else and there would be no second chances. He needed to regroup and deal with the loss.

Footsteps neared the door. Opening his eyes, he stood with his hand at his side, near his weapon.

The stranger walked in alone, nodded at him and shut the door. Without any greeting, he waved Tex to the chair he'd just sat in as he moved toward the TV.

"I want you to see this and tell me what you think." Tex nodded as he returned to his chair.

Moments later, Tex masked his surprise at the scene on the screen. Anna, Brenda's sister, was tied to a chair. Her head lolled from side to side, her hair was stuck up in patches and her busted lip was swollen to twice its size.

"I told you I don't know nothing." Anna's voice sounded hoarse from overuse.

"Why did you go to the nursing home?" a masculine voice asked from off-camera.

"I only did that a couple of times. I thought I could work an angle with my sister's ex-boyfriend, get him off my back."

"What kind of deal?"

"I'd get her to come see our aunt and then give her to him so he'd leave me alone."

"Were you afraid of him?"

"He's going to kill me." Tears rolled down her face.

"Why?"

"I really liked him, but he liked my sister. I set him up. A lot of stuff happened; he blames me. It's just a matter of time," she mumbled.

"Where's your sister?"

"I don't have a sister," she screamed. "I don't have a sister. That's so fucked up." Tex sat forward, confused.

"What do you mean she's not your sister?"

"Mable's not Brenda's mama. A guy Mable knew paid her money to adopt Brenda. He was married and didn't want his wife to know he had another child by his girlfriend. The girlfriend had skipped town and left the baby with him. He made sure Brenda got everything she needed as long as he lived. After he died, Mable lost interest and money."

Tex's hand covered his mouth and chin; he couldn't believe this bullshit. If this were true, Brenda would be devastated.

"Who picked her up from the airport?"

Anna growled. "I told you I don't know. I didn't even know she was coming to town."

"When was the last time you visited the nursing home?"

Anna screamed, a long, tortured sound. "I hate her! I hate her! I wouldn't be here if it weren't for her."

"Answer my question and then you can rest."

"I only went to the nursing home twice, maybe six or eight weeks ago." The screen blanked. Tex continued to stare at the screen.

"What do you think?"

Tex glanced at the man sitting nearby. "I don't know what to think." He wasn't interested in having a conversation with someone who refused to identify himself.

"Do you think she speaks the truth?" Keen eyes watched him.

Tex exhaled, shaking his head. "Like I said, I don't know. It's possible." He shrugged gazing at the carpet. Neither man spoke for a few moments.

"I am seeking information for a friend. I have promised to deliver the culprit behind this entire ordeal, but I must get to the bottom of the matter, Si?"

"Who are you?" Tex asked, staring at the well-dressed man. He figured they were close in age, similar in height and build.

"Julio." The haughty tone said Tex should know him.

Tex didn't relax, but the tension eased from his shoulders. "How can I help?"

"Tell me your thoughts on what you just saw," Julio snapped.

"I believe her."

Julio stared at him for a moment. "Why?"

"Because she hates Brenda, it's unnatural. I never understood why. From what I was told, Brenda went to private school when she was young. She went on trips, saw things. If you talk to Anna for five minutes, you'd know they didn't share those experiences." He paused tapping his chin with his fingertips. "Let's just say, I believe she believes what she's been told, not that what she's saying is true. Her mama's one of the biggest liars in town."

"She was jealous of the little one, I understand. But you do not think she arranged this travesty?"

"It's possible. But I don't see Anna having the patience for a plan like this. She may have started it, but someone else finished it." *Who?* He wondered.

"The Hispanic woman who picked up Brenda from the airport? What is her role?"

Tex chuckled. "Truthfully. I thought she and Anna were lovers."

"Truly?" Julio sounded intrigued although he didn't move.

"Yeah. The little one was very protective of Anna over at the warehouse. The way they were holding each other and shit, I thought they were a couple."

"But she had a crush on you. That is what she says."

Tex frowned, remembering Anna's confession. He shook his head. "I don't believe that unless it was one of those, I want him cause she's got him, things. Like I said, she hates Brenda with a passion. Why would any man want a woman who could hate that hard?"

Julio nodded.

"I mean, she'll flip it on you one day. Maybe she flipped to women, I don't know."

"She knew you meant to kill her."

"Good."

Julio chuckled and glanced at his watch. "It's time, come with me." He pointed to the DVD. "Bring that, please."

Tex nodded, withdrew the disk and then followed Julio out the door.

Chapter 18

Brenda sat in the rear of the church surrounded by Denise, Cherise, and Veronique. Wedding rehearsal was scheduled to begin in ten minutes, so they took this time to catch up. As the bride, all conversation should've evolved around Denise and her fabulous wedding plans. When Brenda tried to redirect the flow of discussion, Denise balked.

"I want to know what happened when Donald told Roark about psycho bitch. I can't believe she broke into y'alls' house to chill." Denise sat forward, engrossed in her thoughts. "I mean, who does that? Breaks into somebody's house to be around his stuff. Plus, he's got his woman living with him." Denise threw up her hands, as Cherise and Veronique nodded in agreement. "That's major drama right there."

"I saw the tape, and it was sad," Brenda said. "She kept trying to climb the stairs, but either the braces on her legs wouldn't bend or her arms were too weak. She fell every time, and would stare upstairs like it was a mountaintop she had to climb." Brenda shook her head. "It was weird."

"What's going on, Chicas?" Vianca asked in greeting as she hugged everyone before sitting down. She glanced at Smoke, who walked over to the guys. "Who we talking 'bout?"

"Brenda was telling us about this woman back home who broke into their house while they were out here. There's some crazy women out there." Cherise shook her head and shifted in her seat.

Veronique looked at her and smiled. "Roark said Donald worked out a deal with her family. She's getting help."

"Si," Vianca said, in a high-pitched snort. "They locked her ass up in some mental place. She must've been bad off for her parents to do that."

"She was, you gotta see the tape," Denise said. "Flipping the subject a bit, I heard the elder O'Connor are in town." She looked at Brenda and Veronique. "From what I understand, they're expecting another announcement from one of their sons. Anybody wanna share?"

Veronique burst out laughing, but covered her mouth when Frank looked at her. She waved him down and looked at Denise. "You're bad, girl. Don't start any mess with *your* in-laws. This is your special time; you already yanked me into walking down the aisle with Frank as a bridesmaid."

"My cousin canceled."

"Sure she did. I smell Frank's hand in this." Veronique waved Denise's lie down. They both laughed.

"Yuck, Ma. You did not say you smelled his hand." Cherise scrunched her nose and pulled on her dress.

"My, you're mighty sensitive these days, Chica," Vianca said her eyes wandering over Cherise. "Plus your ass is spreading like wildfire. If you pull that dress any more it's gonna rip at the seams. Anything *you* wanna share?"

Cherise's eyes watered. "My ass is not spreading." She looked at Veronique. "Is it, Mama?"

Smiling, her mom patted the back of her hand. "No, Baby Girl, it's not spreading." Brenda, Denise and Vianca stared open-mouthed at Cherise and Veronique.

"Oh no, you didn't," Denise said pointing at Cherise. "Did you see that? They working in tandem over here. Mama and daughter working on a big ass cover up. Oops, didn't mean it how it sounded."

Denise covered her mouth, her eyes twinkling as a grin escaped.

Veronique tapped Denise on the arm. "Watch it."

Cherise stood and stalked toward Ross. Brenda, Denise, and Vianca laughed as he met her half-way, bent down to listen to her whining, and finally held her close. He gazed at them and shook his head, a small grin dimpling his cheek.

"Y'all wrong for that," he said as he walked Cherise to a chair and sat next to her.

"Well, it looks like next year's gonna be a busy one for you, Ms. Veronique," Denise said, watching Cherise lay her head on Ross's shoulder as Red talked to the minister.

"Hmmm, I'm afraid to ask why? But I'll bite. Why?" Brenda watched Denise lean into Veronique as though she had a huge secret.

"A Nana, a bride and a mother all in the same year. Sounds busy to me." Denise leaned back as Vianca's mouth dropped open.

"No, Chica. I say Brenda will be the next mother and wife."

"Frank's older and ready to settle, he'll be next, watch." Denise looked at Brenda and then Veronique. Each of them stared at her as though she were on drugs.

"Did you say a mother?" Veronique squeaked and then coughed, clearing her throat. "I know you didn't just wish that on me."

"Ms. Veronique, you know you gonna give that man at least one baby, stop fronting," Denise said with all the authority of a bride about to walk down the aisle. "Frank's ready to settle down, you'll be married next, which leads me back to my and your future in-laws. They'll be here soon and I wanted to give you a heads up." She eyed Brenda and then Veronique. Vianca sat back wearing a grin, enjoying their discomfort.

"Sean, the old man, is pretty quiet until he gets drunk. Allie, Red's mom. She's a pepper and a half. Never, ever agree with Red's mother when she cracks on her sons. If she says Roark is a slob, never agree."

"He's not a slob."

"Doesn't matter. You ever heard of those mamas who can talk shit about their kids, but get pissed when you do?"

Brenda nodded. Most mamas, hers being the exception, were like that. "Yeah." She glanced at Roark. An older man stood nearby talking to them. She wondered who he was.

"Listen to me." Denise tapped Brenda's arm. "I'm trying to help you."

"Okay, got it. Never agree with negative things about Roark. Although there's really nothing—"

"We know, he's perfect," Vianca drawled.

"No, not perfect." She looked away, uneasy, not wanting to get into putting him up so high she'd shatter if he ever failed.

Veronique took her hand and squeezed. "He's perfect for you." She winked. "I know the feeling."

"Awww," Denise said, laughing as the wedding coordinator breezed into the sanctuary, followed by Denise's dad and Roark's parents. Red's mom waved at the men and headed for Denise and her court.

"Hello, little one." She hugged Denise tightly and kissed both cheeks before stepping back. "He has been taking good care of you, I see."

"Yes, he has. My baby's been on point." Denise turned and looked at Red. He winked and turned to his father.

"Good, at least he's good for something other than making babies." Brenda's face warmed as the jolly woman turned and waved her forward. "It has been a long time since you've come to my house to visit. I tell Roark to let you out of bed long enough to sit down to eat some food." She squeezed Brenda's arms." You have lost weight. It is not good to make love and not eat. He must feed you." She turned and glared at Roark.

Brenda's eyes widened and her face burned. What could she say? She glanced at Denise for instructions and the heifer smiled. Okay, she was on her own. She could do this.

"I tell you what you must do," Roark's mom continued. "You must put your foot down. It is not good to allow him his way all the time. Okay."

"Yes, ma'am."

"Good, you're good girl. He'll take better care of you or I'll kick him. He's knows this. I raised my boys to be men who take care of their women." She patted Brenda's cheeks and turned to Veronique, who'd remained seated. Brenda glared at Denise, who shrugged and watched the interaction between the two older women.

"My son tells me he is in love with you." Allie and Veronique squared off. Brenda stood next to Denise, listening.

"I love him as well." Veronique said in a well-modulated tone. Not quite her professional voice, or her social tone. More like somewhere in between.

"He wants children."

"That is something he and I will discuss and decide."

Denise and Brenda looked at each other in surprise. The chill in Veronique's voice said back up and butt out.

"I understand you are older than him. By two years."

Veronique nodded. "Yes, I am." Her chin remained strong as she stared Allie in the eyes. Even from where Brenda stood, she read the warning.

"That does not bother you?"

"No. Should it?"

Allie stared at Veronique a moment longer and smiled. A real one that warmed her eyes. "Not at all. I am happy to meet you and glad my son has found a woman to handle his arrogant ass."

"Like I said, I love him, ass and all." Veronique glanced at Brenda and winked.

Allie snorted and covered her loud laugh. "Oh, I love it. This is going to be fun. Frank is so accustomed to running everyone else's life." She leaned forward, speaking softer than before. But Brenda could still hear.

"He always thinks he has to take care of everyone, he neglects himself. I hope you won't allow him to do that anymore."

"I love him the way he is. It's what makes him unique. I don't have as much time to spend on myself as I used to because I'd rather be with him. So he may not be as available, but he'll probably always have a strong connection to want to fix things for his family." Veronique shrugged. "That's just who he is."

Allie clasped her hands together as though she'd recite a prayer or something. Instead, she nodded at Veronique. "You get him. That has always been my prayer that he meets someone who sees him as he is and loves him in spite of it all."

Brenda coughed to cover her laugh. Denise laughed without restraint as she walked away to the meet with the coordinator. Veronique nodded as she smiled.

****

Roark stared at Brenda sitting in the back of the church with Denise and all the women. From the glances sent his way, he figured she'd told them about Paula and the break-ins. He'd told Red and Frank on the phone. Neither could believe the video when he sent them copies of the security cam's DVD. Although Roark didn't wish any harm on Paula, he was glad that she was out of his life. One of the conditions of the settlement was that Paula would never live in the same state as him. Her father had agreed, and as far as he knew, they'd moved.

Initially, Brenda had been furious to learn Paula had been snooping around their things, until she watched the DVD. Paula's pitiful attempts to climb the stairs brought tears to Brenda's eyes. It hurt to watch. There was no question Paula needed professional help.

Sean O'Connor was as tall as his sons, although not as wide. He clasped Roark on the shoulder and pulled him close, slapping his back. "Good to see you, boyo. I hear everything worked out fine." Releasing Roark, they both glanced in the direction of the women. "Is that your lass standing next to me Denise?" He pointed to Brenda.

Roark groaned at the fumes of alcohol wafting from his dad. Tonight would be long. "Yes, that's her."

"You lost her? How'd you lose your woman?" His Uncle Nate met up with them, glancing at his brother.

"I didn't lose her, Uncle Nate. Why would you ask me that?" Roark growled at the insensitivity of the subject. He was not going to have this discussion with two drunken men. Instead, he glanced at Brenda and noticed his mom sitting next to Veronique. Now that was probably an interesting conversation. He wished he could be a fly on the wall to hear those two.

Frank walked up behind him, his eyes following Roark's. "I'll be damned," he whispered.

"Scared?" Roark teased.

"Of course, I love my mama." He slapped Roark on the back. "Come on, the minister wants to talk to us."

Roark followed, his face blank. His uncle's words hurt. Worse, he still didn't know who had kidnapped her from the airport, or why. That person still lurked somewhere out there. He tried to hide his fear that this whole situation wasn't over yet. After talking to Vianca's partner, they all agreed they needed a little more information. Roark would never use Smoke's contact again, the twelve hour thing had soured him. So, he found an agency to gather the tidbits of information they had and pull threads to gather more. He wouldn't rest easy until the threat to Brenda was eradicated.

Chapter 19

Skin prickling, Brenda glanced behind her and caught a glimpse of movement. Someone had been watching them leave the church after rehearsal. She'd sensed something similar yesterday when she and Denise went to the mall to buy shoes for the twins. Roark's arm wrapped around her waist and she leaned into him, glad he'd come outside.

"Ready to go?" He asked, walking toward their car.

"Yeah." Her teeth worried her bottom lip while she struggled with her suspicions. True, the kidnapping had left her jittery, but she didn't want to jump at shadows. The feeling of someone looking at her hadn't abated since she and Roark had arrived two days ago. As far as she knew, Anna could be around the corner, waiting for another opportunity to finish what she started. Brenda's hand touched her neck, and although the marks were gone, the memory of them lingered. And what if her sister hadn't been the one who'd held her all that time. By the time she and Roark reached the car, her heart was pounding with fear and dread.

Eyes closed, she sat breathing heavily while Roark walked around to his side of the car. When he sat beside her and cranked the car, she blurted. "I think someone's following me."

His hand froze on the steering wheel. The heat of his stare seared her face. "Why?" His voice was curious and pissed, an odd sound which warmed her.

"I felt it yesterday at the mall, this creepy feeling you get when someone's eyes are on you. You know what I mean?" She swallowed the acrid taste of her fears. He grabbed her hand, stilling the tremors running through her, and clasped her face in his hand.

"Baby, I'm here. Don't be scared." His lips brushed against hers. "I won't let anything happen to you, I promise."

At hearing his words, her heartbeat returned to normal. Air filled her lungs and left in a rhythmic pattern. But in the corner of her mind, the place where doubts hide in the shade, apprehension lurked. "Okay. I just wanted to tell you. This is all about our lives and not a TV show. I'm not going to hide what I think no matter what. That cool with you?"

"Definitely." He started the car and looked over at her. "No matter what, big or small, you tell me, okay?"

She nodded, feeling lighter as a load of *you're-seeing-things* lifted from her chest.

****

The wedding was the next day. The sun shone bright, offering a stamp of approval on the festivities. Brenda and Denise sat in one of the rooms in the basement of the sanctuary, completing last minute touches. Allie, Red's mom, and Linda, Denise's mom, had just left, giving the two women a moment of privacy.

Denise pressed a small box into Brenda's hand. Surprised, Brenda looked at the navy blue box and then at Denise. "What's this?" She tried to read Denise's face, but for the first time in a long time, her girlfriend effectively masked her emotions. Brenda opened the box. Her hand flew to her mouth, covering her gasp. Lying on a light blue satin pillow lay an exquisite gold link charm bracelet, with one charm.

"Dee, this is … oh, look." Eyes welling with tears, Brenda held the delicate bracelet up to the light so they could see the charm. Inscribed on a heart were the words, "Maid of Honor."Choked, Brenda couldn't speak. They'd each gone through major drama in their short lives, had stood in the gap for each other numerous times, took some hard knocks and yet, remained standing.

"You made me cry." Brenda dabbed her eyes and looked at her best friend. "You know I love your crazy ass, right?"

Denise's eyes glazed over and she blinked repeatedly, fanning her face with her hand. "I'm getting married and I will not cry. I will not mess up this expensive ass dress or my make-up," she muttered.

Brenda laughed at the typical Denise remarks before she took Denise's hand, "You look beautiful. Irish is going to fall over himself at the altar. Thank you for the beautiful bracelet, you have no idea how much it means to me. All these years..." Unable to say more, Brenda shook her head and raised her arm. "Would you lock it on me?"

Denise placed the bracelet around Brenda's wrist and connected the link. They hugged carefully and stood at hearing the knock on the door.

"You ready?" Denise's father, Rev. Brown, asked before peeking in. Brenda straightened Denise's gown, pulling the train straight, and handed her the bridal bouquet.

"I think she is," Brenda said and stepped around the dapper-looking man to head upstairs toward the sanctuary. Denise and her dad had finally come to terms with the wedding, and from the looks of things just now, he was happy for his only daughter. Brenda was happy for her friend; she knew it bothered Denise to be at odds with her daddy over her decision to marry Red. Reverend Brown and Red would never be friends, that was stretching it, but they'd settled into a truce of sorts. Basically, they ignored one another with a smile. It wasn't perfect, but it worked.

As Brenda reached the landing, someone rounded the corner and almost knocked her down. "Watch it," Brenda snapped, readjusting her flower arrangement and stepping to the side without bothering to look at the other person.

"I need to talk to you," Mable said. Her eyes were bright as they searched the area. Startled at seeing her mother in a church in general, and waiting for her in particular, she paused, unable to speak right away.

"Seriously?" Brenda moved around to pass, seeing the wedding coordinator waving at her. "I'm in a wedding, kinda busy right now."

Mable's hand flew out, grabbed her around the wrist and stopped her in her tracks. "You'd better listen to me, I need a few minutes of your time. It's important. The wedding can wait." She tried to pull Brenda toward the corner.

Growling, Brenda snatched her arm away and pushed Mable hard. The woman stumbled backwards, tripping in her high-heeled pumps. Pointing at the fallen woman, Brenda's teeth clenched as she spoke. "Never, ever touch me again," she panted.

"Brenda come on, you're next." The wedding coordinator waved at her, interrupting the scathing remark she meant to give her mom. Nodding, she headed in the direction of the chapel. When she reached the entrance, she looked back and Mable was gone.

****

Brenda sat at the bridal party table next to Roark. The wedding had been beautiful. After Red kissed his bride, he picked up their daughters, and kissed them as well. The audience gave him a standing ovation while the twins curtsied. Brenda glowed with pride. It had been an 'awwww' moment for sure.

Stomach full, Denise needed to hit the bathroom. Since Vianca had just left, she told Roark she'd catch up with her, so she wouldn't be alone.

He hesitated, and for a moment she thought he'd insist on going with her. Since she'd told him of her fears, she hadn't been far from his side. He nodded and she hurried to catch up with her friend. She thought she saw a flash of cobalt blue, the color of their bridesmaid's dresses. "Vee," she called, moving faster, but didn't see her friend ahead. Still flushed by the excitement of the day, she failed to see the man walking toward her from the side.

"Ms. Washington? Brenda Washington?" The tall Caucasian man asked, his voice cordial.

Caution was the rule of the day. "Why?"

"I've been trying to locate you on a matter of importance. Do you have a few minutes?" His smile seemed genuine, she didn't get a weird vibe from him, but she wasn't taking any chances.

"Sure, let me go to the bathroom and I'll meet you back here in a few minutes." She forced her voice to remain stable, hoping Vianca was still in the bathroom. Otherwise, she'd stay in there until someone came to get her.

He nodded and moved to the side.

Moving at a concise pace, she accessed the bathroom and called out. "Vianca? Vee?" No one answered. *Shit.* Looking around, she realized she'd just painted herself into a corner if he decided to come inside. She ran into a stall, closed the door and used the facility while thinking of a way out of this mess.

The outer door opened and she heard a feminine voice hum an offbeat tune. Brenda breathed a sigh of relief that it was a woman, not the man from outside. Finishing, she opened the door and stared into the face of her mother, who stood with her hands behind her, leaning against the sink, legs crossed at the ankle.

Brenda frowned. "I've seen more of you this month than the last five years. You following me?" Brenda washed her hands, while staring at Mable. There was something off. She couldn't pinpoint it, but her spidey senses had gone past tingling, now they clanged.

Mable shook her head slowly. "I'm trying to talk to you about something important. You've always been a difficult child."

Brenda stiffened at the jibe, but didn't get a chance to respond.

Mable continued as if she hadn't been offensive herself. "You said some hurtful things at the funeral. You think you know shit, but you don't.

You have no idea why I was the way I was or why I did the things I did. Like everyone else you judged me without all the facts."

Brenda went from tense to livid under the unexpected assault. It didn't take long for the memories of her childhood to flood her. Enraged that Mable would try to shift the blame, she pointed a finger at her and said. "I lived through it. I told you what I experienced. That's not judging, that's testifying. You can't rewrite stuff now. You failed big time as a mother, don't try to pull the family card now."

Mable stared at her a second longer and sighed. "No matter. You hate me and that's cool. I'm not too fond of you either right now."

"Fond? Did you use the word, fond?" Brenda asked, as she placed her palm on her chest. "Since when did you start talking like that? Or dressing like this?" Brenda waved at the expensive looking form-fitting dress and matching shoes Mable wore.

"You think you're the only one who can talk properly? Or knows how to dress to fit a role?" She chuckled, but it didn't sound right. More like Mable needed to convince herself she was still in control. *But of what?*

Mable continued talking. "Nah, see that's where you're wrong. I can make myself over into whatever's necessary to survive." She pointed at Brenda. "You're more like me than you want to admit. We're both survivors."

"What do you need to tell me? I've got to do the toast." Mable's words had hit a chord of truth no matter how much Brenda wished otherwise. For years, it'd been her biggest fear, crippling her repeatedly. Time with Roark helped her realize she *was* a survivor, but not a predator. She didn't use people to survive.

"Your father died recently."

The words fell like a bomb in a quiet suburban area, unexpected with no time to prepare, snatching the breath from Brenda's lungs. She struggled to breathe. Of all the things she expected, that wasn't on the list. "What?" she gasped. "My father died ten years ago." The room spun as Mable fidgeted.

"No, he died four months ago." Mable slid further away as Brenda's world tilted. This bitch had lied to her all these years.

"You told me he died years ago; that's why I went to live with Aunt Robin." The pain in her chest robbed her of her wits. She had no defense.

Not knowing her daddy had been a sore spot between mother and daughter for most of their lives. In the back of her mind, she'd always felt there had been someone else who'd cared for her. A male who'd rubbed her knee and fed her ice cream. Whenever she'd asked Mable about the vague memories, the woman scoffed and said her father had left them before she was born. For Mable to stand there and blithely say her father died recently, crossed the line.

"I know, there were some problems— "the door opened and a tall handsome guy rushed in. He went straight to Brenda. Before she could blink, speak or protest, her mouth and nose were covered with something. Her world darkened as she inhaled something potent. Mable grabbed the man's arm and he dropped Brenda, but she couldn't move or speak. The last thing she saw was the man's fist connecting with her mama's jaw.

Chapter 20

Roark glanced at his watch while his dad gave his toast to the couple. Sean O'Connor could talk for a moment when he made friends with a bottle.

"Me youngest son decided to be the first to tie his bonnie Denise to his side. I'm grateful that he has convinced her at last. She took him on a merry chase, but in the end, Benjamin claimed his prize." The old man lifted his bottle, while everyone lifted glasses in a toast to the bride and groom. A cheer rose as Roark's mother walked to the podium, kissed his dad and escorted him off stage.

Brenda had been gone for over fifteen minutes, which worried Roark; he skimmed the crowd for anyone who might be a danger to his woman. It was a futile exercise. He didn't recognize many people. Knowing how Brenda and the other women in the wedding liked to talk, he tried not to grow overly concerned. She knew he worried when she wasn't nearby. The idea of someone stalking her, particularly with his recent experiences, made his blood boil. He and the guys planned to get together after Red and Denise left later tonight. One way or another, this madness had to end.

A minute or two later Vianca returned to the table. Roark watched the entryway for Brenda. A feeling of dread rolled over him. His heart slammed in his chest as he stood up in the middle of Ross' toast to the bride and groom, walked over to Vianca and whispered in her ear.

"Did you see Brenda? She left to catch up with you when you went to the bathroom." Gut churning with fear, he sensed Smoke's attention. The frown of concentration on her face said more than words, she hadn't seen Brenda. His heart sank.

"No. I met up with an old client in the hallway, we got to talking and I walked with her to the other bathroom." She stood and followed hot on his heels out the exit.

"There are two bathrooms?" He asked her looking down the corridor in both directions, unsure which way to go.

"Yeah," she said pointing down the left hallway as Smoke came up beside her. "There's a closer one down there."

Roark pivoted, and made Olympic strides to the restroom. Without waiting, he pushed open the door, walked inside and stopped short. A body lay prostrate on the floor. He pulled his hair and stared at the ceiling in an attempt to stop the yell of rage and frustration from surfacing. "No, no, no."

"Who's that?" Vianca asked circling the woman on the floor.

"That's…" Roark's throat worked several times before he could speak, the pain of failure ripped through him. "That's Mable, Brenda's mom."

"Oh shit," Vianca murmured. "Baby, turn on the water for me." She glanced at Smoke and then looked at the woman on the floor. Smoke complied without a word. Vianca cupped her hands, filled them with water and threw it on Mable's face. The woman groaned and moved slightly. Vianca threw another handful of water on her, and then another. Mable blinked, and rolled to the side, holding her jaw. Whoever hit her, packed a powerful punch, her jaw had swollen to twice its size. If Brenda weren't missing, he might care that this woman was in pain and crying.

Bending beside her, he held her shoulder. "Where's Brenda?" Tension coiled in his neck when she didn't respond. His fingers flexed.

"Ow," she murmured. He released her shoulder. He hadn't realized he'd been squeezing until she spoke.

"Where's Brenda?" he asked again, terrified he'd be too late this time.

Vianca pulled her dress up to her knees and straddled the woman. Roark leaned back; surprised at the ferocious look she wore.

"You will tell me where my friend is or I will cut your ass." She waved a blade beneath Mable's neck. Mable's eyes widened and she tried to scoot upward. Vianca leaned forward, placed her hand around the woman's neck, and squeezed. "I don't have all day to play with you. Tell me what I want to know."

Shocked, Roark watched mild-mannered Vianca turn into a vicious tigress. Mable talked so fast he couldn't understand a word she said. Moments later, Smoke lifted Vianca up and away from her prey, even as she continued to threaten the woman in another language.

Smoke pulled a wad of paper towels from the dispenser, placed them on the floor and kneeled beside the woman. When he spoke, it was a calm, soothing tone. His hand rested on her brow. "Mable, I know you're in pain, the ambulance has been called and you'll get some help soon." The woman's eyes latched onto Smoke as though he were the Messiah. She nodded, releasing a breath. Roark barely contained his snort. Vianca rolled her eyes and leaned against the counter fondling her knife while Smoke worked his magic.

"We have to find Brenda. Do you know where she is?"

"Rafe, he took her."

"Who the hell is that?" Roark roared, frustrated with the delay. Vianca nodded in agreement while Smoke continued to draw information.

"Is he a friend of yours?" Smoke asked.

"He was." Her hand lifted and fell. "He did this. Asshole."

Roark wanted to shake the answers from her; Brenda didn't have time for this. "Smoke?" he growled wanting answers.

Ignoring Roark, Smoke spoke gently. "Where would Rafe take her? Do you know where they are?"

"He bought me a place," she whispered. "But I doubt he'd go there now." Mable tried to sit up and grimaced. "Hand me my purse." Vianca looked around and shook her head.

"I don't see a purse." Smoke took her hand to help her stand.

Turning to the side, she looked around. "That bastard," she snapped and winced. Leaning against the counter, she inhaled. "He took my cell and keys. Maybe he went to the condo." She wiggled her fingers at Smoke. "Write this down." Roark whipped out a pen from his inner coat. Smoke had a pad. They gave them to Vianca to write down the address Mable rattled off. Roark looked at the address and headed for the door, Smoke behind him.

"I can't believe the son of a bitch did this." Mable touched her jaw and winced.

"What were you doing in here with her?" Vianca asked. Roark and Smoke paused at the exit and looked back at the two women. He'd wondered that himself, but had been sidetracked finding her on the floor.

"I'd been trying to tell her about her father."

"What?" Roark turned and stepped in front of her. Brenda told him her dad died when she was a teenager. His opinion of Mable sunk through the floor.

"Yeah, he died about four or five months ago. I think I told her five. There's a time limit on her accepting his estate. At least that's what I heard."

"His estate?" Roark sputtered. Things had stepped into the twilight zone. "He's been alive all this time and she didn't know?"His tone clearly said what he thought of her.

Mable waved him down. "I'm a bitch. Yeah. I know. But I *am* her mother."

"No, you are just the woman who carried her a few months and spit her out. But you're no mother," Vianca spat in her face. "You would sell your own child and put her in harm's way. That is not a mother, you are right, that is a bitch."

"Whatever." Mable turned to Smoke. "When is the ambulance coming?"

He grinned and followed Roark. "Soon. Wait here."

Outside, Veronique and Frank were busy directing traffic to the other bathrooms. Frank took one look at Roark and stepped in his path. "Brenda?"

"Yeah. Some asshole named Rafe took her. I got an address, I'll tell you about it on the way." Frank nodded, and almost knocked over a tall white male who'd walked by.

"Excuse me," Frank said as he moved around the fellow to follow Roark.

"No problem." He nodded at Frank and stopped Veronique. "Have you seen Ms. Brenda Washington? I've been waiting to talk to her. She went into the bathroom and left before I had an opportunity to discuss some important matters with her." He pointed at the bathroom they'd just left.

Roark and Frank stopped, turned and stared at the man. Had this man been following Brenda? "My name is Veronique Walters, I'm Brenda's attorney and this is her fiancé." Veronique pointed at Roark.

"And I'm her mama," Mable said from behind them. "What they won't tell you is she isn't here. Rafe took her so she can't fulfill the agreement of the will." By the time she reached them, she was wheezing.

Ignoring Mable, the thin man stretched his hand toward Veronique. "My name is Walter Chalmers. I am the attorney and good friend of Bernard Shaw. Is there somewhere we can talk privately?" He didn't spare Mable a glance after his eyes widened at the state of her face.

"Hey, I'm her mama; you should be talking to me." Mable moved forward.

Vianca blocked her path, grinning evilly at her. "You're not invited."

"Yes, please come this way." Veronique led Mr. Chalmers to the front of the Country Club. "As you know there is a wedding going on and we need to be discreet." She nodded at Roark.

Relieved to hand those matters over to someone qualified to deal with them, he turned to leave.

"What's going on, boyo?" His father strode in his direction, looking at the three men.

Groaning at the delay, Roark slowed, but didn't stop. "I've got to make a run, I'll be back in a few."

Sean glanced at Smoke and Frank, who flanked Roark, and barked an order. "Stop."Roark ceased moving as his father and Uncle Nate moved quickly across the hall. "I willna' keep ye, but why ya leaving?" The more his dad drank the stronger his brogue.

"I have an address to pick up Brenda." Roark stepped aside to leave.

"What? Ye lost your gal again?" his drunken uncle yelled, causing people to stare in their direction.

Roark's face burned, he couldn't speak. Frank placed his hand on Roark's shoulder, pushing him forward.

"Why can't these young'uns hang onto their women, I ask ye? It be a miracle iffen she dinna run off with someone stronger." His uncle said, watching Mable walk closer. He swaggered in her direction.

"Me boyo knows what he's bout. Go get your lass, son." His dad waved him on.

Roark stalked out the building, his uncle's words boiling in his gut. He rushed to the side of the building and released the food he'd eaten earlier. By the time he'd cleaned up, Smoke sat in the car in front of the building. Roark sat in the front, a weird cocktail of anger and embarrassment riding him. No one spoke as they navigated the streets to the address Mable had given them.

As they walked into the entry, Smoke turned on the charm as he spoke to the guard on duty. "Sam, my man, what's up?" The security guard's face lit up in genuine pleasure when he realized it was Smoke.

"Nothing much." He bumped Smoke's fist. "What's going on with you?"

"Going to visit a friend, that's all. It's a surprise."

The guard nodded. "Got it. All surprises need to ride elevator four, you remember where it is."

"Yeah, sure do."

The guard slapped Smoke's palm. "Good seeing you. I hate I missed the wedding, I'm sure the guys will tell me about it at work on Monday."

"No doubt." Smoke nodded and walked around the corner, and then another. They followed him down a long corridor to another hall and then to the elevator. Smoke used the key the guard had put in his palm to take them to the third floor.

The unit was in the middle of the floor. Just as they turned the corner, two well-dressed men walked around the other corner. Roark didn't recognize either man, but it became apparent by the huge smile on Smoke's face that he knew at least one of them.

"Hey man." Smoke reached forward and embraced the Hispanic man in a hug. They slapped one another on the back a couple of times before stepping away. "It's damn good to see you. You involved in this?" he asked Julio.

Julio nodded. "I have learned that when you have problems, they often impact my business. That is why I do not hesitate to look into the matters." He glanced at Roark and Frank. "These are Red's brothers. He was married today. I know he is relieved."

Roark grew antsy and went to pass the men.

Smoke grabbed his arm. "Is Brenda here?" Roark tensed and stared at the two men in confusion. Why would either of these men know his woman? His eyes landed on the tall, muscular, black male. He appeared upset in reaction to Smoke's question. That bothered Roark. How do they know Brenda? They shouldn't unless…Roark's jaw tightened as he realized who they were.

"Are you Tex?" Roark growled at the black man who stood beside Smoke's friend. The man returned his stare and didn't speak.

Smoke stepped in front of Roark, his hand on his chest. Tex's jaw clenched and unclenched. Smoke looked at Julio, a question in his eye.

"She is here in her mother's unit. The man with her is small-time with big ideas. My men will take him in…" he glanced at his watch, "one minute." He glanced at Roark, who stared back at him.

"A minute?" Roark snorted and pushed forward. "A lot can happen to her in a minute."

"It will take you that long to reach the unit, longer to open it, and longer to dodge the bullets he will have aimed at you. Make no mistake; he is expecting you. He is not expecting me." Julio's voice hardened as he returned Roark's glare. "You will not interfere. I have promised my friend to assist in this matter and I have done so. Do not push me or mine." He tipped his head toward Tex and glanced at his watch.

Furious at being dismissed, Roark glared at the man he believed was Brenda's ex. The dam broke when the man winked at him. Frank placed a restraining hand on his shoulder. It was lukewarm at best. Fighting enemies was in their blood.

A minute was all he needed. He shrugged it off and charged, knocking Tex to the ground. Unleashed anger roared through Roark. Jealousy ripped across his heart. This man once held a place in his woman's bed and heart. He punched Tex in the jaw with all the fury of a man staking a claim on the ass of a rival. The sound of flesh pounding flesh echoed in the hall. Tex rolled him over and punched him twice, once in the face, the other in his side. Stars raced across his vision as he blocked the next hit. Evenly matched, both got in good hits until they ran out of steam. Roark's vision blurred, he had no doubt his eye was swelling. A glance at his adversary lifted his spirits. The man didn't look so GQ anymore. His jaw had swollen, along with his eye. Staggering, each man stood on his own, albeit wobbly, feet, eying one another.

Tex rolled his jaw, wincing. "I'll always love her."

Roark nodded, happy he'd inflicted some pain on his adversary. "I understand. But don't ever touch her."

"She chose you." And that said it all. Tex extended his hand. Roark stared for a moment and then accepted it. "Take care of her, she's good people."

"I know," Roark snapped, pissed that Tex knew Brenda in the biblical sense." He tempered his tone, knowing he wouldn't have allowed Brenda to leave him if he'd been in Tex's shoes. He pumped the man's hand again. "I will." Roark had to respect a man who still admitted to loving a woman after he'd gotten his ass kicked. At least, he believed Tex got his ass handed to him, and that's what mattered.

"Are you two finished? There is a woman down the hall to be rescued, but we will wait until you pull yourselves together." Julio's sarcasm wasn't lost on either man. Julio and Smoke walked down the hall.

For a minute or two, Roark's jealousy had pushed everything from his mind. "Damn, she's going to kill me," he muttered as he tried to fix his clothes and tame his hair. There was nothing he could do about the bruises he knew were forming on his face and other parts of his body. He hoped she wouldn't be too angry.

"Here." Frank handed him the royal blue cummerbund from his tuxedo, it had come off during the fight. He took it and moved slowly behind Smoke and Julio.

"I didn't take her," Tex said walking beside him. He shook his head as though he still couldn't believe something.

"But you know who did." Roark didn't know why he said that, but somehow he knew it was true.

"Yeah. I used to work for him. He was stealing from his own operation to cheat the rest of us out of our cut. They shut him down, but he didn't stop doing side deals."

"Why'd he drag Brenda into this?" Roark asked as they neared the unit.

"I don't know. It has something to do with Brenda's mom. She's a bitch plus some. She told Anna some lie about Brenda belonging to someone else. Drove the girl crazy."

Julio waved Tex over. The two men talked briefly and Tex left the hall for a few minutes. Roark stared at the door, wondering what was going on. Tex returned, talked to Julio before going to the door and unlocking it. He pulled out his gun and went inside.

Roark tensed. He didn't want the first person Brenda saw to be her ex. He headed toward the door, Frank behind him. As they reached the door, Tex walked out, stared at Roark and then went to Julio. Since no one stopped him, Roark strode into the unit and searched for Brenda.

He found her in the front bedroom. A sigh of relief escaped his lips as he watched the rise and fall of her chest. His legs buckled as he knelt on the side of the bed and said a silent prayer of thanks. Frank looked in, and then left them alone. There were footsteps in the other rooms, instructions delivered and more movement. Through it all, Roark remained steadfast by her side, waiting for her to wake up.

"How is she?" Tex asked from the doorway.

"She's breathing, no fever, I think she'll be fine." He didn't bother looking up.

"Brenda is a fighter, she'll get over this." Tex stepped inside the room but stopped at Roark's snarl. Brenda stirred, grabbing the attention of both men.

"Tex?" she murmured, her forehead furrowing.

Roark froze. His arm suspended enroute to hold her tight. Did he hear correctly? Had she called out to her ex-lover? Roark's eyes locked with Tex, daring him to respond.

"Tex?" This time her voice was stronger although she hadn't opened her eyes. Her uncoordinated hand and leg movements concerned Roark; something had her agitated. As much as it hurt to hear another man's name on her lips, Roark refused to interfere. He looked toward the door; Tex had left and in his place stood Frank.

"She okay?" he asked as though he hadn't heard her calling for another man. Roark shrugged, unsure what to say or do.

"Tex?" Brenda screamed and shot up from the bed. Smoke and Julio came to the door.

"What's wrong?" Smoke asked in a low tone, looking at Brenda and then Roark.

"Help, help," she cried out, eyes open but unseeing.

Roark's heart ached for her; he pulled her to his chest and rubbed her back. She pushed against him, thrusting a dagger into his heart. She hadn't called his name and although the only thing that should matter is her safety, it bothered him that she had not recognized him yet.

"Help him; they're going to kill him," she cried. Julio turned and ran from the room, Smoke on his heels.

"Roark." Her breath hitched. She inhaled deep and long. "Roark," she said again, appreciation inherent in her tone, as if his name was akin to the air she breathed.

"Brenda?" Roark whispered unsure if she was alert or speaking under the influence of something.

"They planned to kill him. This is crazy, crazy," she muttered relaxing into his hold. "It's so stupid, men are so stupid." She pulled him close, her face buried in his neck.

"Brenda, you with me?" Roark asked still in the grip of uncertainty.

She nuzzled into his chest. "Roark," she said on a long sigh. "I prayed you'd find me." She leaned back, her eyes not as clear as they should be, but close enough to ease his fears. "You found me. You came."

"Where else would I be? You hold my heart." The words were ripped from his soul.

"I was scared," she whispered against his chest. "I thought…I figured this was too much. I wasn't sure you'd come this time. Thank you, I'll make it up to you."

Roark pulled her from his chest, and stared into her eyes. "Brenda." He waited until she looked up at him. "Do you have any idea how much I love you?"

Her eyes filled.

"If you had a clue what you meant to me, you'd have never doubted for a second that I'd find you. I'll always come for you. Never thank me for that. You're the sunlight in my world."

"I…I'm sorry there's so much happening."

"Baby, it's not your fault. We'll work this out. Just promise me one thing."

Her large eyes snared his and he saw her fear, doubt, and most importantly, hope. Gravitating to the last emotion, he waited for her to respond.

"What?" she stared expectantly.

"Love me."

Her eyes widened. Seconds ticked as she searched his face. "I do," she whispered as a smile rose like the morning sun on her face.

"I love you, too. I plan to spend the rest of my life showing you how much. Can you say the same?"

Her answer was interrupted by gunshots. Roark leapt up and covered her, keeping her down. Running footsteps and shouts filled the distance. Beneath him Brenda tensed and tried to move. Roark wouldn't budge.

"They're trying to kill Tex," Brenda said, her words choppy from trying to get more air.

Roark may respect the man, but he didn't give a damn. Brenda was his priority and he wasn't about to allow her to enter the fray.

"Smoke's out there." She'd have to be satisfied with that.

She pushed again. "Can you give me some room? I can't breathe."

He slid to the side, but kept his hand on her waist. Staring at him, her fingertips traced the bruises on his face. He released a sigh of relief inwardly, the tension in his back easing immediately. She slapped his chest; he winced. His muscles were sore, but he wore a smile on his face.

"You got hurt."

He remained still as she examined him, he had no idea what he looked like.

"What the hell happened?" Her eyes met his briefly.

He glanced away. "I got into a fight with lover boy." He knew he was being unfair. It still stung that the first name she called out hadn't been his. It pissed him off more that Tex hadn't stuck around to take advantage of the situation. He would have.

Her brow rose. "Lover boy?" She yanked his hair.

"Ow." He moved back, but she stopped him.

"You deserved that for messing up this face." She leaned forward, and kissed his lips. "Now I can't suck your face the way I want to." She pouted.

"I don't know about that," he challenged as she tried to sit up.

"It's a shame, too. I had so many kinky things I wanted to try, with," she pointed at his face, "you know, your mouth." She released a long sigh, her eyes twinkling.

"Demon." He pinched her hips as she stood.

"Name calling? Has it come to that?"

"You guys okay?" Frank asked. As he entered the room, Roark stood. Brenda moved forward, but Roark stopped her.

"I'm not going out there, I just wanted to know what was going on." She looked at his hand on her arm, waiting for him to release her. He simply stepped closer and looked at Frank.

"What happened?" Roark asked, ignoring Brenda's frown. There was not a chance in hell he'd be allowing her out of his sight any time soon. She'd have to adapt.

Frank raked his hand through his hair. "Brenda was right, someone took a shot at Tex."

"Whoa," Brenda said, frowning at Frank. "I said that?" Frank and Roark glanced at each other and then at her.

"When you were waking up, you called out his name." Roark refused to call the name himself.

She frowned. "Who?" She looked at him. "Tex?"

He nodded, still pissed.

"Why? What'd I say?" She looked at Frank.

"You said someone wanted to kill him or something like that."

"And someone shot him. I wonder…" She looked at Roark. "That's right. That man was mad at Tex. Something about Tex ruined his life. Some deal went bad. I think he used Mable, he hit her hard."

Roark nodded. "I found her in the bathroom when I went looking for you. She mentioned your dad and that somehow all of this was connected."

"She didn't get to say much before he walked in on her and took me. I still can't believe all of this happened, and I don't know why." Glancing at Roark and then Frank, she asked. "Does anyone know why this is going on?"

Smoke walked in and waved them out. "Let's go, the cops will be here soon and we don't need to be here."

Chapter 21

Allie and Sean O'Connor were standing outside in front of the country club when they drove up. The moment Roark assisted Brenda out of the car, his mom wrapped her in her arms, cocooning her with warmth.

"It's cold out here, Mama, let's go inside." He tugged on Brenda's arm to free her from his mama's grip.

"Why're you and daddy standing out here?" Frank asked, wrapping his arm around his mom's waist. His dad pushed him away and took his place.

"Go find your own woman," he grumbled.

Frank laughed. "I plan to do that as soon as you tell me why you're standing out front in the cold." He looked at his mother, whose lips had tightened.

"Now, Allie, don'cha be like that. I apologized all right an proper," Sean said, trying to pull his wife closer.

She wasn't having it and pushed him to the side. "No, Sean O'Connor. I'm tired of you misbehaving and embarrassing me when you drink." Frank, Roark, and Brenda stopped at her inflexible tone. As kids, they knew what that meant, but had never heard her use it on their father.

"He had no right to say what he said." Roark's father argued.

Nervous, Brenda glanced at Roark, but he had no clue what had happened and knew better than to interrupt with questions.

"He's her father! Just as you mouth off at the boys, he—"

"But I don't mean most of it." He waved at Frank and Roark, who tried to become invisible. "They know I don't mean any harm."

"What if her father is like you?" she yelled, pointing at him. "You had no right to hit him." Roark's eyes flew opened. Brenda turned to leave, no doubt to find her best friend, but Roark wouldn't release her hand.

"Wait," he said, still listening to the exchange between his parents.

"He disrespected my son."

"Your son is grown and that is his father-in-law. They're family." She threw up her hand and stalked away. As she passed Roark, she pointed. "I want to know what happened to your face."

He groaned, wishing he'd left earlier. Frank walked over to his dad and the two men talked low. Roark and Brenda went inside. He glanced at his watch; Red and Denise should've already left, and he hoped Smoke and Ross were somewhere around. He had a few questions to ask Smoke.

Roark was surprised to find the reception in party mode. The ballroom was still full. When he and Brenda entered, people stopped and stared. He'd forgotten about his bruises and Brenda didn't look as neat as before. He nodded at Smoke and slipped through one of the side doors, searching for one of the smaller rooms, so they could talk before he and Brenda left for their hotel room. He was feeling the effects of the fight and wanted to get comfortable.

The small blue salon near the ballroom suited his purposes. After making sure Brenda was comfortable, he searched the smaller room for something to drink. Just as he handed Brenda a glass of water, the door opened and the bridal party filled the room.

Veronique, Cherise and Vianca swarmed Brenda with hugs and kisses before they sat down. Frank picked Veronique up and sat her on his lap, claiming there weren't enough chairs. Ross and Smoke followed suit.

"Brenda, I don't know how much you know about your father, but his attorney was here earlier and he left his card for you to contact him. He's flying back to California tomorrow afternoon. I really think you need to talk to him in the morning. There are a lot of things you need to know."

"You mean a tall white man, the one hanging around the bathroom? He was really a lawyer?" Brenda asked.

"Yes, he's been trying to close out your father's estate," Veronique said.

"I wished I'd known, he was the reason I ducked into the bathroom. I thought he was someone stalking me. Instead it was somebody else."

"Tex said it was a guy he worked for." Everyone looked at Roark as he repeated what Tex had said.

Smoke whistled. "He was stupid not to stop when they bought him out. He paid for it with his life."

"I still don't know how I got mixed up in this. Why did they take me?" Brenda asked.

"It wasn't just one thing," Smoke said, deep in thought. "It sounds like a series of events, some related, most wasn't. For instance, Anna started the impersonation with your Aunt. She must have told someone what she was doing, because someone else continued the charade after she stopped.

Someone Rafe hired, and Mable gave pertinent information so the scheme would work."

"I wondered how they'd been able to fool your Aunt Robin, now we know. Her own sister set her up," Veronique said in disgust.

"That's probably why she cried at the funeral, she knew what she did," Brenda said. "I hope I never see that bitch again."

No one spoke, although Roark was sure everyone agreed.

"What happened to Anna?" Brenda asked Smoke.

"She moved."

"Huh?" Brenda frowned. Roark squeezed her shoulder as the other men looked down. "When?"

Smoke shrugged. "When I asked, I was told she moved. I don't know where or when."

Roark coughed, drawing the attention to himself, changing the subject. "What was Rafe's plan and why'd he need Brenda?" Although he suspected he knew the answer, he believed an explanation was necessary for closure.

Smoke looked at him for a second. "According to my sources, Rafe stole from his own business, made a lot of money on the side to finance some other deals. He used a warehouse to store the merchandise, without the owner's consent. His contact was a Puerto Rican woman named Lola. She was the one who picked Brenda up from the airport. Rafe lost everything when Tex did his job and got the merchandise back. The owners of the warehouse were angry that their premises had been used, but were impressed with the way Tex handled everything. In fact, he saved Rafe's life. The way it was explained to me, had Tex handled anything differently, every person who worked in that small group would've died. They offered Tex a better position, closed down the smaller operation and released Rafe. Instead of being grateful, he blamed Tex for losing everything and decided to kill him. That was hard because of who Tex now worked for. Apparently, Rafe knew Brenda was Tex's only weakness and used that connection to pull Tex from under his protection. It almost worked."

"Me?" Brenda swallowed hard, as she gripped Roark's hand. "I was kidnapped so this sick fool could catch my ex-boyfriend, someone I hadn't seen in, what, two whole years?"

Smoke shrugged. "He bought Mable a place, set it up in exchange for information to get you. Rafe was fixated on his revenge. It doesn't make sense, especially when you factor in how much everyone is watched in the organization. They knew Rafe was up to something and gave him enough rope to hang himself. When I called about Brenda missing, it was the tool they needed to sink his plan, and cement Tex to their side."

Brenda shook her head, baffled at first, and then angry. "I don't fucking believe this shit." She looked at Smoke, then Vianca, Cherise, then Ross. Her gaze went to Veronique. "Somebody choked me, drugged me, and left me high and dry as bait? Tex didn't even know I was in town until I ran away from the house. What? Are they fucking insane? In the first grade?" she screamed in pain. Roark rubbed her back.

"Did they catch Rafe?" Vianca asked.

"He's no longer a threat," Smoke said.

"What about Mable?" Cherise asked. "She needs her ass checked as well for lying to her own kid like that. No wonder Anna's so messed up."

"I believe she moved away also," Smoke said avoiding Brenda's eyes.

"Good," Brenda said.

"Mable's beginning to make Paula look good," Frank said.

Roark groaned as Veronique chuckled. "Not even," Roark said.

"I wonder what did Rafe think he'd do if he took out Tex?" Ross asked. "He had to know his life would be over."

"His wife's missing, has been for six months. Rumor has it he planned to disappear. Although that doesn't make sense. He had to know the people Tex worked for wouldn't allow this to pass." Smoke shrugged.

A tepid knock hit the door, Allie opened it and looked inside. Her eyes brightened when she saw her children. "There you are." She looked around and stopped at Roark's face. "How does his face look?"

"Worse," Frank answered before Roark could speak.

Allie nodded. "Blaine and Donald are upset you left them to deal with the wedding and the guests. Should I tell them you are in here?" she asked, her eyes sparkling.

Ross stood, taking Cherise's hand. "That's our cue to leave."

"When is the baby due?" Allie blurted, stopping Cherise and Ross.

"Good question," Smoke said, smiling at Ross's reddening face.

"In six months," Cherise said, a smile lighting her face.

Allie clapped in joy. "Great, when's the wedding?" Everyone froze.

Ross looked at Cherise.

"Wedding?" Cherise looked ill. "We…we don't know yet."

"Well, I hope you decide soon," Allie said, her hand on her hip. "Your mother will be marrying my oldest so that makes you my grand-daughter and I'll not be having my first great-grand born out of wedlock. We've had enough of that in this family, that's for sure."

Ross paled at Allie's speech.

"So I suggest you get to talking and make this happen before my great-grandchild makes an appearance." Allie pointed at Ross and smiled at Cherise.

"Mama," Cherise whispered, a thread of desperation in her voice. Veronique looked at her daughter and shrugged. Frank pulled his woman against his chest.

"You and Ross need to talk, Cherise," Veronique said.

Cherise nodded and waved good-night to everyone.

"I'm going to head to the hotel and take care of this eye and a few other things." Roark stood, hoping to escape Allie's tongue lashing.

"Brenda has had a rough day, Roark. Don't be pushing up on her tonight, let her rest." His face burned as Smoke and Vianca burst out laughing. Even Brenda chuckled.

"Ma!" She was incorrigible.

Chapter 22

Brenda looked at the card Veronique had given her. She'd put it down several times that morning. She wanted to know, and then she didn't. Ignorance being bliss and all that. Denise would call it her ostrich move. She called it self-preservation. Closing her eyes, she inhaled and decided to make the damn call and find out who was her father.

Mr. Chalmers was on his way to her room. He planned to leave from there for the airport. Nervous, Brenda sat on the sofa reading the newspaper as she waited to discover the identity of the man responsible for her existence.

When the knock came, she froze. After the second knock, Roark came from the bedroom, looked at her strange and answered the door.

"Hello, I'm Walter Chalmers, I'm here to talk with Ms. Washington." He glanced at Brenda. Roark moved so the older man could enter and closed the door behind him. "Just a moment." He rolled in a large cardboard box on a dolly and placed them to the side, before turning to Brenda.

He extended his hand, and she stood and shook it. "Hello, thank you for seeing me," he said.

"Thank you for coming so far." Licking her dry lips, she glanced at the box and then him. "I'm nervous. I thought my father died years ago, so this is a surprise." She didn't miss the frown that flashed across his face at her words.

"I've met your mother and can only imagine what she's told you over the years. First off you need to know your father had no idea where your mother had taken you, she kept moving around."

"I know, I lived through it." She hadn't meant to sound curt, but it was a sore point for her.

"Yes, she was somehow able to always stay ahead of the private investigators searching for her. She stayed off the radar."

"She didn't work or have anything in her name," Brenda said slowly, rethinking Mable's motives. "Why was she hiding from him?"

"Bernard, that's your father, won custody of you and she stole you away. She didn't want him to raise you with his lover."

Brenda's head whipped around. "What? His lover? Why not?"

Mr. Chalmers straightened. "Your father was a well-known performer in San Francisco. He'd met your mother when he was still discovering his sexuality. No one was more surprised than him when she told him about her condition. He didn't remember being with her that way." The man's face reddened as he plowed through the story.

"My father was gay?"

"Yes."

" A gay drag queen?" She guessed.

"Yes. A more crude term, but not outside the ballpark."

Brenda looked at Roark and chuckled. "You can't make this shit up, can you?" Roark shook his head as she returned to her guest.

"I'm sorry, just a little surprised."

"I can imagine," he said, his voice tight. Brenda realized she'd offended him, but was unsure how, so she remained silent.

"After the DNA tests proved his parentage, he wanted to take care of you, but your mother became unreasonable in her demands."

"I know she didn't want to marry him." Mable was many things, but she'd never marry a man who liked men.

"No, she wanted him to keep you away from his lifestyle. He didn't know how to do that. She took him to court for child support, which he paid. I'm not going to get into everything other than this, Bernard loved you and it broke his heart when she stole you away. He spent most of his energy and money trying to find you, there's not much left."

Brenda laughed at the irony. "Mable wanted money. She did all this thinking to get more money."

"Maybe recently, but she hid you because although Bernard was, shall we say, effeminate or passive, his family was not. Your uncle Roger, his brother, threatened to kill her if she took you and she believed him. I don't think she knows he died three years ago, either." He shrugged and stood. Opening his briefcase, he handed her a large manila envelope. "Here are the things Bernard wanted me to give to you. He wanted you to know he was sorry he missed all the milestones in your life and that even though he wasn't here, you were always loved and in his thoughts. He left some things for you in this box." He pointed to the cardboard box near the table and shook his head. "It seems unfair that a man with the capacity to make so many people happy, was shortchanged in his personal life. I don't believe he ever thought he'd be a father, but once you arrived, he was over the top.

He loved you fiercely. I hate that you'll never get to meet him. He was an incredible guy."

Tears filled Brenda's eyes. "Wow, thanks. I appreciate this, I really do." She stood, looked at the box, and hugged him. "I don't know what to say."

He squeezed her arm. "It's okay. He was a good man and a great friend. He would've done this for me." He waved goodbye as he headed for the door.

"Wait!"

He stopped at the door and looked at her.

"What did he die from?"

Walter shook his head. "He was crossing the street and a car hit him."

Brenda's heart hurt. "I'm sorry to hear that, sorry I didn't know him."

"Be good." He smiled and left them alone with the folder.

"Mable is full of surprises." Brenda sat and opened the envelope. The first thing she pulled out was a sequined mask. Roark laughed.

"Don't laugh," Brenda said, pulling out other stage items and laying them on the coffee table. "This is my legacy from my daddy." Together they looked at the gold sequined mask, the pink feather boa, a long gold chain and a key ring with a small key. A letter sat at the bottom of the package. Laughing at her inheritance, Brenda broke open the letter and read.

"*My dearest Felicia.*"

Brenda frowned at the paper and said, "This letter is addressed to Felicia, is that my real name?" She glanced at Roark, who looked over her shoulder at the note.

"Could be, Mable probably changed your name while she was on the run." He kissed her ear. "I'll call you Felicia when we make love, okay?"

Laughing, she elbowed him backward. "You have a one track mind. Be good so we can go through the box." She returned to the paper, impressed by the neat cursive writing. Her father had been neat and precise.

If you are reading this, then we will never meet on this side. You may not remember me or the great times we shared. I used to ride you piggy back in the back yard, we built sand castles on the beach, but like those castles, the tides of time washed away your memories of me. The years we've been separated have been hard and long. I hope you've been treated well and have prospered. It hurts to think otherwise. I have left you a few things that have served me well.

A golden mask: there will be times when it is necessary to hide who you are inside to survive. It doesn't change you, only someone else's perception. It's important to always remain true to yourself. Thus the mask, easily put on and taken off, without affecting the wearer.

A feather boa: it accents and diverts attention. Let's face it, who's paying attention to the wearer, when a stream of pink feathers float in front of them. I'm not saying hide, but never show everything that you are, distractions have their place.

The gold chain is the first piece of jewelry I purchased with my own money. It never broke and I've never lost it. There's value in the things you do for yourself. Hard work has its own reward. I'm not ashamed of how I labored, I was my own man, able to go where I wanted and do what I needed to do.

The key on the ring is symbolic. It is the entryway to my heart. In the box are pictures and memorabilia from over the course of my life. When you're ready, open the box and get acquainted with your old man. Let me warn you, some are pictures of me at work and some are pictures of you and me when you were small. They are my most precious gifts and I leave them to you.

Your daddy,
Bernard

Roark held her tight as she stared at the letter, tears rolling down her cheeks. It sounded as though he'd lived a covert life, hiding who he was, except for the pink feathers. She fingered them and picked up the gold chain.

"He sounded like a nice guy. If nothing else, your life would've been colorful with him," Roark whispered.

She snorted. "No doubt. Many days I could've used his words of wisdom. I wish I knew him. Mable deserves her ass whooped for what she did. She only thought of herself." Brenda wiped her face with the back of her hand. "She was probably pissed he preferred a man over her."

"It was probably the money. If he had custody, she wouldn't get any money from him." Roark rubbed her shoulders.

"For a gay man to get custody of a small child back then, she must've done something really bad."

Roark agreed. "No telling with her." He moved Brenda to the side and pulled the box closer. "Ready to get to know your dad?"

Brenda inhaled. A mixture of sadness, happiness and fear assailed her. Finally, this part of her life would be settled, but she missed knowing of her daddy. What if she couldn't handle all that he'd been? "Yeah, let's do it."

Roark pulled out a knife and sliced the tape.

"Do you always carry one of those?" She pointed to the blade.

He looked at it and smiled. "Yeah." He proceeded to pull back the flaps so she could see inside. There were several photo items and packs of letters, tied in various colored ribbons. Some had faded over time.

Her heart caught at the implication, warily she reached for a pack of letters near the top and looked at the name it was addressed to. *Felicia Shaw*. Brenda's hand shook as she dropped the bundle. He'd written to her and she never knew. All these years, there'd been someone in the wings, prepared to take care of her and she'd been shuffled from person to person while Mable shacked around. Tears filled her eyes as she remembered those strangling feelings of abandonment. She had cried and asked God why she'd been born if nobody cared or wanted her, but someone had. Through the years, she'd buried the pain from her childhood to survive, now it surged with a vengeance at the knowledge she'd been cheated.

Turning, her forehead hit Roark's chest and she cried. Loud, body wracking, sobs. No one knew of her nightmares of being left behind again, an afterthought, forgotten. Her hunger not only for food, but for love and affection. As a child, she'd craved it all, and had been rejected time after time.

"Baby…"

She heard the agonized whisper from Roark, but couldn't respond. Everything hurt. Her heart ripped with pain for the child she'd been, always trying to be whoever, whatever was necessary, so she wouldn't be put aside. Her mind bucked at the knowledge her mother denied her the one person in the world who'd loved her unconditionally. *Who did things like that?* Her throat tightened and breathing became difficult. She needed to tell him she'd be okay, but she couldn't speak around the knot of pain lodged in her chest.

"No matter what, Bren, I love you. I've wanted you from the moment I laid eyes on you in the restaurant. I didn't know your father, but from what I can see, looking at all these letters, knowing he wrote them to you, he was pretty cool." His lips brushed her ear. "The letters and pictures aren't to make you sad, but a way to make you even stronger than you are. I bet when you read his letters, you'll find pieces of yourself. The best parts. We know you didn't get those from Mable."

Brenda sniffed and smiled a little.

"The words in the first letter are his legacy to you. I'm sorry you don't remember him, maybe some of the pictures will jog your memory." She sighed as he rubbed her back and kissed the top of her head.

"Most importantly," his voice deepened, "I'm here. We'll go through everything together. You may not have had him fighting your battles when you needed, or offering advice. But I'm not going anywhere without you. I'm here, Baby. You can always come to me for anything."

Brenda's heart melted and strengthened. "I love you. How'd I get so lucky?" she asked, pulling him in for a kiss.

"I don't know if it's luck." He snuggled closer. "I'm just glad you're here, and that you're mine."

Brenda kissed his forehead, wondering if Bernard would've approved of the woman she'd become. He sounded like a kind-hearted man. She hated she couldn't remember their time together; her childhood years were a blank. Mable told her the tidbits she knew, and now she doubted they were true. The one thing she'd always wanted was to be loved. Her heart clenched at the inexplicable pang of loss of her father.

"No. It's not luck, it's who you are, a man I can always run to when things get hard, but who allows me to stand on my own." She kissed him, content with her choices in life for the first time in a long time.

-The end.-

Erosa Knowles has a love for the written word. She lives in the Southwest with her husband and son. Her favorite pastime is reading and people watching. Coming from a large family, most of her stories incorporate extended families, realizing it takes a village to raise a child. Please visit her website: www.erosaknowles.com for more information. The following books are in the Men of 3X CONStruction series: www.menof3xconstruction.com.

Have I Told You Lately
Ready for Love
Where There's Smoke
Not This Time
* Run to You

The following excerpt is from her next book in the Men of 3X CONStruction series, Not This Time - Frank and Veronique's story.

Chapter 1

There was nothing special about the small hotel lounge other than it smelled clean. Not a pine scent or anything commercial like that, in reality it was more what it didn't smell like that grabbed her attention and appreciation. The absence of stale cigarette smoke and unwashed bodies overrode the lack of décor, the limited liquor selections and insufficient seating. Three large flat-screened TVs droned on in the background with various news and sports programming. It was the sort of place where you could chill in peace at the end of a long day if you weren't a smoker.

"Another rum and coke." Veronique motioned to the bartender as she set her empty glass on the bar. Without looking, she scooped up a handful of peanuts from the half-full basket on her left. It had been a long day. She needed a quick drink to unwind before she reclaimed her hotel room. Her married sorority sister, Pam, had borrowed her suite earlier to engage in illicit relations with a man she'd met at their sorority's ball last night. In other words, her girl was humping like a rabbit and didn't want her husband or any of the other women to know of her loose morals. Obviously, she didn't care that Veronique knew. What the hell should she think of that? She tried to muster interest at the question and realized she didn't care. Why waste time thinking about her friend's immorality when she'd be on her back as well, if she'd met someone interesting enough to place her there. Glancing at her watch, she grunted. Hell, it'd been two hours. If they were still at it, her girl would be on stage and she'd be the audience. She was tired and her well of benevolence was bone dry. Glancing around at the half-filled tables, she spotted an empty one by the door.

"Here you are." She took the drink, left a five on the bar and headed for the table. After a few excuse me's, she reached her goal, and placed her purse on the table. Once seated, an unheard sigh echoed in every quadrant of her weary body. Her feet hurt, her stomach growled, and her head sent signals of its unhappiness. Shit, she was getting too old for these events. Next year, she'd pass on her sorority's annual gala and after-party.

This afternoon's step competition had showcased the best and the brightest from every fraternity and sorority. What made her think she and her contemporaries could still get down with those young, boneless newbies? Her cute red and white pumps had screamed stop-this-shit right now, the entire time. Payback was a mutha, and her feet had taken her prisoner.

One foot toed off her shoe. "Ummm..." She sighed in exquisite bliss. Then that foot did the honors for the other foot. Wiggling her toes, she'd swear they tingled in joy, expanded in the open air, and wept merrily for their new freedom.

Sipping on her drink, she looked around the bar. The room was filling up. Lots of men dressed in suits, with precision haircuts and buffed nails. There had been a time when those men drew her like ink to paper. But it didn't take long to realize she didn't like soft, well-manicured hands. Or someone who read the labels on their shampoo and conditioner. And a man who took longer than her to match his attire, worried her last nerve.

Nope, she'd moved most of her colleagues to the 'admire from a distance column,' it made for better friendships. Who'd that leave? A woman had to be realistic, if she wanted a man. Since becoming an attorney, and then going through her divorce, she'd never paid much attention to blue-collar workers. But then her daughter, Cherise, had met a man in construction. Tall, rock solid, good head on his shoulders, with a don't-mess-with-me persona. It seemed those kind of men ran in packs. The men who worked for Three X Construction were mouth-watering in so many ways. Not to mention their women, the few she'd met, all seemed to have silly smiles on their faces. Her daughter glowed with so much happiness and contentment; she'd thought they had a baby on the way. Although Cherise denied being pregnant, it wouldn't be long, not with the way Ross stayed on her.

Hedrick, her ex, was military. He missed both the professional and the blue collar columns. Military men had a column all their own, a definite breed apart. For the past two months, they'd been playing tag. Him tagging her ass and her allowing him to. His frustration that she wouldn't allow them to move past the casual sex phase irritated her. Casual was all she wanted right now, especially with him. Sex between them had always been good, but trusting him in another relationship, that was off the table as far as she was concerned. Not only had he cheated on her, but he'd married the bitch just a few months after their divorce. Cheaters who lied, and then married the Cheatees, didn't get second chances with her heart; too bad her body wasn't as discriminating. Thoughts of him and their past sent her spirits into a downward spiral.

"Hell, I can be depressed in my own room. Time to go." Placing her glass on the table, she leaned over to pick up her shoes and bumped into a pair of jean-covered, rock solid long legs. Pushing back quickly, she bumped her head on the table.

"Ow." She rubbed the bruised spot.

"I'm sorry, didn't see you... down there." The deep cadence of his voice reignited her long-held crush of Barry White. She'd bought every record that dark chocolate god had released. His music had been her panty-wetting-let's-screw anthem. Eyes closed, she basked in the memories of days and nights of fast and hard loving with Barry crooning "can't get enough of your love," in the background.

"Are you okay?"

The deep sexy-as-sin voice shot straight to her core. Damn. Now visions of tangled sheets and long nights ran through her mind with the voice. And she hadn't even seen the body it came from. Sitting back up in her chair, she eyed him while she rubbed the side of her face. *Damn, he's fine.*

"I'll live."

"Can I get you another drink?" The dark eyes pinned her to her chair. A flutter of interest rose in her breast.

She nodded, her pussy tingled at his look of interest.

"What're you drinking?" He smiled. And Veronique, defense attorney extraordinaire, swore the sun had just come from behind a dark cloud, making her world seem brighter. Sappy, but true.

"Oh, a glass of zinfandel will be fine." Any buzz she'd had earlier evaporated under the heavy dose of lust that'd swamped her. Although he wore jeans, his shirt was professional grade. Could he be in the gray area? A professional with blue-collar tendencies. Hmmm, watching him weave through the crowd, she marveled at his size. Tall, broad shoulders, dark hair and eyes. All-around nice package. Her lips puckered and smacked, wanting a taste.

God, please let him be capable of a halfway decent conversation. No matter how hot and horny he made her, she'd long passed the stage where she screwed dumb men. Even brief flings had to bring more than solid meat to the table. Placing her shoes into her large Coach bag, she watched him maneuver the crowd while holding her wine and a beer.

He handed her the glass as he sat next to her.

"Thanks, I appreciate it. I'm Veronique by the way." She looked at him from beneath her lids as she took a sip of the cool liquid.

"I'm Frank. Your name's different. Are you from Philly?" He took a pull from his bottle. The weight of his gaze warmed her.

"No, I'm here for a conference. Two more days to go." She gazed at his dark eyes, and the heat singed her core. His eyes blazed as he watched her lips on the glass. *Yep, he was he interested.* "Is this home for you?"

"I live an hour away, but I had some business in town, and came in here to unwind before heading out." He looked at her and winked. "Glad I did."

Me, too. "How about that? I was on my way out when you bumped into me. Must be kismet, huh?" She smiled as he placed his bottle on the table, and leaned toward her.

"Yeah, kismet works for me. Let me buy you dinner before you leave. You seem like an interesting person, Veronique. I'd like to know you better."

Tingles shot down her spine when he said her name. "I am." She stood, and picked up her purse.

He followed. "Is there anything you prefer?"

"Lean meats." She smirked as her eyes roved slowly over his muscular frame. Did she say he was fine? Regardless, his body demanded another bravo for fineness.

He placed his hands in his pocket and walked behind her. "Lean meats? Hmmm, lean and juicy, I hope."

"Juicy works. Nobody likes dry meat." She stopped and looked around the hotel lobby for the entrance to the in-house restaurant. Spotting it, she headed in that direction. "We can eat here."

"Sounds good. I like lean and juicy myself." He grinned. They entered the restaurant, and the hostess sat them in the back after Veronique explained the problem with her shoes.

After they'd been seated, she glanced at Frank over her menu. Damn. The man was handsome. Thick, dark shiny hair touched his collar, a small close-cropped beard, and a nice smile. He reminded her of Russell Crowe and Mel Gibson combined into a delicious package. A package she planned to unwrap before the night was over.

Frank O'Connor slid the bulge in his pants, in search of a comfortable spot. The woman sitting next to him had his mouth watering, an unusual occurrence for him. Her smooth chocolate complexion reminded him of his favorite candy, Milky Way. He couldn't wait to taste every delectable inch of her. She wore her hair pulled up in the back, showing off her long neck, while curls framed her face. It seemed like a lot of work to accent to an already beautiful countenance. Large eyes stared at him with a teasing challenge that ripped into his calm facade.

This woman seemed secure enough to take him on for the short time she'd be in town. That rocked for him. Without her shoes, the top of her head reached his nipples. The red dress accentuated her curves, especially her ass. Nice, high, round and firm-looking. His cock twitched in excitement. Black women's ages were always harder to gauge. He placed her in her mid-thirties, much younger than his forty-one. Sharp, intelligent eyes peered from her heart-shaped face. A full lower lip, slightly larger than the upper, teased his imagination, he wanted to taste all of her right now. *Patience.* What was it about her that drew him like an infant to a nipple? Sitting across from her, he pretended to read his menu. He'd have the steak dinner, he'd had it before. Only this time, she'd be dessert. He just had to convince her to be on the menu.

"Have you eaten here before?" She asked in a husky tone.

No, I've never been between your legs, but I hope to be real soon. "Yes, the steaks and chicken dishes are pretty good. Can't go wrong with those." He shifted to get comfortable.

"Thanks. I think I'll have the chicken picata with a salad." She nodded and placed the menu to her right.

He nodded as the waiter placed two glasses of water and a basket of warm rolls on the table. "We're ready to order." The waiter nodded and took out his pad. Frank waved at her, signaling she should go first. He wanted to hear the huskiness of her voice again. It called to something in him. It'd made him sit his big ass down in a bar, when he knew he needed to leave before nightfall. He'd been in too many late night driving accidents to leave this late, it wasn't his favorite thing.

Yet, something dark and primitive unfurled when he gazed down at her. His mind drew all sorts of erotic images. Seeing her so close to his cock in the bar had sealed her fate for the night, he liked the visual and decided her lips around his rod was the right thing to do. He hadn't counted on her being so damn sexy and hungry. Her full lips tilted at the corners at his stare, letting him know that having her in his bed tonight wouldn't be automatic. She was no submissive.

So, he'd revised his strategy. Now they sat at dinner, but all he could see was his cock between her breast, in her mouth, and then the tight sheath below. Conversation, although a necessity, bored him. Action, the need for it, prompted him toward civility and the niceties. He didn't consider himself a Dominant, like his twin brothers who lived an alternative lifestyle. A slave or submissive didn't interest him, especially 24/7, but he admitted, to himself at least, that all of the O'Connor men were dominant to a point.

There was a baseness in them, almost primitive, that pushed them to conquer. As the oldest, he'd like to think he was more level-headed, more polished, more flexible. Then there were times like this, when all he wanted was to pick this woman up, sling her over his shoulder and take her to a quiet spot, and screw the challenge out of her. The need burned in him. The more she acted as though it didn't matter, as if tonight might not happen between them, the harder his need pressed to prove her wrong. Damn. He was in trouble. In the few minutes of their acquaintance, he knew they'd butt heads.

"Sir?"

Frank heard the waiter over the rushing wind of his growing need. "I'll have the steak, medium rare – juicy." He winked at her. "Veggies, no potato." He handed the menu to the waiter, then took a sip of water to cool his raging hard on. The pain in his groin increased. There was no more room in his pants. A quick glance around the near empty room eased his tension. Fewer eyes to see his condition. It'd been years since anyone had evoked such a strong reaction from him. For that alone, he owed her a good, solid fuck.

They sat staring at each other as if they were in a poker game. Neither moved nor spoke. A loud crash from the kitchen area broke the stare-fest.

"What are your plans for the evening?" he asked, although anything other than being with him was the wrong answer.

"I'm going to get some rest; it's been a long day." The huskiness of her voice soothed and aroused him.

Although her mouth spoke, his eyes fastened on the twin pointed peaks on her chest. "Tired?"

"Not really."

"Good. I'd hate for you to be worn out so soon." He smiled as her brow rose.

"So soon? It's been a long day." Her lips tilted at the corners letting him know she was game, but he'd have to work for it.

"Perhaps, but the day wouldn't be complete without seeing some of Philadelphia's better sights."

She leaned forward slowly, licking her lips. His eyes followed the trail of moisture glistening in the dim light.

"Better sights, is that what they're calling it these days?" The teasing glint in her eye set off a spark in him. He liked this one.

"Yeah, you should see Liberty Hall at night," he said straight-faced. "There's nothing quite like it."

"I have. And you're right, it's ridiculously beautiful. Oh well, since I've already seen it, my night will be less eventful." She glanced up as the waiter placed their drinks on the table.

"Part of the beauty is buried in the guide, the one that unleashes the untapped depths of our relics. You haven't seen anything in Philly, if you haven't seen it with me." He trapped her with his gaze. Tonight belonged to them, his eyes dared her to refuse.

Veronique enjoyed the cat and mouse banter with the hunky stranger. For a moment, she felt young and carefree. It'd been a while since she'd been so ardently pursued; it did wonders for her ego. Most of the men of her acquaintance lacked the hard-core alpha appeal that rolled off her dinner date in waves. No one she knew would throw out such a challenge.

"You're probably right," she agreed.

He nodded and visibly relaxed. "I'd like to spend more time with you tonight."

Really? I hadn't guessed. "Are you married?"

He frowned and held up his hand. "No."

She waited a beat. "Aren't you going to ask me?"

He shook his head. "You're not the type to cheat. I think you'd say fuck it and walk away."

Since he was right, she didn't comment. "Children?"

"Not yet."

"I'm here for two more days. What do you think you can show me that I haven't already seen?"

His eyes darkened as they stripped her naked.

Exposed, she battled the panic rising inside her. It wasn't fear that he'd hurt her physically, she wouldn't have accepted his dinner invite if she'd picked up those vibes. It was his uncanny ability to pinpoint her needs that rattled her. Her week had been hellacious and for numerous reasons, many she'd blocked from her mind, she didn't want to be in charge. Tonight, she needed a strong, assertive man. Someone confident in himself to chart their course and give her what she desired. So far he'd hit the ball, the only thing left was to reach the bases.

"Veronique." His voice deepened. Her thighs clenched. "I'm not sure if two days between your legs, tasting and pounding your pussy, will satisfy your hunger for this cock I plan to give you tonight, but it'll be a start."

Erosa Knowles

CPSIA information can be obtained
at www.ICGtesting.com
Printed in the USA
BVHW041727011218
534537BV00003B/202/P